PATRICIA WENTWORTH

Born in Mussoorie, India, in 1878, Patricia
Wentworth was the daughter of an English
general. Educated in England, she returned
to India, where she began to write and was
first published. She married, but in 1906
was left a widow with four children, and returned again to England where she resumed
her writing, this time, to earn a living for
herself and her family. She married again in
1920 and lived in Surrey until her death in
1961.

Miss Wentworth's early works were
mainly historical fiction, and her first mystery, published in 1923, was *The Astonishing Adventure of Jane Smith*. In 1928 she
wrote *The Case is Closed* and gave birth
to her most enduring creation, Miss Maud
Silver.

BOOKS BY PATRICIA WENTWORTH

WICKED UNCLE

Patricia Wentworth

HarperPaperbacks
A Division of HarperCollinsPublishers

This is a work of fiction. The characters, incidents, and dialogues are products of the author's imagination and are not to be construed as real. Any resemblance to actual events or persons, living or dead, is entirely coincidental.

HarperPaperbacks   *A Division of* HarperCollins*Publishers*
10 East 53rd Street, New York, N.Y. 10022

This book was originally published in hardcover in 1947 by J. B. Lippincott Company.

A trade paperback edition of this book was published in 1993 by HarperPerennial, a division of HarperCollins *Publishers.*

Cover illustration by Paul Cox

First HarperPaperbacks printing: June 1996

Printed in the United States of America

HarperPaperbacks and colophon are trademarks of HarperCollins*Publishers*

❖ 10 9 8 7 6 5 4 3 2 1

CHAPTER 1

When Dorinda Brown came into the Heather Club at four o'clock on January eighth she hadn't the slightest idea that she had just made the first step upon a road which was going to take her into some curious places. If anyone had told her so, she would have laughed. She laughed easily, to be sure, with a backward tilt of the head, eyes crinkling at the corners, and a generous display of excellent white teeth. Anyone less good-tempered than Dorinda might have been annoyed with Justin Leigh's remark that when she was really amused he could count them. Dorinda had only laughed again and said, "Well, they're all there."

The Heather Club wasn't really a club. Penny plain it was a boarding-house, and twopence coloured it was a private hotel. Miss Donaldson who presided over it felt that she was combining patriotism and refinement by calling it a club and displaying a large bowl of Scottish heather in the little dark hall. It was, perhaps, better not to drag in the word private, since privacy was one of the things which the Club was quite unable to offer. It was a big house in a locality which had come down in the world, and its big rooms had been cut up so small that they resembled slices from a once ample joint, each slice just wide enough to take a narrow bed and leave room for the occupant to get in and out. Some of the slices shared a window, others had a narrow slit which let in no air when it was hot and poured an icy draught down the back of your neck when it was cold. Dorinda had a slice with a slit.

As she passed through the hall she encountered Miss Donaldson, tall, bony, and austere of feature. The austerity was all in the shop window. It daunted newcomers, but took nobody in for long. Behind that formidable manner, that tight hair, those rugged eyebrows, there lived a simple, genial creature who asked no more of life than to be able to pay her way.

"Oh, Miss Donaldson," said Dorinda—"I've got it!"

"The job you were inquiring after?"

Twenty years in London had done nothing to deprive Euphemia Donaldson of her Scottish tongue.

Dorinda nodded.

"I've got it!"

"It wouldn't be in Scotland?"

Dorinda shook her head.

There was a wistful gleam in Miss Donaldson's eye.

"I was thinking if you'd relatives there, it would be nice—"

Dorinda shook her head again.

"But I haven't."

Miss Donaldson looked disappointed.

"That's strange too, and you so young. Now take me—it's more than twenty years since I came south, and I've five-and-thirty relations in Scotland—counting third and fourth cousins." The r's were like a drum-roll.

Dorinda laughed.

"I wasn't counting cousins."

"Ah, your mother was English, you were telling me—that would account for it. Now that Mr. Leigh that was calling for you once or twice, he'd be on your mother's side?"

"A long way off," said Dorinda. "You know—the sort that's a cousin if you want them to be, and not a relation at all if you don't."

Miss Donaldson commented on this with the old Scottish word "Imphm," which can mean almost anything. In this case it implied that she knew what Dorinda meant and disapproved of it, adding with a fresh roll of drums,

"Relations can be awful disagreeable, but blood's thicker than water and they'll stand by you at a pinch."

Dorinda felt that honour was now satisfied. She smiled her wide, attractive smile and moved on.

"I was just going to telephone."

Miss Donaldson said, "Imphm," and withdrew into the dismal hole which she called her office.

Dorinda bounded into the telephone-box and shut the door. This was the one place in the house where you could talk without being overheard. In the slicelike cubicles you could hear every sound made by every other person within the four walls of what had once been a very fine room. In the hall, in the passages, in the dining-room, in the lounge, there were always people coming and going and listening—especially listening. Some of the old ladies had no other interest in life. They put together all the things they heard and exchanged them as they sat in a solid bank round the fire in the evenings. Even if you had a bath, they could hear the water run in, and gurgle out again, so they knew at once if anyone was taking more than her fair share. Tongues had become very sharp over Judith Crane who had actually had two baths a day, but fortunately she had left at the end of a week.

The telephone-box really was soundproof. It always

amused Dorinda to see people talking behind the glass, opening and shutting their mouths like fishes in an aquarium, but when you were shut up inside it yourself it felt rather nice, as if you were in a private world of your own. And not alone there, because you had only to magic with the dial and you could have anyone you liked to share it with you—well, anyone in reason.

Dorinda flicked the dial, put her pennies in, and waited. If anyone had been passing they might have thought she made a pleasant picture. There are so many sad faces, so many tired, lined, cross, difficult, irritable faces that it is pleasant to see a cheerful one. Dorinda nearly always looked cheerful. Even on her solitary visit to a dentist, when she had secretly been a good deal daunted by the unknown and rather terrifying apparatus which appeared to be lying in wait for her, she had contrived to smile. She went through life smiling, sometimes resolutely, but for the most part in a pleasantly spontaneous manner, and when she smiled her eyes smiled too.

They were quite ordinary eyes, with quite ordinary lashes. They had a way of shining and looking golden when she was pleased or feeling fond of anyone. Her hair was golden brown and very thick. Justin Leigh once said that it was walnut-coloured. He explained kindly, and a little condescendingly, that he didn't mean the colour of the nut but of the polished wood. Dorinda, who was ten years old at the time, went and stood for a long time in front of the walnut bureau in the drawing-room trying to make up her mind whether Justin meant that he liked her hair. She held her plait against the wood and gazed at it. The hair certainly had the same colours in it as the wood, and when it was well brushed it shone in very much the same way. After that she made a point of brushing it a great deal. But she didn't like the plait, because all the other girls at school had short hair. So in a good-tempered but perfectly determined manner she took her Aunt Mary's cutting-out scissors and removed it. She had smiled equably through the painful family scene which followed, secure in the fact that they couldn't put it back. She had a bright rosy colour, two dimples, and a wide, generous mouth which was really quite red enough to do without lipstick. For the rest, she was five-foot-five in her stocking feet, and she had the kind of figure which has agreeable curves without being fat.

The telephone buzzed and Justin Leigh said, "Hullo!" in the cultured and rather *blasé* manner in which it was his habit to address telephones.

"It's me," said Dorinda, throwing grammar to the winds.

"*I.*"

"No, *me*. Listen—I've got a job."

"Oh? What is it?"

He sounded bored. But it was impossible for Dorinda to believe that anyone could really be bored when she herself was feeling all lit-up and excited. She began to pour everything out in a rush.

"It was an advertisement. One of the other girls showed it to me in the lunch-hour—I mean her lunch-hour, not mine. She's in an office—"

"Don't you have lunch?"

"Well, I do as a rule, but I hadn't time today because she showed me the advertisement and I rushed straight round to the address, which was Claridge's—and when I got there, there were about six other girls waiting there too, and no one very pleased about it, if you know what I mean. So I thought, 'Well, if this has been going on all day, I haven't got an earthly.' "

"And had it?"

"Well, I think it had, because I was the last to go up, and Mrs. Oakley said it was making her feel quite giddy. There was a red-haired girl coming out as I went in, and she stamped her foot at me in the corridor and said in one of those piercing whispers you can hear all over the place, 'Pure poison—I wouldn't take it for a thousand a year.' Then she grinned and said, 'Well, I suppose I should, but I should end by cutting her throat and my own, and anybody else's who was handy.' "

Justin sounded quite interested—for him.

"What does one say to a total stranger who bursts into confidences about throat-cutting in a corridor at Claridge's? These exciting things don't happen to me. You intrigue me. What did you say?"

"I said, 'Why?' "

"How perfectly to the point!"

"And she said, 'Go and see for yourself. I shouldn't touch it unless you're absolutely on your uppers.' And I said, 'Well, I am.' "

"And are you?"

In a tone of undiminished cheerfulness Dorinda said, "Just about."

"Is that the reason why there wasn't time for lunch?"

He heard her laugh.

"Oh, well, it doesn't matter now, because I've got the job. I went in, and Mrs. Oakley was lying on a sofa with most of the blinds down, all except one which made a spotlight where you had to go and sit and be looked at. It gave me the sort of feeling of being on the stage without any of the proper clothes, or make-up, or anything."

"Continue."

"I couldn't see much to start with, but she sounded fretty. When I got used to the light, she had a lot of fair hair which she was being rather firm with—not letting it go grey, you know. Fortyish, I thought. And she hadn't ever got out of being a spoilt child—that sort. And the most heavenly pale pink negligée, the kind people have in films, and a little gold bottle of smelling-salts."

"Who is she?"

"Mrs. Oakley. Her husband's name is Martin, and he's a financier. They've got pots of money and a little boy of five. His name is Martin too, but they call him Marty, which is pretty frightful for a boy, don't you think?"

"I do. Go on."

Dorinda went on.

"Well, first she moaned at me and said all these girls were making her giddy. And I said didn't any of them do? And she said no—their voices were wrong. She had to have a voice that didn't jar her nerves, and the last girl was a volcano. I said what about my voice, because I thought if it jarred her like the others, it wasn't any good my sitting in a spotlight wasting time. She had a good sniff at the smelling-salts and said she thought I had a soothing personality. After that we never looked back, and she's giving me three pounds a week!"

Justin showed a disappointing lack of enthusiasm.

"What is this job—what are you supposed to do?"

Dorinda giggled.

"She calls it being her secretary. I think I do all the things she's too fragile to do herself—writing notes, doing the flowers, answering the telephone when it's someone who insists on speaking to her. She took quite a long time telling me about that. There are times when it jars her too much even to hear the voice of an intimate friend, and she has to be fresh for Martin in the evenings. And then I keep an eye on Marty when his nursery governess gets an afternoon off, and—oh, well, that sort of thing."

"And where does all this go on—at Claridge's?"

"Oh, no. She's got what she calls a country cottage in Surrey. As there's her, and him, and Marty, and the nursery governess, and me, and a staff of servants, and they mean to have house parties every week end, I expect it's something pretty vast. Anyhow it's called the Mill House, and we go down there tomorrow."

After a pause Justin said with notable restraint,

"It sounds damp—water in the cellars, and mildew on your shoes in the morning."

Dorinda shook her head.

"It's not that kind of mill—she said so. It's on the top of a hill. There used to be a windmill, but it fell down and somebody built this house. I'll write and tell you all about it. Did you hear me say I was going down tomorrow?"

"Yes. You'd better dine with me tonight."

Dorinda laughed.

"I don't know that I can."

"Why don't you know?"

"Well, I was dining with Tip, but I told him I wouldn't unless he let Buzzer come too, and I don't really know—"

Justin said in his most superior voice,

"Cut it out! I'll call for you at half past seven."

CHAPTER 2

Martin Oakley came out of Gregory Porlock's office and shut the door. He stood with his hand on the knob for about half a minute as if he were half inclined to turn it again and go back. A tall man of a loose, rangy build, with a sallow skin, receding hair, and dark, rather veiled eyes. As he presently made up his mind and went on down the stairs without waiting for the lift he was frowning. If Dorinda Brown had been there she would have been struck by his resemblance to the cross dark little boy whom she had encountered briefly as she came away from Mrs. Oakley's suite. But Dorinda wasn't there—she was telephoning ecstatically to Justin Leigh from the Heather Club. There was, therefore, no one to remark on the likeness.

Inside the room which Martin Oakley had just left, Gregory Porlock, with everything handsome about him, was holding a telephone receiver to his ear and waiting for Mr. Tote to say "Hullo!" at the other end of the line. Everything in the office was suavely and comfortably the best of its kind. Mr. Porlock called himself a General Agent, and nobody who entered this room could doubt that he made his agency pay. From the carpet on the floor to the three or four paintings on the walls, everything declared that solid balance at the bank which needs no vulgar advertisement but makes itself felt along the avenues of taste. The richness was a subdued richness, Gregory Porlock's clothes were part of it. Admirable in themselves, they not only did not have to atone for nature's defects, but actually gained from nature's bounty. He was an exceedingly personable man, rather florid of complexion, in marked and becoming contrast to the colour of his dark eyes and a head of very thick iron-grey hair. He might be in his middle forties, and he might be, and probably was, a couple of stone heavier than he had been ten years before, but it was not unbecoming and he carried it with an air.

The line crackled and Mr. Tote said, " 'Ullo!"

It is not supposed that Mr. Tote was in the habit of dropping his h's. If he had ever done so, it was a long time ago, but like a great many other people he still said, " 'Ullo!" when confronted by a telephone.

Gregory Porlock smiled as affably as if Mr. Tote could see him.

"Hullo, Tote—how are you? Gregory Porlock speaking." The telephone crackled. "And Mrs. Tote? I want you both to come down for the week-end. . . . My dear fellow, I simply won't take no for an answer."

The telephone crackled again. With the receiver at his ear, Gregory Porlock was aware of Mr. Tote excusing himself.

"I don't see that we really can—the wife's none too well—"

"My dear fellow, I'm sorry to hear that. But you know, sometimes a change—and though the Grange is an old house, we've got central heating everywhere and I can promise to keep her warm. There will be a pleasant party too. Do you know the Martin Oakleys?"

"I've met Oakley."

Gregory Porlock laughed.

"But not his wife? Then we're in the same boat. They won't be in the house-party because they've just moved into a house of their own quite near me. Horrible great barrack of a place. But don't tell Oakley I said so—he thinks it's bracing. I'll get them to come over and dine. They're my nearest neighbours, so I must contrive to meet Mrs. Oakley. I'm told she's pretty. Well now, you'll come—won't you?"

Mr. Tote was heard to swallow.

"I don't know that we can—"

"My dear Tote! Oh, by the way, you have that memorandum I sent you? The address? And the date? Well,

I have one or two more that might interest you. I thought we might talk the whole thing over in a friendly spirit if you came down. I really think it would be a good plan—don't you? . . . Oh, splendid! I shall look forward to it so much. Goodbye."

He hung up, and almost immediately dialled another number. This time it was a woman's voice that answered.

"Moira Lane speaking." A pretty voice, a good deal farther up the social scale than Mr. Tote's.

Gregory Porlock announcing himself, compliments were exchanged. Miss Lane was invited to join the week-end party, and accepted with alacrity.

"I'd love to! Who else have you got?"

"The Totes. You won't know them, and you won't want to. I want to talk over a bit of business with him."

"Isn't he one of our Newest Rich?"

"That's it. Her jewellery has to be seen to be believed."

Moira laughed. It was a pretty sound.

"What is she like?"

"A white mouse."

"My dear Greg!"

"You needn't talk to her. The others in the house will be a Mr. and Miss Masterman—brother and sister—just come in for a lot of money from an old cousin."

"Some people have all the luck," said Miss Lane in a heartfelt manner.

He laughed.

"Perhaps there'll be enough to go round—you can't tell, can you?"

"Anyone else?"

"Oh, yes—Leonard Carroll for you."

"Greg, *darling!* Why for me?"

"The nearest approach to a fellow bright young thing."

"My poor sweet! We're both of us going to be thirty as soon as makes no difference."

He laughed.

"A delightful age. If I may use a nursery metaphor, you have got past the bread and butter and begun on the cake."

He could hear her blow him a kiss.

"Is Len really coming? Last time I saw him he told me he was booked up for months. What it is to be a popular Entertainer!"

"*The* popular Entertainer, isn't it? I don't think he'd care about that 'a' somehow. But—oh, yes, he'll come. Well, I'll be seeing you."

He hung up, smiling pleasantly.

After a moment he dialled again.

"Is that the Luxe?"

"Yes, sir."

"Oh—has Mr. Leonard Carroll finished his turn in the cabaret?"

"Well, sir, I think he has, just about."

"Could you send someone to tell him I'd like a word with him? . . . Gregory Porlock. I'll hold on."

He had a little time to wait. He beguiled it by humming the air of an old Scotch song. Presently the humming broke into words:

> "*The love that I had chosen*
> *Was to my heart's content.*
> *The salt sea shall be frozen*
> *Before that I repent.*
> *Repent it will I never*
> *Until the day I dee,*

*But the Lowlands of Holland
Have twined my love and me."*

A lovely minor air, rendered softly in an agreeable baritone. There was time to repeat the refrain before Leonard Carroll said, "Hullo!"

Gregory Porlock noted that he seemed a little out of breath.

"My dear fellow, I hope I haven't hurried you."

"Not at all. What do you want?"

"My dear fellow!" There was some good-humoured protest in Gregory's tone. "But there—I expect you are up to the eyes. No time for me—eh?"

"I didn't say that."

Gregory laughed.

"Well, I hope you didn't mean it. Joking apart, I've rung up to find out if you'll come down to my place for the week-end."

"I can't possibly."

"My dear Carroll, you're so impulsive. You know, I've got a feeling that it's overwork, and that if you are not careful you'll be finding you are having to take a very long rest. In your own interests you shouldn't let it come to that—the proverbial stitch in time. I'll be expecting you on Saturday."

"I tell you, I can't come." Carroll really wasn't troubling to be polite.

Gregory continued to smile.

"What a pity! By the way, if you ever have time for reading, I've got something that's right up your street. Fellow called Tauscher. Extraordinary revelations. But there—I don't suppose you've time."

There was rather a long pause before Carroll said in a slow, dragging voice,

"Not unless I get away for a week-end."

"Well then, my dear fellow, it's easy—come along down to me on Saturday and I'll fix you up with Tauscher."

There was another pause. The slow voice said,

"All right."

Gregory Porlock heard a click at the other end of the line. Leonard Carroll had hung up.

He had one more call to make. When a woman's voice answered he asked for Mr. Masterman. The voice replied without bonhomie,

"He's engaged. I can take a message."

Gregory Porlock gave a laugh of the lighter social kind.

"Of course—it's Miss Masterman! How stupid of me! I didn't recognize your voice. It's Gregory Porlock."

"Oh, yes. What is it, Mr. Porlock?" There was some slight evidence of a thaw.

"Well, I just rang up to say how much I'm looking forward to seeing you at the week-end. I hope you can get down to tea?"

"I don't know—I shall have to ask my brother—"

"All right, I'll hold on if you don't mind. Will you tell him that with regard to the matter of business he was consulting me about, I think I've worked out a very satisfactory solution. I really don't think he need worry about it any more."

A telephone is a very sensitive instrument. Miss Masterman was quite five miles away, but Gregory Porlock distinctly heard her catch her breath. He might have been mistaken, but he did not think so. The sound told him something which he wanted to know. It informed him that she was in her brother's confidence. He had thought so, but it was always better to be quite sure of your ground.

When she came back presently and said that they would try to be down at the Grange by four o'clock, he was the delighted, genial host.

"Splendid! I hope you'll like the party. All pleasant people, and one famous one. Leonard Carroll is coming, so we oughtn't to be dull. Then there's a very charming girl, Moira Lane. And the Totes—nice simple people. And some near neighbours thrown in. Well, all the best to your brother."

Miss Masterman said, "Thank you," and sounded as if she meant it.

Gregory Porlock hung up and burst out laughing.

CHAPTER 3

Justin Leigh took Dorinda to one of those places which is just going to be the rage. When it actually did become the rage he would probably say it was vulgar and go somewhere else. He was a beautiful and immaculate young man on the opinionated side of thirty, with a job in the Ministry of Reconstruction. No one, to look at him, could have believed it possible that he had spent nearly six years in a more or less constant condition of being dirty, unshaved, and soaked to the skin, with excursions into being baked and frozen. There were also considerable periods when his immediate surroundings were going up in smoke. If you survived, it left you even filthier than before. All very incredible when you looked at the dark *soigné* young man with his air of careless elegance and the poise which always gave Dorinda a slight feeling of being back in the schoolroom. She didn't give way to this feeling, because if you once let yourself start an inferiority complex with Justin, he would become simply intolerable, and that would be a pity because, umpteenth cousin or no, he was the only relation she had left.

She could feel his eye on her dress. It was a blue dress, and she had bought it because she liked the colour, and of course that was a mistake. If you've only got one dining-out dress, it's simply got to be black, and no matter what else you do without, it's got to be good. Then you just go on wearing it until one of you dies.

She met the eye with firmness mitigated by the dimples.

"It's no good—I know it all by heart—it hasn't got any line, and line is what sees you through. But it's a nice colour, isn't it?"

"My child, it's a disaster."

Dorinda was not lacking in spirit.

"What's the good of saying that when I've got it on? The pink one was worse—I've given it away. And you can say what you like, this one suits me. Tip said it did."

"Tip Remington is in the maudlin state of mind in which he would say anything."

"Buzzer said so too."

"Did he?"

Justin's voice was completely uninterested in Buzzer Blake. He was consulting the menu, and proceeded to catch the headwaiter's eyes. After an intimate and technical discussion he turned back to Dorinda, who was solacing herself for her lost lunch by thinking that it sounded as if it was going to be a heavenly dinner, and said,

"Are you engaged to either of them?"

She came out of a lovely dream of food and met his eyes frankly.

"Well, I don't know—"

Justin's eyebrows rose, as at a social solecism.

"Hadn't you better find out? I should hate to interfere, but you can't marry them both."

"Oh, I'm not marrying them. I don't want to marry anyone for a long time."

The soup arrived. It smelt heavenly. It was very difficult to take it slowly enough, but Aunt Mary's iron training held. One of the last things she had said to Dorinda was, "Well, I've only got fifty pounds a year to leave you, but I've taught you how to behave like a gentlewoman." There were moments when she found it inconvenient. This was one of them. She was very hungry.

Between sips she imparted her views on matrimony.

"You see, it lasts such a long time, unless you go in for divorce, and that always seems to me rather nasty, unless you've simply got to."

Justin looked faintly amused and said,

"It can be overdone."

Dorinda pursued the theme.

"Suppose I married Tip. He's twenty-four, and I'm twenty-one. It might go on for about fifty or sixty years. It's a frightfully long time. Of course he's got plenty of money. He's in his uncle's office and he'll be a partner in a year or two, and it would be rather nice to have one's own flat and a car, but I've got a feeling I'd get tired of being married to Tip—" She broke off to help herself to *sole meunière*.

"Then I shouldn't do it."

Dorinda said, "Oh, I'm not going to—at least I don't suppose I shall, unless the Oakleys really do turn out to be pure poison like the red-headed girl said. Do you know, she looked nice. I wouldn't have minded knowing her."

"It isn't the slightest good trailing red-headed herrings across the path. The point is not what you either think or don't think about getting married, but what these wretched lads think you are thinking. Have you, or have you not, given either or both of them to suppose that you will marry him?"

Dorinda beamed.

"Justin darling, this is *the* most lovely fish I've ever tasted. I'm so glad I didn't have any lunch."

He looked at her severely.

"Neither red herrings nor soles, Dorinda. Have you, or have you not?"

"Do you think I could have some more?"

"You can if you like, but you'd better see what's coming."

After an earnest study of the menu she sighed regretfully and said perhaps she had better not—"It all sounds too lovely."

"Well then, perhaps you'll answer my question."

Whilst the waiter was changing their plates she gazed at Justin, and he had occasion to observe that the offending dress really did make her hair look very bright. To the callow taste of Tip Remington and Buzzer Blake it would doubtless appear that it was becoming. On the other hand, it was improbable that they would notice or appreciate the fact that her lashes were of exactly the same golden brown. If she ever started darkening them, he would have to speak to her about it, because it was a very unusual colour and from the purely aesthetic point of view she couldn't be allowed to play tricks with it.

When they had helped themselves to chicken *en casserole* with mushrooms and all sorts of other exciting things in the gravy, he put his question again.

"Well," said Dorinda, "I might say, 'What has it got to do with you?'" Her tone was perfectly friendly.

"Are you going to?"

She laughed.

"I don't suppose I am. The trouble is—"

"Well?"

"It's so hard to say no."

This had the pleasing effect of making Justin laugh. On the rare occasions when that happened Dorinda always felt that she was a social success. Her eyes became several shades darker and her colour deepened.

"Well, it is," she protested. "I like them both dreadfully. If anything, I think I like Buzzer best, but perhaps that's only because he hasn't got any money, which gives me a fellow feeling. But I don't really want to marry someone who has absolutely nothing, because when I do get married I should like to have some children, and if one hadn't got anything at all, it would be a bit difficult to bring them up."

"It might be."

"Oh, it would. I've thought about it a lot. You see, I think two boys and two girls would be nice. And there's not only bringing them up, with shoes, and school books—even if all the education is free—but it's putting them out in the world and getting them jobs. So I don't think it would be a good plan to marry Buzzer even if I wanted to. And I should feel a bit low if I married Tip just because there would be enough money."

"My good child, if you attempt to marry either of them, I shall come and forbid the banns."

Dorinda evinced a frank interest.

"How do you do it?"

"I've no idea, but I shall make it my business to find out. You'd better stiffen the backbone and practise saying no for five minutes every morning in front of the looking-glass. You can't marry everyone who asks you."

"Nobody has except Tip—not really. Buzzer just said he couldn't—not until he got a proper job, but would I wait for him. I don't know if you'd count that or not."

"I shouldn't count either of them. Look here, will you promise me something?"

Dorinda possessed a vein of caution. It prompted her to ask,

"What is it?"

"Don't get engaged to anyone without asking me. And don't be in a hurry. Generally speaking, I should say the idea is not to get engaged unless you mean to get married, and not to get married unless you feel you must. Didn't your Aunt Mary ever tell you that?" There was a slight quizzical smile in his eyes.

Dorinda said candidly, "She told me never to get married at all. You see, she had a complex about men. Because of the Wicked Uncle."

"I never met your Aunt Mary, but she sounds a most unpleasant woman."

Dorinda did her duty by the dead.

"Oh, she wasn't really. It was frightfully good of her to bring me up, you know. Nobody else wanted to, but she thought it was her duty and she did. I was only two, and I must have been a lot of trouble."

If Justin had a softened thought of Dorinda at two, smilingly unconscious of being a nuisance, he showed no sign of it. He simply disliked the late Mrs. Porteous a little more.

Dorinda pursued the theme.

"The Wicked Uncle really was an uncommonly bad lot. He used to go off and run riot, and then come back, take anything she'd got, and go off again."

"There's a Married Woman's Property Act. Why did she let him?"

"Well, she told me about that when she was ill. I think she was a bit wandery and didn't quite know what she was saying, but she meant it all right. She said, 'Don't ever get married, Dorinda. It's just giving a man the power to wring your heart.' And another time she said, 'He was bad through and through.' She asked me if I remembered him. I said I remembered calling him Uncle Glen, and that he had dancing dark eyes, and a round white scar on his wrist. And she said in a dreadfully bitter voice, 'He had what they call charm. And he'd take anyone's last drop of blood and their last penny and laugh.' Then she told me that he'd had all her money except her annuity and the fifty pounds a year she was leaving me. And she said never to let him have a penny of it."

"He isn't dead?"

"She didn't know. And right at the end when she was very wandery she wanted me to promise I'd never marry, but of course I wouldn't."

"You can refer the applicants to me."

"Justin, do you know, I believe you've got something there. It really is frightfully difficult for a girl to go on saying no all on her own. I've often felt it would be useful to have a stern parent or guardian or someone in the background to say it for you. Would you—really?"

"I would—I will. You can come and watch me if you like. I feel I'm going to be good at it. Are you going to have ice pudding?"

Dorinda looked at him reproachfully.

"Of course I am! Justin, it's a lovely dinner!"

"Enjoy it, my child. And now listen. I've been finding out about your Oakleys. He made a lot of money in the war. Theoretically the Excess Profits Tax made this impossible. Actually quite a lot of people did it. Martin Oakley is one of them."

"Yes, I told you he'd got a lot of money—Mrs. Oakley said so. She's that sort—she tells you everything."

Justin laughed.

"Then Martin Oakley probably takes care she doesn't know anything to tell. Anyhow he's supposed to be financially sound, and there's nothing against her, so there seems to be no reason why you shouldn't take the job."

An agreeable glow made Dorinda's colour rise. Justin had actually taken the trouble to find out about the Oakleys because she was going to them. It was frightfully nice of him. She said so.

"Because there isn't anyone else to do it, is there—only me. And of course it's much nicer to have the stern parent or guardian or whatnot to do it for you—it gives you a background, if you know what I mean."

Justin smiled rather nicely.

"I definitely refuse to be a parent."

Dorinda regarded him with thoughtful appreciation.

"No, you're much more the right age for a brother—aren't you?"

She was surprised and a little startled at the warmth with which he said,

"I'm damned if I'll be a brother, Dorinda!"

In her own mind she put it down to the unlucky blue dress. Justin's sister would certainly never have bought it just because she liked the colour. She would have had perfect taste, and would never have made him feel ashamed of her in public. She said with artless candour,

"Of course if you'd had a sister she wouldn't have been a bit like me."

Justin had retreated behind an enigmatic smile.

"I'll be a whatnot," he said.

CHAPTER 4

Dorinda travelled down to the Mill House next day in a very large Rolls which contained Mrs. Oakley, the nursery governess whose name was Florence Cole, Marty, herself, and, in front beside the chauffeur, Mrs. Oakley's maid, who looked like an old retainer but had actually only been with her for a week. Nobody seemed to have been with her for very long except Marty. Florence Cole had done about ten days, and if Dorinda was any judge, she was rapidly working up to leave at the end of the month. The pay might be good, but Marty was definitely poison. As he bore no resemblance to his little fair-haired wisp of a mother, Dorinda concluded that he must take after Mr. Oakley, in which case it was perhaps not surprising that the latter had emerged from the war in the odour of prosperity. Marty was the most acquisitive little boy she had ever had the misfortune to meet. He wanted everything he saw, and bounced up and down on the well-sprung cushions demanding it at the top of his voice. If he didn't get it he roared like a bull, and Mrs. Oakley said fretfully, *"Really,* Miss Cole!"

The first thing he wanted was a small black goat tethered by the side of the road, which they passed in a flash but which he lamented loudly until his attention was caught by Dorinda's brooch. His mouth, which had been open to the fullest extent, fell to, cutting off a sirenlike scream half way up the scale, and a quite normal little boy's voice said, "What's that?" A grubby finger pointed.

Dorinda said, "It's a brooch."

"Why is it?"

"Why are you a little boy?"

Marty began to bounce.

"Why is it a brooch? I want to see it. Give it to me!"

"You can see it from there quite nicely, or you can come over here and look. It's a Scotch brooch. It belonged to my great-grandmother. Those yellow stones are cairngorms. They come out of the Cairngorm mountains."

"How do they come out?"

"People find them lying about there."

"I want to go there and find some—I want to go now."

Dorinda kept her head.

"It would be much too cold. There would be deep snow all over the place—you wouldn't be able to find the stones."

Marty had continued to bounce.

"How deep would the snow be?"

"It would be four foot six and a half inches. It would be right over your head."

Marty was a plain, dark little boy. A dull red colour came into his face. He bounced harder.

"I don't want it to be!"

Dorinda smiled at him.

"The snow will go away in summer."

He bounced right out of his seat.

"I want to go now! I want your brooch! Undo it, quick!"

"I can't do that."

"Why can't you? I want it!"

Mrs. Oakley, who had been leaning back with her eyes shut, now opened them and said in a hopeless tone,

"If he doesn't get it he'll scream."

Dorinda regarded her with interest.

"Do you always give him things when he screams?"

Mrs. Oakley closed her eyes again.

"Oh, yes. He goes on screaming till I do, and my nerves won't stand it."

Dorinda wondered if anyone had tried what a good hard smack would do. She almost asked the question, but thought perhaps she had better not. Marty was opening his mouth. A roar was obviously imminent. Her fingers tingled as she unfastened the brooch and held it out. With a carefree smile he took it, jabbed the pin into her leg as far as it would go, and with a shriek of laughter tossed the brooch clean out of the top of the window, which happened to be two or three inches open. By the time the car had been stopped it was extremely difficult to identify the spot. After a half-hearted search they drove on, leaving Dorinda's great-grandmother's brooch somewhere by the wayside.

"Marty has a marvellously straight eye," said Mrs. Oakley. "Martin will be so pleased. Fancy him getting right through the top of the window like that!"

Even Dorinda's sweet temper found it difficult to respond. Florence Cole had obviously given up trying. She was a pale, rather puffy young woman who had been brought up to breathe through her nose, however difficult. Whenever the car stopped she could be heard doing so.

Marty continued to bounce and scream—for a wild rabbit whose scut glimmered away into a hedgerow, for an inn sign depicting a white hart on a green ground, for a cat asleep inside a cottage window, and finally for chocolate. Upon which Miss Cole, still breathing hard, opened her bag and produced a bar. He went to sleep over it after smearing his face and hands profusely. The resultant peace was almost too good to be true.

He slept until they arrived at the Mill House. There was a lot of shrubbery round it, and a dark, gloomy drive overhung with trees went winding up to the top of the hill, where the house stood in the open, exposed to every point of the compass except the south. It was a very large and perfectly hideous house, with patterns of red and yellow brick running about at random, and frightful little towers and balconies all over the place. Mrs. Oakley shivered and said the situation was very bracing. And then Marty woke up and began to roar for his tea. Dorinda wondered whether she would be having nursery tea, and felt selfishly relieved when she found that she wouldn't. But she no longer expected Florence Cole to leave at the month. Her only doubt now was whether she would catch the last train tonight or the first tomorrow morning. In which case—no, she would *not* look after Marty—not for thousands a year—unless she had a free hand.

She had tea with Mrs. Oakley in a distressingly feminine apartment which she was thrilled to hear her employer call the boudoir. Dorinda had never encountered a boudoir before except in an old-fashioned novel. It lived up to her fondest dreams, with a rose and ivory carpet, rose and ivory curtains lined with pink, a couch with more cushions than she had ever before seen assembled at one time, and a general air of being tiresomely expensive.

Mrs. Oakley, in a rose-coloured negligée covered with frills, nestled among the cushions, whilst Dorinda sat on a horribly uncomfortable gold chair and poured out. Just as they were finishing, a knock came at the door. Mrs. Oakley said "Come in!" in a rather surprised voice, and Florence Cole, still in her outdoor things, advanced into the room. She wore an air of dogged purpose, and Dorinda knew what she was going to say before she opened her mouth. She said it in quite a loud, determined voice.

"I'm sorry, Mrs. Oakley, but I'm not staying. There's a train at six, and I'm catching it. I've given that child his tea, and left him with the housemaid. She tells me his old nurse is in the village, and that *she* can manage him. I can't. If there's anyone who can, you'd better have her back. He's just tried to pour the boiling kettle-water over my foot. If you ask me, he's not safe."

"He has such high spirits," said Mrs. Oakley.

"He wants a good whipping!" said Miss Cole. A dull colour came into her face. "Are you going to pay me for the ten days I've put up with him, Mrs. Oakley? You're not legally bound to, but I think anyone would say I'd earned it."

Mrs. Oakley looked bewildered.

"I don't know what I did with my purse," she said. "It will be somewhere in my bedroom—if you don't mind, Miss Brown. Perhaps you and Miss Cole could look for it together. It will be in that bag I had in the car."

When they had found it, and Florence Cole had been paid a generous addition to cover her railway fare, her manner softened.

"If you like, Mrs. Oakley, I can stop and see Nurse Mason on my way through the village. Doris says I can't miss the house."

Mrs. Oakley fluttered.

"Oh, no, you can't miss it. But perhaps she won't come back. My husband thought Marty was getting too old for a nurse. She was very much upset about it. Perhaps she won't come."

"Doris says she'll jump at it," said Florence Cole. "She says she's devoted to Marty." Her tone was that of one confronted by some phenomenon quite beyond comprehension.

Mrs. Oakley continued to flutter.

"Well, perhaps you'd better. But my husband mayn't like it—perhaps Miss Brown—"

"I couldn't possibly," said Dorinda with unmistakable firmness.

Mrs. Oakley closed her eyes.

"Well then, perhaps—yes, it will be very kind if you will—only I hope my husband—"

Florence Cole said, "Goodbye, Mrs. Oakley," and walked out of the room.

Dorinda went out on to the landing with her and shook hands.

"I hope you'll get a nice job soon," she said. "Have you anywhere to go?"

"Yes, I've got a married sister. Are you going to stay?"

"I shall if I can."

Florence Cole said, "Well, if you ask me, it's the kind of place to get out of."

Dorinda remembered that afterwards.

CHAPTER 5

It was about an hour and a half later that Dorinda knocked on what had been the nursery door. A voice said, "Come in!" and she had no sooner done so than she became aware that after a brief unhappy interlude as a schoolroom it had quite firmly reverted to being a nursery again. All Marty's clothes were airing in front of a fire, Marty was putting away his toys in a toy-cupboard, and a large, firm, buxom woman whom no one could have taken for anything but a nurse, was sitting up to the table darning socks. The scene was peaceful in the extreme, but there was an underlying feeling that if anything broke the peace, Nurse would want to know the reason why. Dorinda knew all about nurses. She had had a very strict old-fashioned one herself in the days before so much of Aunt Mary's money had been disposed of by the Wicked Uncle.

She said, "Good afternoon, Nurse," very respectfully, and then explained that Mrs. Oakley had asked her to find out whether she had everything she wanted.

Nurse Mason inclined her head and said in a tone which was more non-belligerent than neutral that what she hadn't got she would see about, thank you.

Marty stopped with a headless horse in his hand.

"Nannie says she never did see anything like the way my things is gone to rack an' ruin."

"That will be enough from you, Marty! You keep right on putting those toys away—and shocked I am to see the way they've been broke."

Marty thrust the mutilated horse out of sight and turned round with a cheerful smile.

"I've been a *very* naughty boy since you've been away, haven't I, Nannie?"

"You go on picking up your toys!"

With an armful of wreckage, Marty continued to discourse.

"I frowed her brooch out of the car"—he appealed to Dorinda for confirmation—"didn't I? And I digged a pin into her leg to make it bleed. Did it bleed, Miss Brown?"

"I haven't looked," said Dorinda.

Nurse had fixed a penetrating eye upon the culprit.

"Then you say you're sorry to Miss Brown this very

minute! Digging pins into people to make them bleed—
I never heard such a thing! More like naked heathen
savages than a child brought up in any nursery of mine!
Go and say you're sorry at once!"

Marty dropped all the toys he had gathered, advanced two paces, clasped his hands in front of him,
and recited in a rapid sing-song,

"I'm sorry I was a naughty boy and I won't do it
again."

There was a little talk about the brooch, Nurse being
much shocked on hearing that it had been a legacy from
a great-grandmother, and Marty contributing a few
facts about cairngorms and finishing up with,

"I frowed it as hard as shooting from a gun."

"I don't want to hear no more about it," said Nurse
with decision.

"And I frowed water out of the kettle on to Miss
Cole, and she put on her coat and hat and went away."

"That's enough, Marty! If those toys aren't back in
ten minutes, you know what will happen."

He bent strenuously to the task.

Dorinda turned to go, but just as she did so something caught her eye. When Marty dropped his armful it
had really been more of a throw than a drop. The
lighter things had scattered, amongst them a bent carte-
de-visite photograph. Dorinda picked it up and began
to straighten it out. At just what instant everything in
her began a landslide, she didn't know. She heard Nurse
say sharply,

"Marty, wherever did you get that photograph
from? Is it one of your mother's?"

And she heard him say, "It comed out of a box."

"What box did it come out of?"

"A box. And it was all crumpled up and stuck in
underneaf."

WICKED UNCLE • 31

Dorinda heard the words, but she didn't make anything of them. She was sliding much too fast. By making a simply tremendous effort she managed to say, "I'll see it's put back," and she managed to get out of the room.

Her own room was just across the landing. When she had locked herself in she sat down on the bed and gazed in unbelieving horror at the crumpled photograph. There wasn't any mistake. The name of the photographer was glaringly legible—"Charles Rowbecker and Son, Norwood." It was the twin photograph of the one in Aunt Mary's album. It was, incredibly but indisputably, a photograph of the Wicked Uncle.

CHAPTER 6

It was certainly a shock. Practically everyone has a relation whom they hope never to see again. There never has been, and probably never will be a time when this would occasion any particular remark. Dorinda sat and looked at the photograph and told herself what a perfectly ordinary thing it was to have a Wicked Uncle, and to find his photo doubled up among the nursery toys of your employer's brat. She had the feeling that if she could convince herself of the ordinariness of what had just happened she would stop feeling as if she might be going to be sick. The fact was that she had always had what she chose to call a complex about Glen Porteous. A very, very long time ago that famous charm of his had charmed her too. And then one night she woke up and heard him talking to Aunt Mary, and all the charm turned to bitter poison. She couldn't have been more than six years old, but she never forgot lying there in the dark and hearing them in the next room. The door must have been open, because she could hear quite well, and she never forgot, because it was the first time that she had heard a grown-up person cry. Aunt Mary had cried bitterly, and Uncle Glen had laughed at her as if she was doing something very amusing. After that he went away for about two years. Aunt Mary didn't cry any more, but she got very strict and cross.

Dorinda came back out of the past. It was dead, and Aunt Mary was dead. But was the Wicked Uncle dead too—that was the question. It wasn't a question to which she had any answer. His last appearance had been about seven years ago, when he had blown in and blown out again, leaving Aunt Mary noticeably more economical. She had rather taken it for granted that he was dead because he hadn't come back, but that might only have been because he thought that there wasn't any more to be had. As a matter of fact there was the fifty pounds a year which Dorinda had now, but he mightn't have known about it, and the rest of what Aunt Mary had being an annuity, he couldn't, even with the worst intentions in the world, put it in his pocket and walk off with it.

She stared at the photograph. It was the exact twin of the one in Aunt Mary's album. It showed a good-looking man with dark hair and very dark dancing eyes. The hair curled a little too visibly. The teeth showed in a smile which everyone who knew him had considered charming. Dorinda wondered when it had been taken. Not later than about fifteen years ago, because after that he only came to get what he could out of Aunt Mary, and he wouldn't have gone to a local photographer and given her a copy. She thought it must have been done when they were living at Norwood. Before the Row.

It was a long way from the time before the Row and Charles Rowbecker and Son to Marty's toy-cupboard and the Mill House. The most frightening idea came suddenly into her head. Suppose the Wicked Uncle was Martin Oakley. She was too sensible to encourage it, but it lurked. Hastily assembling reasons to disprove it, she recalled that Nurse had given the photograph no name. If it was a picture of Martin Oakley, wouldn't she have said, "What are you doing with your father's picture all crumpled up like that?" She stopped feeling sick and her spirits began to rise. After all, the very worst that could happen would be that she might have to leave her job. But she wouldn't have to—she felt quite reassured about that. Everyone has got old photograph albums full of junk. Aunt Mary had forgotten the names of a lot of people in hers. Uncle Glen's photograph was neither here nor there. It hadn't the slightest importance. It was just something out of a junkery. She was wearing a dress with large patch pockets. She slipped the photograph into one of them and went down.

It ought to have been the easiest thing in the world to walk into the boudoir, slap the photograph down in front of Mrs. Oakley, and say, "Marty had this knocking about in his toy-cupboard. I told Nurse I'd bring it down." But it wasn't. When she thought about doing it she couldn't even open the door and go in. It was too stupid. If Doris, who was one of the housemaids, hadn't come along the passage, she might have just stuck there and grown into the floor. As it was, she got herself inside the room and found it empty. Voices from the bedroom next door proclaimed that Mrs. Oakley was dressing for dinner.

With a feeling of relief, Dorinda put the photograph

down upon a gimcrack writing-table and ran upstairs to assume the despised blue dress.

When she came down again Mrs. Oakley had exchanged the sofa for the most comfortable of the armchairs. Her fluffy draperies were still pink, but of a different shade. The photograph was nowhere to be seen. No reference was made to it, which suited Dorinda very well. Anyone who had known Glen Porteous might have just as good reasons as she had herself for not wanting to talk about him.

They had a delightful meal on a tray. Dorinda told herself that there were going to be far too many meals, and all much too good, but it was a very pleasing change after the economical dullness of the food at the Heather Club.

They had no more than finished dinner, when the telephone bell rang. As it had been explained to her that her most important duty was to stand between Mrs. Oakley and the telephone, Dorinda went to it. The instrument stood upon the writing-table where she had put the photograph. She lifted the receiver and said,

"Mrs. Oakley's secretary speaking."

A man's voice said, "Will you tell Mrs. Oakley that Gregory Porlock would like to speak to her?"

She replaced the receiver and repeated the request. With her back to her, Mrs. Oakley murmured,

"I don't speak to anyone except Martin or someone I know very well indeed—never, never, *never*. He must talk to you, and you can tell me what he says."

Dorinda took up the receiver again.

"I'm sorry, Mr. Porlock—Mrs. Oakley asks me to explain that she never speaks on the telephone. I'm new, or I should have known. If you will tell me what you want to say, I will pass it on."

She heard Mr. Porlock smother a laugh. Well, that was better than getting his back up. He said,

"Will you tell her I saw her husband this afternoon? I'm having a week-end party, and he promised that he and his wife would join us for dinner on Saturday night. He said it would be all right, but as I haven't had the pleasure of meeting Mrs. Oakley yet I don't want to seem to be taking too much for granted."

Dorinda repeated this, and received the fretful reply that if Martin had said they would go, she supposed they would have to. The words were so barely audible that there were grounds for hoping that they would not carry as far as the Grange.

Dorinda conveyed a polite acceptance, and heard Mr. Porlock say, "Splendid!"

The word rang a bell somewhere. It reminded her of something or someone in one of those flashes which are so vivid whilst they last, and so impossible to recall when they are gone. She came out of a dizzying moment to hear him say,

"Now this is where I ought to be talking to Mrs. Oakley, because I want to ask her to be very kind and bring you along. Miss Brown, isn't it? . . . Yes, I thought that was what Martin Oakley said—Miss Dorinda Brown. Now will you be as persuasive as I should be myself and tell Mrs. Oakley that I am a lady short and I am particularly anxious to make your acquaintance."

Dorinda fixed a grave, frowning gaze upon the instrument. She considered Mr. Porlock's manner to be on the familiar side. She repeated his invitation in the baldest possible way.

"He says he is a woman short on Saturday, and will you bring me. He seems to have fixed it up with Mr. Oakley."

There was a murmur of assent. Dorinda put it into

words, again heard Gregory Porlock say, "Splendid!" and hung up.

When she came back to her seat she found herself the object of Mrs. Oakley's attention.

"What about an evening dress, Miss Brown? Have you one that will do?"

There really must be something wrong about that wretched blue dress, because Mrs. Oakley simply didn't consider it for a moment.

"Oh, no—that was what I was afraid of. Martin telephoned while I was dressing, and he said I must see that you had something suitable."

Dorinda wouldn't have been human if she had been pleased. She said in a restrained voice,

"There is no need for me to go."

Mrs. Oakley's face puckered up as if she were going to cry.

"Oh dear—now you are offended—and Martin will say I have no tact. And it isn't that I haven't really, but I do think being tactful is the most utterly exhausting thing, and my nerves won't stand it. It will be so much simpler if you just won't be offended. Because of course we couldn't expect you to have clothes which you didn't know you were going to want. And of course we shouldn't expect you to be put to any expense, if you know what I mean."

Dorinda knew quite well. She wasn't Dorinda Brown—she was an Appanage, an outward and visible sign of the Oakleys' financial standing. They could no more go out to dinner with a shabby secretary than with shabby liveries or an elderly broken-down car. Her Scottish pride stiffened.

And then she became aware that Mrs. Oakley was frightened. She was actually leaning forward, and the hand on the arm of her chair shook.

"Miss Brown—please don't be offended. You are quite a young girl—why should you mind if we give you a frock?"

A real person had emerged from behind the frills. Not a very grown-up person—not at all accustomed to letting go of its props, and very shaky without them. Dorinda's sweet temper reasserted itself. She said,

"But of course, Mrs. Oakley—it's very kind of you."

When Mrs. Oakley had gone to bed she rang up Justin Leigh.

"Look here, I'm coming up to town tomorrow. . . . Yes, I know you thought you'd got rid of me—I did too. But you haven't. There's going to be a reprieve—or perhaps you'll feel as if it was a relapse."

Justin's voice sounded cool and amused.

"I don't know that I should go as far as that. Is this leading up to the fact that you will lunch with me tomorrow if I press you very hard?"

"Yes—at one o'clock. Because I'm being sent up to buy a dress to dine out in on Saturday, and if we lunch together I can show you what I've got, and if you thought it wouldn't do, I could go back and change it."

"Nothing doing. I don't know where you're in the habit of lunching with Tip and Buzzer, but in my high-toned circles you can't try things on between courses."

Dorinda gave a sort of wail.

"Justin, sometimes I do think you are a beast!"

"Far from it—I am a noble hero. I shall wangle my lunch-hour between twelve and one and meet you at—where are you going?"

"Mrs. Oakley said any one of these . . ." She read from a list of names.

"All right, we'll take the big shop first. It will be easier for you to wait about for me there—let's say the glove counter. A connoisseur's eye can then direct your choice. What time do you get up?"

Dorinda was thrilled.

"Oh, Justin—will you really? I get up at half past ten. But that doesn't matter—I've got things to do for Mrs. Oakley. I can put in the time all right—in fact I shall want it. I'm to be at Mr. Oakley's office at a quarter past two, and he'll drive me down. It will be more peaceful than it was today—at least I hope so."

"Why, what happened today?"

She began to tell him about Marty and her brooch. If she made an amusing story of it, perhaps Justin would laugh. It appeared quite soon that he wouldn't. He actually sounded angry as he exclaimed,

"Your great-grandmother's brooch!"

"The only one I've got," said Dorinda ruefully. "I shall have to buy a gold safety-pin to fasten the things that just have to be fastened. I know where I can get one for seven-and-six."

"Then it won't be gold."

Dorinda giggled.

"You're so lordly. It won't be real of course—only rolled."

Justin lost his temper quite suddenly. She had never heard him do it before, and it surprised her very much. The odd thing was that she heard it go, like something breaking at the other end of the line. He couldn't have banged a door, but there was that kind of effect about it. After which he said in quite a violent tone, "I never heard such nonsense in my life!" and jammed the receiver back.

Dorinda went to bed a good deal heartened.

CHAPTER 7

Miss Maud Silver was choosing wool for a set of infant's vests. After the khaki and Air Force yarn she had knitted up during the war, to say nothing of useful grey stockings for her niece Ethel's three boys, it was a real pleasure to handle these soft blush-pink balls—all ready wound, and so much better than you could wind it yourself. Ethel's eldest brother, who had been abroad for so long, had come home some months ago, and his wife was expecting her first child. Quite an excitement in the family, because they had been married for ten years and the empty nursery had begun to have a discouraging effect upon Dorothy. Miss Silver felt that something rather special in the way of vests would be appropriate. This pale pink wool was a most charming colour, and so soft and light. She paid for her purchase, and stood waiting for her change and the parcel.

The wool was heaped in a profusion of delightful shades upon a large three-tiered stand where four departments met. Straight down the way she was facing there were stockings, gloves, handkerchiefs—behind her a long vista of inexpensive gowns. To the right, past a stand festooned with umbrellas, she had a view of pull-overs and knitwear. Whilst to her left a display of glass flowers, bead chains, and necklets conducted the eye to the millinery department. Miss Silver thought it all looked very bright and pretty. It was nice to see the shops filled up again after the lean years when even the cleverest window-dressing would not make things go round.

Someone else was admiring the chains and necklets. There were little bunches of flowers in glass and bright enamel—violets, daisies, a spray of holly, a spray of mimosa. The girl who was looking at them lingered over the mimosa. She had rather bright golden-brown hair, with eye-lashes of exactly the same colour, and she was wearing a loose coat of honey-coloured tweed. It was rather shabby, but it had been well cut, and it suited her. Miss Silver thought the mimosa spray would look very well on it. The girl evidently thought so too. She looked, and looked again, and then with a regretful sigh prepared to pass on.

It was just at that moment that a number of people began to stream forward from the stocking counter in the direction of Millinery. To do this they had to pass the girl in the tweed coat. She became entangled amongst them. Miss Silver watched with interest and attention. The attention became very alert. She saw the girl in the tweed coat disengage herself and move in the direction of the handkerchief counter. Miss Silver observed a small dark woman in the group emerge upon the other side of it and go up to the assistant behind the counter. She appeared to say something in rather a hurried manner, after which she hastened in the wake of her companions and was lost to view.

Miss Silver turned to receive her parcel and her change. She then hurried in the direction of Handkerchiefs. She was not in time. Dorinda Brown, with an expression of astonishment upon her face, was being shepherded down the aisle by a very imposing shopwalker. As they turned first to the left, and then to the right, and then to the left again, this look changed to one of frowning intensity. She didn't know what was happening, but she didn't like it. Why should she be asked to step round to the manager's office? She didn't want to see him, and she could think of no possible reason why he should want to see her.

They arrived at a door of marvellously polished wood, so bright that you could see your face in it, and the next moment Dorinda was walking into a very grand office with a large and quite bald-headed man sitting at a table and looking coldly at her through horn-rimmed glasses, while a voice from behind her said,

"Shoplifting, sir."

A wave of indignant scarlet rushed right up to the roots of Dorinda's hair. You may have the sweetest temper in the world, but to be called a thief by a perfectly strange shopwalker is just pure dynamite. The temper went sky-high, and Dorinda stamped her foot and said,

"How dare you!"

The manager appeared to be completely unimpressed. He said in what Dorinda considered a very offensive voice,

"Will you hand the things over, or will you be searched?"

The voice over the top of Dorinda's head said,

"I expect they'll be in the pockets of her coat."

At this moment Miss Silver walked into the room without knocking—a dowdy little woman who looked as if she might have been somebody's governess during the early years of the century. She wore a serviceable black cloth coat which had only done two winters, and a little yellow fur tippet of uncertain ancestry. Her hat, which had been new in the autumn, was of the kind which looks the same age for about ten years and then falls to pieces. It was made of black felt with a purple velvet starfish in front and a niggle of black and purple ribbon running all round the crown. Under the hat Miss

Silver's neatly coiled mousy hair preserved the early Edwardian fashion. An Alexandra fringe in a net cage surmounted her neat elderly features and the small greyish hazel eyes which, according to Detective Sergeant Abbott of Scotland Yard, always saw a little more than there was to see.

The manager's horn-rimmed glasses were turned upon her in a petrifying stare.

Miss Silver showed no sign of being petrified. With a slight introductory cough she advanced to the edge of the table.

"Good-morning."

"Madam, this is my private office."

Miss Silver inclined her head with so much dignity that an awful doubt entered the managerial mind. Dowdiness did not always imply poverty or a lowly status. Sometimes the very wealthy or the very celebrated affected it. There was a dowager duchess of dreadfully formidable character—

Miss Silver was saying, "If you will allow me—"

He stopped trying to place her and in quite a polite tone enquired her business.

Miss Silver coughed again, graciously this time. No words had passed, but there had been an apology. She accepted it. In the days, now happily left behind, when she had been a governess, she had maintained a firm but gentle discipline among her pupils. The habit persisted. The authority was in her voice as she said,

"My name is Maud Silver. I was completing the purchase of some pink wool, when I happened to witness the incident which has, I think, resulted in this lady being requested to come to your office."

"Indeed, madam?"

Dorinda turned her eyes upon the little woman in

black. They burned with indignation. Her colour burned too. She said in a young, clear voice,

"You couldn't possibly have seen anything—there wasn't anything to see!"

Miss Silver met the indignant gaze with a steady one.

"If you will put your hands in your pockets you will, I think, see reason to change your mind."

Without an instant's hesitation Dorinda drove both hands into the pockets of her tweed coat. They were deep and capacious. They should have been empty. They were not empty. The fact struck her a blow which was as hard as it was unexpected. She felt as if she had missed a step and come down in the dark. Her eyes widened, her colour rose brightly. Her hands came up out of the pockets with a scatteration of stockings, handkerchiefs, and ribbon.

The shopwalker said something, but it didn't reach Dorinda. She stood looking at the silk stockings, the handkerchiefs, the trailing ribbons, whilst the bright angry colour in her cheeks drained away until it was all gone. Then she stepped forward and put all the things down on the table and felt again in the pockets of her coat. There was one more pair of stockings, and the mimosa spray which she had thought would look so nice on the lapel of her coat. She put it down with the other things and said steadily,

"I don't know how these things got into my pockets."

The manager looked at her in a way that made her Scottish blood boil.

"Oh, you don't, don't you? Well, I think we can make a pretty good guess. We shall charge you with shoplifting. And if this lady will kindly give us her address, we can call her as a witness. Perhaps you won't mind saying what you saw, madam."

Miss Silver drew herself up.

"I have come here to do so. After completing a purchase I was waiting for my parcel and the change, when I saw this lady standing looking at the display of glass flowers and necklets at the corner leading to the millinery department. She seemed to be admiring that little bunch of mimosa, and I thought perhaps she was going to buy it. It would certainly have looked very well upon her coat. She was just about to turn away, when a number of people came from the direction of the stocking counter. I do not know whether they were all in one party. By the time they reached her this lady had moved away from the place where she had been. I should like to state quite definitely that the mimosa spray was still in its place when she had moved at least a yard away from it and was heading in the opposite direction. There were two young women in the party from the stocking counter. They closed up on either side of this lady. By this time there were quite a number of people coming and going between the departments. Sometimes they were between me and the two young women, and sometimes they were not. I am prepared to swear that this lady never turned back, and that she could not possibly have taken the mimosa spray. I was interested in her, and there was never a time when I could not see at least the top of her head. She could not have reached the mimosa spray from where she was, and she did not turn back. That is the first point. The second one is this. As the people moved on, there were naturally gaps between them. Through one such gap I saw one of the two young women I have mentioned in the act of withdrawing her hand from this lady's coat pocket. At this moment the attendant at the wool stall offered me my parcel and the change I had been waiting for. I saw the young woman say something to an assistant behind the counter and hurry away. By the time I had taken my parcel there were a good many people between us. When I arrived at the counter both young women had disappeared and the assistant was making a somewhat agitated communication to the shopwalker. I noticed that the mimosa spray was gone. When I saw the shopwalker address this lady, who was by then approaching the handkerchief counter, I realized that my evidence would be required and decided to follow them."

The manager was leaning back in his chair. He said in a sceptical voice,

"You say you saw a young woman put her hand into this girl's pocket?"

Miss Silver coughed in a hortatory manner.

"I stated that I saw her in the act of withdrawing her hand from this lady's pocket. I am perfectly prepared to swear to what I saw."

The manager raised his eyebrows.

"Very convenient for the young woman, I am sure. Quite a good idea, if you're going shoplifting, to have someone handy to swear you couldn't have done it."

Miss Silver turned upon him the look before which the hardiest of her pupils had been wont to quail. It was a look which had daunted the evil-doer on many an occasion. Since then Chief Detective Inspector Lamb himself had been halted by it and brought to unwilling apology. It went straight through the manager's self-esteem and stripped him to his bare bones. He found them chilly and uncertain of their footing. When you have been kept together by conventions and clothed with observances, it is very disintegrating to be left without them.

"I beg your pardon," said Miss Maud Silver.

The manager found himself apologizing. She had spoken quite quietly, and he knew now that she was neither an eccentric duchess nor any lesser member of the aristocracy. But the authority behind that quiet tone had him rattled. He paused in his not very well chosen phrases and discovered that he was being addressed. He had the quite unwarranted feeling that he was being addressed from a platform. He had the unusual feeling of being something rather lowly in the scale of creation.

Miss Silver treated this frame of mind with firmness.

"You would, perhaps, care for me to furnish you with proofs of my credibility as a witness. This is my business card."

From the shabby black bag which depended from her left wrist she produced and laid before him a small, neat pasteboard rectangle. It displayed her name in the middle—*Miss Maud Silver,* with, in the left-hand bottom corner, an address, *15 Montague Mansions, S.W.,* and in the corresponding right-hand corner, the words, *Private Enquiries.*

As he absorbed this information, Miss Silver continued to address him.

"If you will be so good as to ring up Scotland Yard, Chief Detective Inspector Lamb will tell you that he knows me well, and that I am a person to be believed. Detective Sergeant Abbott, or in fact any of the officers on the detective side, will be able to assure you that I have the confidence of the police. If, of course, you are prepared to admit that a mistake has been made, and to offer to this young lady an unqualified apology, we need not trouble Scotland Yard."

The manager, thus baited, turned with ferocity upon the shopwalker. His diminished ego obtained some helpful support from having a subordinate at hand to bully.

"Mr. Sopeley!"

"Sir?"

"On what evidence did you act? This lady says that one of the assistants came up and spoke to you. Who was it, and what did she say?"

Mr. Sopeley began to see before him the unenviable rôle of the scapegoat. An elderly survivor of the war period, his tenure was not so secure that he could afford to have it shaken. With a feeling that his collar had suddenly become too tight for him, he stumbled into speech.

"It—it was Miss Anderson. She said a lady had whispered to her that this—" he paused and swallowed—"this young lady was filling her pockets, and she thought she ought to mention it."

"Then why is she not here as a witness?"

"She said she had a train to catch," said Mr. Sopeley in an ebbing voice.

The manager's bald head became suffused with an angry flush.

"Miss Anderson should have detained her."

Perceiving a possible ram in a thicket, Mr. Sopeley agreed that Miss Anderson had been very remiss, though just how she could have detained a determined customer in full flight to catch a train, neither he nor the manager was prepared to say. In a tone of virtuous indignation he remarked,

"I spoke to her quite severely on that point, sir."

Miss Silver intervened.

"It is perfectly clear that this woman who brought the accusation and then disappeared is the person who placed the stolen goods in this young lady's pockets. I would press you now to ring up Scotland Yard. A full and unqualified apology is due to this young lady, and I shall not be satisfied until it has been offered."

Chief Detective Inspector Lamb lifted the receiver

from the instrument on his office table. The voice of Sergeant Abbott came to him.

"I say, Chief, here's a lark! I've got the manager of the De Luxe Stores on the line, wanting to know if Maudie is a credible witness! He's asking for you. An offensive fellow—perhaps you'd like to crush him yourself."

Lamb grunted.

"What's it all about?"

"Case of shoplifting. Maudie says the girl was framed. Says she saw a woman put a hand into her pocket, afterwards skipping to an assistant to lay information, and then vanishing from the scene to catch a train. Shall I put you through?"

Lamb's grunt must have conveyed assent. It was followed by a click and the impact on his ear of a voice which he thoroughly disliked. A shrewd and experienced observer of human nature, he deduced the man who has made a bloomer and is trying to bluster his way out. He stemmed the current by announcing himself.

"Chief Detective Inspector Lamb speaking." Every syllable slowly and ponderously fraught with authority.

The manager had to begin all over again, and didn't like it. He began to wish that he had apologized to Dorinda Brown and left Scotland Yard alone.

The Chief Inspector stopped him before he had got very far.

"I have nothing to do with what happened in your shop. If you wish to charge anyone, it is a matter for the local station. In so far as your inquiries relate to Miss Maud Silver, I am prepared to deal with them. I know her very well and can assure you that she is an entirely credible witness. She has been of great use to the police on many occasions, and if I may say so, you would be well advised to be guided by her opinion. If she says this girl is innocent, you'd better believe her—she knows what she's talking about. One moment—I will speak to her, just to make sure of her identity."

In the manager's office Miss Silver took up the receiver with a preliminary cough.

"Chief Inspector Lamb? How very pleasant to hear your voice! You are well, I hope? . . . And Mrs. Lamb? . . . And the daughters?"

When the compliments were over Lamb was pleased to relax into a chuckle.

"What have you been up to?"

"My dear Chief Inspector!"

The chuckle became a laugh.

"Had to come to the police to get you out of it—eh? Now, you know, that's very pleasant for us—isn't it?"

"I am always quite certain that I can rely upon you," said Miss Silver gravely. She handed the receiver back to the manager, whose bald head had now assumed the colour of a beetroot, and stepped back.

Made aware of the change, Lamb said briskly and ungrammatically,

"There's only one Miss Silver, and that's her all right."

CHAPTER 8

Justin Leigh was a little puzzled by his Dorinda. She had remembered to wear clothes which he had once commended. She appeared to be in perfect health, and she seemed to be extremely pleased to see him. But all the same, there was something. Her attention wavered, and he missed the zest which should have accompanied the selection of a fur-below at somebody else's expense. Mrs. Oakley's ideas on the subject of what should be paid for an evening frock seemed to be thoroughly sound.

Dorinda, who had never scaled such giddy heights, ought to have been leaping from peak to peak with carefree enthusiasm, instead of which she remained aloof. It wasn't until The Dress had been extracted from some inner shrine and reverentially displayed that she seemed to be taking any interest at all.

The Dress had a compelling effect. She said "Oh!" and her colour rose. Justin remarked that she had better try it on, and she retired to do so.

When she came out in it there were of course no doubts. It was It. It had that magic touch so impossible to describe. It moulded, and it flowed. It was dead plain. By some subtle art the unrelieved black made her hair look richer than gold. It brightened her eyes, it brightened her skin.

Justin said in rather an odd tone,

"That's the ticket. Go and take it off, or there won't be time to have any lunch."

When the dress had been packed up and a vast sum paid for it, they took it away with them.

Justin had found a new place for lunch, their table pleasantly retired in a shallow recess. It being now possible to converse, he looked at her very directly and said,

"What's the matter?"

He was a good deal concerned when she turned very pale and said with a shake in her voice,

"I nearly got arrested for shoplifting."

Concern became something more as she poured it all out.

"If it hadn't been for Miss Silver, they would have

arrested me. It's given me the most frightful sort of giddy feeling—like thinking you're on quite an ordinary path, and all of a sudden your foot goes down and there isn't anything there. I expect you've done it in dreams— I have, often. But it's never happened when I was awake—not till this morning."

When the waiter had come and gone he made her tell it all over again.

"Had you ever seen any of those people before?"

"No. Miss Silver wanted to know about that. We went and had coffee together after they had apologized. She's a marvel. She knows everyone at Scotland Yard, so of course they had to listen to her. She simply flattened that awful manager."

The memory cheered her a good deal. "But, Justin, she said was there anyone who would like to get me into trouble, or get me out of the way, and of course I said no. Because it couldn't—it simply couldn't have anything to do with the Wicked Uncle—could it?"

"What do you mean?"

"Well, there was a photograph of him all crumpled up in Marty's toy-cupboard."

"Dorinda!"

She nodded.

"Well, there was. It was the twin of the one Aunt Mary had—Charles Rowbecker & Son, Norwood. And I put it on Mrs. Oakley's writing-table, and I didn't say anything to her, and she didn't say anything to me. Justin—it couldn't be that!"

He looked handsome and remote. A dreadful feeling that perhaps she was boring him came over her. She said in a hurry,

"We needn't go on talking about it."

Still handsome but not so remote, he frowned and told her not to be silly.

"But, Justin, you looked bored."

"That's just my unfortunate face. The brain was getting to work. Look here, Dorinda—why did you go to that shop at all?"

"I had some things to do for Mrs. Oakley."

"My good child, you're not going to tell me that Martin Oakley's wife shops at the De Luxe Stores! Modes for the Million, and a Brighter and Better Bourgeoisie!"

Dorinda giggled.

"Not for herself, she doesn't. But someone told her they'd got luminous paint, so she told me to go there and see. Because Marty's got his old nurse back and she isn't a bit pleased because he's been allowed to chip all the stuff off the night-nursery clock and she can't see what time it is when she wakes up in the dark. So I was to go there and see if I could get some."

"Who knew that you were going there?"

"Well, Mrs. Oakley—and Nurse—and Doris, who is the girl who does the nurseries—and—well, I should think practically everyone else in the house, because Marty kept telling everyone I was going to buy him some shiny paint because he had been a *very* naughty boy and had scraped it off the clock. And every time he said it Nurse came in with how difficult it was to get, but she did hear they had some at the De Luxe Stores. But I don't know who told her."

Justin's frown deepened.

"If that was a frame-up, it was arranged by someone who knew you were going to the damned shop. Are you sure you had never seen anyone in that crowd before?"

Dorinda shook her head.

"Oh, no, I hadn't."

"Well, it doesn't sound as if it could have been a case of having to get rid of the stuff because the thief was under suspicion. She would never have risked speaking to the assistant if it had been like that. Look here, I don't like it. I think you'd better clear out of this job. You can ring Mrs. Oakley up and say that an acute family crisis has arisen, and that you have been called to your Aunt Jemima's death-bed."

"Justin, I couldn't. Even if she didn't know—and she does—that I haven't got an aunt in the world, I couldn't possibly. I've just spent twenty pounds of her money on a dress, and I've got to work it out."

Justin looked angrier than she had ever seen him.

"You can take the damned thing back!"

"They wouldn't give me the money," said Dorinda with conviction. "They'd just say they would put it to Modom's credit, and that wouldn't be any use at all, because Mrs. Oakley wouldn't shop there for herself— she told me so. She said they had very nice inexpensive little frocks for girls, but of course she had to pay a great deal more for her own things. So you see, I can't possibly."

Justin leaned across the table.

"Dorinda—let me lend you the twenty pounds."

Gratitude made Dorinda's eyes look exactly like peat-water with the sun on it.

"I think that's absolutely noble of you. But of course I can't let you."

"You must."

"Darling, I can't. Aunt Mary would get right up and haunt me. It was one of her very strictest things—never let a man speak to you unless he's introduced, never let a man pay your debts, never let a man lend you money. And when you've had that sort of thing soaked into you for as long as you can remember, you just *can't*—not even if you try."

"Relations are quite different," said Justin.

Dorinda shook her head.

"Not when they're men. Aunt Mary had a special thing about cousins. She said they were insidious."

Justin burst out laughing, which relieved the emotional strain. Just why there should have been a strain, he wasn't clear. He had felt angrier than he could remember to have done for quite a long time, and when Dorinda began to be obstinate, an urge out of a neolithic past had suggested to him how pleasant it would be to knock her over the head and drag her to a cave by the hair. The suggestion did not, of course, arrive in words, but this was what it amounted to.

The laughter carried it away, but Dorinda's obstinacy remained. She wanted to keep her job, she wanted to keep her twenty-pound dress, she didn't want to go back to the Heather Club, and she was thrilled through and through because of Justin being really angry and really interested. It wasn't Aunt Mary who had told her that a man only scolds a woman when he is fond of her. It was Judith Crane, the girl who had annoyed the old ladies at the Heather Club by having so many baths and going out with so many young men. One way and another Dorinda had learned quite a lot from Judith Crane. Aunt Mary's foundation-laying had been very solid and sound but the lighter touches had been wanting, and having suffered from a Wicked Uncle had, perhaps naturally, given her a poor view of men. They had to be, but the less you had to do with them the better for your peace of mind.

With all this at the back of her thoughts, Dorinda continued to glow with gratitude and to say no to the twenty pounds. She also ate a very good lunch and recurred at intervals to the subject of Miss Maud Silver.

"She gave me her card, and she said if I had any more trouble to let her know at once. I told her I couldn't pay a fee or anything like that, and she said it didn't matter—just to let her know. Justin, she's rather a pet. She patted my hand, and she said, 'My dear, there was a time when I was a young girl earning my living in other people's houses. I have so much to be grateful for that I like to pay a little of the debt when I can.' "

In the end Justin gave up. He had something to give Dorinda, and if he wrangled with her up to the last moment, the atmosphere would be all wrong. Not that there was any wrangling on Dorinda's side. She just glowed, and called him darling, and went on saying no. He began to feel that he must be making a fool of himself. What he wanted for his little presentation was the attitude of the kind, indulgent cousin, but he didn't find it easy to come by.

Dorinda gave him an opening by opining that she would just have time to shop her rolled-gold safety-pin before she had to meet Mr. Oakley at his office. Justin dived into his pocket and produced something in an envelope.

"This will look nicer than a safety-pin—at least I hope you'll think so. It belonged to my mother."

"Oh, Justin!" Her colour changed brightly.

Inside the envelope was a shabby little brown leather case, and inside the case, on a background of ivory velvet which had turned as yellow as the keys of an old piano, there was a shining brooch. Dorinda gazed at it and felt quite unable to speak. The interlaced double circle of small bright diamonds caught the light. She lifted swimming eyes to Justin's face.

"You like it?"

She took a long breath.

"It's much too lovely!"

"Put it on."

Half way to her throat her hands remained suspended.

"Justin—you oughtn't to—I mean I oughtn't to take it. If it was your mother's, oughtn't you to keep it? Because when you get married—" She stopped there, because the idea of Justin getting married hurt so frightfully that she couldn't go on.

There was a curious emotional moment. Justin looked at her rather gravely and said,

"What sort of girl do you think I ought to marry?"

It was of course quite easy to answer this, though it hurt like knives and daggers. Dorinda had always known exactly the sort of girl that Justin would marry, and within the last few months, from being a type, this girl had become someone with a name. Dorinda had seen her photograph in a gossipy weekly—"Mr. Justin Leigh and Miss Moira Lane." She cut out the picture and kept it, and one day when she was feeling extra brave she asked Justin, "Who is Moira Lane?" and got a frown and a casual "Oh, just a girl I know." After that she saw them together once or twice—at lunch when she was out with Tip, and at the theatre with Buzzer. Moira Lane always looked just the same—as if she knew exactly what to do and how to do it. She was very, very decorative of course, but she might have been that and yet all wrong for Justin. It was that look of being dead right and dead sure of being right which ran the splinter of ice into Dorinda's heart. She laid the brooch back on its ivory bed and began to draw strokes on the tablecloth with the tip of her finger.

"Tall, and of course very, very slim, only not thin—you don't like thin girls, do you? And perhaps very fair hair—only I don't know that that matters very much as long as it's beautifully done. And very, very smart, with all the right clothes, and knowing just where to get them. And what you do and what you don't do, and just the right kind of makeup, and when a thing's dead and you just can't be seen with it any more. Because, you know, all that sort of thing is very difficult unless you've been brought up to it, only even then some people are much better at it than others—and you'd have to have someone who was *really* good at it."

"Would I?"

"Oh, yes, Justin. Because you notice everything, and you can't bear it if there's the least thing wrong. You like everything to be perfect, so you would have to marry a girl who would never, never make a mistake."

She pushed the little brown leather case across the table, not looking at it, because her eyes never left his face. He picked it up and put it down in front of her.

"She would probably think my mother's brooch old-fashioned. I think I'd rather you had it. Suppose you put it on."

"Oh, Justin!"

"My darling child, don't be ridiculous. I shouldn't give it to you if I didn't want you to have it. . . . No, that's not right—a little higher up. . . . That will do." He looked at his wrist watch and got up briskly. "I shall have to fly. Be a good child. And continue to report progress."

CHAPTER 9

Mrs. Oakley had been wishing all the morning that she hadn't sent Dorinda up to town. Any of the three houses to which she had directed her would have been only too pleased to send down a selection of suitable frocks in response to a request from Mrs. Martin Oakley. And the De Luxe Stores could have been rung up. There was nothing else that couldn't have waited. As it was, she was going to be alone all day. Martin wouldn't be down till four o'clock at the very earliest, because Dorinda was only to meet him at half past two, and that meant he wouldn't get started till three, and it might be much later than that. Things always seemed to turn up at the last moment in offices.

Her ideas about Martin's office were rather mingled. She hated it because it took him away from her, but if he didn't go to it there wouldn't be any money, and she would hate it if there weren't any money. There had been a time in her life when there had been, first very little money, and then no money at all. There had been only one room, and there hadn't always been enough to eat. She had had to try and clean the room herself, with the result that her hands became exceedingly dirty, and the room didn't seem to get any cleaner. She had had to try to cook, but the results wouldn't bear thinking about. For years she had never let herself think about that time, but today she couldn't help it. The dreadful sordid memories came crowding into her mind. It was like having a lot of dirty tramps in her nice clean house. They went everywhere, and did just what they liked. They had kept her awake in the night, and when she slept they had walked in and out of her dreams.

She oughtn't to have let Dorinda go. There were quite a lot of things they could have done together. There were all those patterns for the new curtains and covers for the drawing-room—they could have had them out and looked at them. It would have taken the best part of the morning. After lunch Dorinda could have read to her or talked to her, and by teatime she could have been looking forward to Martin's arrival.

Whereas now there was the whole empty, dragging day with no one to talk to. Nurse didn't really care about her coming into the nursery. She was very polite, but she and Marty always gave her the feeling that she was interrupting something. She could feel them going back to it with relief almost before she was out of the room. If her new maid had been different, the morning could have been got through quite easily. She had a lot of clothes and it would have been quite interesting to talk to Hooper about them. The trouble was that Hooper wouldn't talk. She knew her duties, and she knew how to carry them out, but that was as far as it went. She said, "Yes, madam," and she said, "No, madam," and if she had to say more than that she cut it as short as possible.

In Dorinda's absence Hooper had to answer the telephone when the bell rang just before lunch.

"Mr. Porlock, madam."

"Ask what he wants, Hooper. He knows I don't come to the telephone."

After a pause Hooper's wooden face was turned towards her again.

"He asks to see you, madam—an important message for Mr. Oakley. He says he will call at two o'clock."

Mrs. Oakley sounded a little fluttered.

"But I ought to be resting—I did not sleep at all well last night. Tell him—tell him—that Mr. Oakley ought to be here by half past four—"

Hooper was replacing the receiver.

"Mr. Porlock has hung up, madam."

At two o'clock precisely Gregory Porlock rang the front door bell at the Mill House. Both as a bell and as an expensive if mistaken piece of workmanship, it could fairly be described as loud. He could actually hear it ringing, just as he could presently hear the footsteps of the butler coming to let him in.

Mrs. Oakley, it appeared, would see him upstairs in her own sitting-room. He was conducted by way of a massive staircase and a landing, where a buhl cabinet contained some remarkably ugly china, to a corridor at the end of which a door was thrown open and he was announced.

"Mr. Gregory Porlock—"

Mrs. Oakley looked up from the book which she hadn't been reading, to see a big man in brown country tweeds. He had a handkerchief up to his face—a brown silk handkerchief with a green and yellow pattern on it. And then the door shut behind him. His hand with the handkerchief in it dropped to his side, and she saw that it was Glen. She was so frightened that though she opened her mouth to scream, nothing happened, because she hadn't any breath to scream with. She just sat there staring at him with the whites of her eyes showing and her mouth like a pale stretched O.

Gregory Porlock put his handkerchief away and mentally commended his luck. She might have screamed before the butler was out of earshot. He had just had to chance it. She wouldn't come to the telephone, and the one maxim of behaviour which he regarded as sacrosanct was, "Never put anything on paper."

He came and sat in the opposite corner of the sofa, after which he put out his hand and said in a pleasant conversational voice,

"Well, Linnet, I thought it would be you, but I had to make sure. It wouldn't have done to have you arriving with Martin to dinner on Saturday and staging a great recognition scene right in front of everyone."

As she continued to gaze at him in frozen horror he took her by the hand.

"My dear girl, pull yourself together! I'm not going to eat you."

Perhaps it was the warm, virile clasp and the dancing light in the dark eyes, perhaps it was the memories which these evoked. Her gaze wavered. She gave a sort of gasp and said,

"I thought you were dead—oh, Glen!"

Gregory Porlock nodded.

"I don't look dead—do I? Or feel dead either."

He had both of her hands by now, and he could feel them quivering and jerking like two little frightened wild things. He kept his hold of them and said,

"Come along, wake up! There's nothing for you to get into a state about. I don't want to hurt you, or to dig up the past. Everything suits me well enough the way it is. You wouldn't have seen hair, hide, or hoof of me if it hadn't been that Martin and I are in on a business deal together, so I knew we'd be bound to meet, and I thought we'd better get it over in private."

Even the weakest creature will fight when it has everything to lose. Linnet Oakley freed her hands with a sudden jerk.

"Why did you go away and let me think you were dead?"

"My dear child, what a question! I had a chance and I took it. We were just about down to bedrock bottom, weren't we? One of the most unpleasant sections of a not uneventful life—there was really nothing to be gained by prolonging it."

She said, "You didn't think what might happen to me."

Gregory Porlock laughed.

"On the contrary, my dear, I was quite sure that my

Linnet would find a new perch. And so she did—a much better, firmer, more substantial perch. How does the song go?

> She's a beautiful . . . something . . . something,
> In a beautiful gilded cage."

Linnet Oakley hit out like a bird pecking. He laughed again.

"Oh, stop being silly! I know it's hard for you, but we haven't got all day. Get this into your head and keep it there. Seven years ago you were seven years younger than you are today, and about ten years prettier. When I faded out and you very sensibly made up your mind to consider me dead, you could be quite sure of that new perch I spoke about. If you do anything silly now and forfeit your present very comfortable position, I don't quite see what's going to become of you. Don't look so frightened—there's no reason at all why you shouldn't go on just as you are. I suppose you told Martin that you were a widow?"

She had begun to cry.

"I thought I was—I thought you were dead—"

The dancing eyes laughed into hers.

"I'm afraid the brutal courts in this country rather expect a death certificate. Naturally you hoped that I had perished, because it was going to be so very convenient for you to marry Martin. But it was rather a case of the wish being father to the thought, and I've got a feeling that the courts wouldn't be very sympathetic about it. Let me see—how long had you been hoping I was dead before you married Martin—six months? . . . Oh, nine? Well, I don't say that I should have expected to be mourned for longer than that. But the law is so conventional that I'm afraid it takes rather a poor view of bigamy."

He wondered whether he had pushed her too far, because she did scream then. It wasn't a loud scream—too frightened for that—but a scream of any kind is quite a difficult thing to explain away. He changed his bantering tone to a frank and simple one.

"Look here, Linnet, you don't have to be frightened of me. I don't want a show-down any more than you do—it wouldn't suit my business plans. Of course I haven't broken the law, and you have. But I don't want my plans upset, so I've no reason to want to upset your marriage. You've got a boy, haven't you?"

She looked at him with a new terror in her eyes.

"Oh—*Marty*—"

"All right, all right—nobody's going to hurt him. Now you just listen to me! Do you think you can hold your tongue?"

"Oh, yes—"

"Well, I shouldn't suppose you could for a moment if it were about anything else. But with everything you've got in this world at stake, you will at any rate try. No sobbing it all out on Martin's shoulder, because if you do, he'll put you out in the street and I'll put you in court for bigamy. The first word you say to him or to anyone, you're for it. Have you got that?"

"Yes, Glen—"

"And don't you go calling me Glen, or you'll do it by mistake one day. Remember my name's Gregory Porlock, and my friends call me Greg. You'd better start thinking about me as Greg and talking about me as Greg until it comes natural and you don't want to do anything else. And for any sake stop looking as if I was going to murder you!"

She did look just like that—like a creature that sees

the knife coming nearer and knows there is no help—
every muscle strained and taut, the fixed terror in the
eyes. There was a sick wincing every time any movement brought him nearer. He made such a movement
now, reaching forward to pat her on the shoulder.

"My dear girl, you never did have much in the way
of brains, but if you'll just take a pull on yourself and
listen to what I'm going to say you ought to be able to
take it in, and once you've got hold of it you'll feel a
whole lot better. Now listen! I don't want to upset your
marriage to Martin Oakley. Got that?"

She gave a brief shaky nod.

"Well, hold on to it! There's no need for anyone to
know we've ever met before. If you hold your tongue,
I'll hold mine. If you go blabbing to Martin, or to any
other living soul, the bargain's off, because the minute
anyone knows, I shall be bound to take proceedings.
Got that?"

Another of those trembling nods.

"It's a bargain which is entirely in your favor. You
keep Martin and Martin's money, you keep your position and reputation, you keep your child and you keep
out of prison. It's quite a lot—isn't it? In return I only ask
you to do two things. The first is to hold your tongue. It
will be quite interesting to see if you can do it. The second—" He paused, looking at her with smiling intensity.

Some of the terror had left her. It was like a pain
which has ebbed, but which may begin again at any moment. As he sat back in his sofa corner and looked at
her in that smiling way, she felt the preliminary stab.

"Listen, Linnet! The second thing is something I want
you to do for me. It's quite simple and easy, and when
you've done it I won't bother you any more. Martin and I
are in a business deal together. Naturally each of us has
his own interest to think of. Now it would be to my

advantage if I knew something which Martin knows. When he comes down this afternoon he will have some papers with him which I very much want to see. They'll be in his attaché case and I want to have a look at them."

"I can't—I can't—I can't!"

"Now what's the use of saying that? It's as easy as kissing your hand. When Martin goes to dress for dinner, where does he generally put that case of his?"

"In the study. But I can't—and the case is locked—"

"The study—that's the room under this?"

"But I can't!"

"My dear Linnet, I don't want to lose my temper, but if you go on with these senseless repetitions I probably shall, and then you won't like it. You never did, did you?"

She shuddered from head to foot. The past came up in small, bright pictures, quite clear, quite dreadful, quite terrifying. No one who hadn't seen Glen lose his temper could possibly believe how dreadful it was.

He laughed.

"All right. You do what you're told and there won't be any unpleasantness. This is what you've got to do. While Martin is dressing you'll take that case with the papers in it and put it outside the study window on the window-sill, and you'll leave the window unlatched. Now that's absolutely all I'm asking you to do. It won't take half a minute, and there's no risk about it at all. The case will be back again on the study table before you've finished your dinner, and Martin will never know it's been out of the house. If you feel like wandering in and fastening the window any time after ten o'clock, it wouldn't be at all a bad thing."

She said in a dreadfully frightened voice,

"I can't do it—"

"Quite easy, you know."

Her hands twisted in her lap.

"I know I'm stupid about money, but I'm not as stupid as you think. If I let you see those papers, you'll be making money, and Martin will be losing it."

"Perfectly correct. Quite a lot of money too. Now just go on being intelligent for a moment. How much do you think Martin would pay to save your reputation and keep you out of the dock? To say nothing about saving his son from being publicly exposed as illegitimate. I should have said he would put his hand pretty deep into his pocket. He's fond of you, isn't he?"

"Oh, yes—"

"And of the boy?"

"Oh, Glen!"

"If you call me Glen, I really will murder you! Just let's have that again, and make it 'Oh, Greg!' "

She repeated it in a terrified whisper.

"That's better! Well now, this sum of money is what Martin is going to pay to keep his wife, his son, and his peace of mind. Do you think he'd grudge it if he knew? You know he wouldn't—not if it was twice as much. Do you know, like a more famous adventurer, I really am surprised at my own moderation."

Linnet Oakley gazed at him. She would have to do it—she had known that all along—she couldn't hold out against Glen. She couldn't lose Martin. And she *couldn't* go to prison. Martin wouldn't want her to go to prison. He would pay anything for her, or for Marty. It didn't really matter about the money. She said in a yielding voice,

"If I do it, will you promise—will you really, really promise that Martin won't know?"

Gregory Porlock laughed heartily.

"My dear, I should think even you would see that I'm not likely to want Martin to know!"

CHAPTER 10

Dorinda had a perfectly silent drive down to the Mill House. Martin Oakley sat in front beside the chauffeur and never uttered. She had the back to herself, with a cushion to tuck into the corner, and a lovely warm rug. As she watched the streets and the people slipping by she had at least one cause for gratitude. Martin Oakley certainly wasn't the Wicked Uncle. He was just Marty grown up and become a very successful business man. There was the sallow skin, the brooding look which meant mischief when Marty had it, the same quick twitching frown. Not, however, the same flow of conversation, which was an added reason for being grateful.

Dorinda felt very glad indeed that she hadn't let Justin drag her out of what promised to be a comfortable job. Even in her short experience it had occurred to her that an aloof and silent employer might be worth his weight in gold. So many of them seemed to be afflicted with a coming-on disposition. She told herself that she was in luck's way, and that it wasn't any good Justin saying things, because there were a lot of girls wanting jobs just now, and if you had got a reasonably good one you would be a fool not to stick to it.

Her fingers went up to Justin's brooch. When she had taken it off and looked at it, and put it on again, she felt all warm and glowing. It was wonderful of him to give it to her. She hadn't thanked him a bit properly, because she had had a dreadful feeling that she might be going to burst into tears. She couldn't imagine anything that Justin would mind more than having you burst into tears in a public restaurant—it was the sort of thing you would simply never live down. So she hadn't really dared to speak. She began to plan a letter to write to him after tea.

When she came to write it she didn't seem able to get it down the way she had planned it. She wasted quite a lot of paper and quite a lot of time. In the end she wrote slap-dash fashion without stopping to think:

> "Justin, I wasn't ungrateful. I do hope you didn't think I was. I've never had such a lovely present. I truly love it. I was afraid I was going to cry because it was so lovely, and if I had you wouldn't ever have wanted to speak to me again.
>
> Your loving Dorinda.
>
> P.S.—Mrs. Oakley likes the dress.
> P.P.S.—Mr. Oakley isn't a bit like the Wicked Uncle. So far the only thing he has said to me is 'How do you do, Miss Brown?' But that's better than being the other sort.
> P.P.P.S—I do love my brooch."

When she had finished she changed into her blue dress, but with an uncertain feeling, because she didn't know whether she was to dine with the Oakleys when Martin Oakley was there or not. She had asked of course, but Mrs. Oakley had merely looked vague and said it would depend on Martin. There was an uncomfortable sense of being on approval, and she felt a passionate preference for a tray in her sitting-room. That was something she hadn't told Justin. She turned back to the letter and added a fourth postscript:

"I've got a sitting-room of my own."

It was across the passage from her bedroom, next to

the nursery on the third floor. Except that the ceiling was lower, it was the same size and shape as Mrs. Oakley's boudoir, and it was quite comfortably furnished, with an electric fire which she could turn on when she wanted to. It was glowing red now and the room was beautifully warm. She thought it must be immediately over the boudoir, but strange houses were difficult until you got your bearings. She began to try and make them out. The boudoir was at the end of a passage on the left, and so was this. She went to the window, dividing the curtains and letting them fall to behind her so as to cut off the light.

At first she couldn't see anything at all. Like another curtain, the darkness hung close up to the other side of the glass, but after a little it seemed to get thinner, to melt away, to dissolve into a sort of glimmering dusk. The sky was cloudy, as it had been all day, but somewhere behind the cloud she thought the moon must be up, because now that her eyes had got accustomed to the changed light she could see where the trees cut the sky, and the dark line of the drive, and the gravelled square on which the house stood. This window looked out to the side. Yes, that was the boudoir window just below, and the study underneath that again. Mrs. Oakley had told her she could go there and get herself a book if she wanted to, and that is how she had described it—"At the end of the passage, right underneath this room." And "this room" was the boudoir.

She could see that there was a light in the boudoir. A faint rosy glow came through the curtains. The study curtains were red. If there had been a light behind them, she wondered whether it would have filtered through to stain the dusk outside. Perhaps it wouldn't. The curtains were very thick scarlet velvet with deep pelmets, and the furniture all chromium-plated tubes, except the desk, which was quite comfortable and ordinary.

She was thinking she would get tired of those surgical-looking chairs and all that scarlet leather, even with a black marble mantelpiece and a black carpet to tone it down, when someone loomed up on the gravel square. One minute he wasn't there and the next he was. She didn't see where he came from, she just saw him against the gravel because it was lighter than he was. She couldn't really see that it was a man, but it never occurred to her for a moment that it wasn't—something about the outline, something about the way he moved—a quick, thrusting way. He came right up to the study window and turned round and went back again. There was hardly a check, there certainly wasn't any pause. He went away across the gravel square and over the edge on to the grass, where she lost him. She thought it was very odd.

As she drew back into the lighted room, Doris came in with a tray.

"Mr. and Mrs. Oakley will be dining together, Miss Brown, so I've brought your dinner up."

Chapter 11

Mr. and Miss Masterman were the first of Gregory Porlock's guests to arrive for the week-end. They were rather better than their word, for having said that they would aim at four o'clock, they actually entered the hall at the Grange as the clock struck half past three.

Gregory Porlock came to meet them with a good deal of warmth.

"My dear Miss Masterman! Now what would you like to do—a little rest before tea? Do you know, I think that would be the thing for you, and your brother and I can get our business over before anyone else arrives. That will suit you, Masterman, won't it? . . . All right then. Gladys, will you take Miss Masterman upstairs and see she has everything she wants." His genial laugh rang out. "I'm afraid that would be rather a tall order for some of us—eh, Masterman?"

Miss Masterman, following a maid in a very becoming dark red uniform, had no answering smile. Her handsome haggard face was stamped with fatigue. She looked as if she had forgotten how to sleep. When Gladys had left her in the comfortable, well-appointed bedroom she walked slowly towards the hearth, as if drawn by the warmth of the fire. She had removed her gloves and had unfastened a rather shabby fur coat. Gregory Porlock had noticed it as she came in—but Gregory Porlock noticed everything. Standing like that, she felt the warmth of the fire beat against the cold of her body. No, it wasn't just her body that was cold. It was something no fire could ever warm again.

There was a chintz-covered chair drawn up to the hearth. She sank down on it and buried her face in her hands.

In the study Gregory Porlock was pouring out drinks.

"Glad you were able to make it early. More satisfactory to get the business out of the way."

Geoffrey Masterman resembled his sister rather strongly. No one seeing them together could be in any doubt as to their relationship. Both were tall, dark, and without quite enough flesh to cover their rather decided bones. Of the two the brother was the better looking, the rather bold cast of the family features being more suited to a man than to a woman. Both had fine eyes and strong dark hair with a tendency to curl. Either might have been just under or just over fifty years of age.

Masterman drank from his glass and set it down. If anyone had been watching him very closely—shall we say as closely as Gregory Porlock—it might have been observed that this simple action was rather carefully controlled. In the result, no one could have said that the hand which set the glass down had shaken—no one could have said for certain whether it did not shake because it had no inclination to shake, or because Masterman had not permitted it to do so. From the depths of a comfortable chair he looked across at his host and said,

"My sister told me that you said you had found a satisfactory solution. I should like to know what it is."

Gregory laughed.

"I told her to say that you needn't worry. I thought you might be having rather a bad time. By the way, how much does she know?"

"Look here, Porlock, I resent that tone. The fact that someone with a hideously suspicious mind thinks they can make money out of a perfectly baseless charge does not entitle you to talk to me as if either I or my sister were involved in anything of a—well, of a discreditable nature."

Gregory Porlock finished his own glass, leaned forward, and put it back on the table.

"My dear Masterman, of course not. A thousand apologies if I conveyed any such meaning. But you see, my dear fellow, it isn't a case of what you say or I think. It's a case of a witness who has just not quite decided whether she will go to the police. If you don't mind her going—well, that's that. But you know how it is, if you get pitch thrown at you, some of it sticks."

Geoffrey Masterman made an abrupt movement.

"Who is this woman?"

Gregory Porlock was lighting a cigarette. He waited till the smoke curled up, and said casually,

"I'm going to tell you. In our previous very short conversation I informed you that owing to an odd set of circumstances I had come into possession of some rather curious evidence with regard to the death of an elderly cousin of yours, Miss Mabel Ledbury. When I said that the evidence was in my possession, I didn't of course mean that literally. What I meant was that I had been consulted by the person who said she had this evidence. Well, of course when you hear a thing like that about a friend you can do no less than let him know. I began to tell you about it and we were interrupted. On receiving your note asking for a further interview—really, my dear fellow, it was extremely incautious of you to write—I thought it best to ring up and suggest your coming down here, where we can, I hope, dispose of the whole thing in the most satisfactory manner."

Masterman reached for his glass, took another drink, and said,

"How?"

"That's what I'm coming to. But before we go any farther I had better just remind you of what this woman says she saw. I think I told you that she was lying in bed with a broken leg in an upper room in one of the houses in the street next to yours. The backs of the houses in these two streets look at each other across short strips of garden. Your cousin occupied a room exactly opposite that in which this woman lay—I will call her Annie. She had all the time in the world, lying there, and she was deeply interested in her neighbours—she used to watch them through a pair of opera glasses. She became especially interested in Miss Mabel Ledbury, and she formed the impression that you were not being very kind to her."

"Ridiculous!"

"Miss Ledbury was not bedridden, but she spent most of her time in bed. Sometimes she got up and pottered about the room. On several occasions Annie saw her rummage in a biscuit tin and produce from under the biscuits a long, folded legal-looking document. Annie says with the glasses she could read the words 'Last Will and Testament' plainly endorsed upon the envelope."

"What's all this flapdoodle?" Geoffrey Masterman's voice was a shade higher than it should have been. He had not put down his glass again, he sat holding it between his two hands.

Gregory Porlock's black eyebrows lifted.

"My dear fellow, don't you think you'd better just listen to what she's got to say? You can't meet a thing in the dark—can you?"

"Oh, there's more of it, is there?"

"Naturally, or I shouldn't have troubled you. Annie says that on the fourteenth of October last she saw you come into Miss Ledbury's room, Miss Ledbury being up in her dressing-gown sitting at the table by the window with this paper which Annie says was a will in front of her. The old lady was deaf, was she not? Annie says she didn't seem to hear you come in, or to know that you were there. She says you stood behind her looking over her shoulder. And she says—if you'll excuse my mentioning it—that you looked like a devil. Women have a natural tendency to melodrama—it compensates for the dullness of their lives."

He paused with his eyes on Masterman's rigid face and allowed a slight deprecatory laugh to escape him.

"To continue with what Annie saw. Really that

would make a suggestive headline, wouldn't it—'What Annie Saw.' I can imagine its having quite a wide appeal. She says Miss Ledbury turned round suddenly and saw you, and that there was what she described as a scene—you very angry, Miss Ledbury very much frightened, and you snatching the will and holding it up out of her reach while she tried to get it back. She says you took hold of the old lady by the shoulders and pushed her on to the bed, and that then the door opened and your sister came in. You went out, taking the will with you, and Miss Masterman did her best to soothe Miss Ledbury down. When she had got her quiet she put on the light and drew the curtains, so that Annie didn't see any more. In the morning the milkman brought the news that Miss Ledbury had been found dead in her bed. There had been a doctor in attendance and he said it wasn't unexpected, so there wasn't any fuss or any inquest. And when the will came to be proved it left you and your sister sole legatees with a hundred thousand pounds to divide. Annie went into hospital on the day of the funeral, and she only came out about a month ago. When she heard that you and Miss Masterman had come in for all the money she wondered what had happened to the will she used to see the old lady looking at. Because when you stood there reading it over her shoulder she didn't think it looked as if it was the sort of will under which you were going to benefit to the tune of fifty thousand pounds. And then she remembered that a friend of hers who used to come in and work for Miss Masterman had told her about six months previously that the old lady up at the top of the house had called her in one day when you and your sister were out. She said she wanted her to witness a will, and she must go and find someone else because there must be two witnesses, and she would give them each a ten-shilling note for their trouble. So this Mrs. Wells ran across the road to No. 17 where she knew the cook, and the two of them saw Miss Ledbury sign a big paper, and she told them it was her will."

There was a sound of breaking glass. Geoffrey Masterman's grip upon the tumbler he was holding had tightened in an involuntary jerk.

Gregory was all concern.

"My dear fellow—have you cut yourself?"

It appeared that he had not. There was no blood upon his hands. Some glass to be picked up, a splash of whisky and soda to be wiped from a trouser leg, and they were back at the point of what Annie might or might not be going to say.

Masterman leaned forward.

"Of course the whole thing's damned nonsense from beginning to end—a pack of lies!"

"Naturally."

"Blackmail—that's what it is—blackmail!"

"Well, my dear fellow, if that's what you think, the only advice I can give you is to go straight to the police. I think the will under which you inherited was several years old. If there wasn't a later will, the whole thing falls to the ground."

Masterman stared past him.

"If there was another will, she destroyed it herself. Old women are always making wills."

"Was there another will?"

"There may have been. How do I know?"

Gregory Porlock whistled.

"That means there was. It's awkward, you know."

"It's rank blackmail!" said Masterman violently.

"My dear fellow, she hasn't asked you for a penny. She is engaged in a struggle with her conscience. If she decides to go to the police—"

Masterman interrupted.

"How did she come to go to you?"

He received a slow, benignant smile.

"Too long a story to go into—far too long. Really a very curious chain of circumstances. But very fortunate for you."

"Was it?" Masterman's voice was savage.

"Undoubtedly—or she might have gone to the police. There is a point at which a woman's conscience simply has to boil over. For the moment I have, as it were, turned down the gas under the pot, but it may reach boiling-point again."

Masterman's control broke. He swore vehemently. He cursed women in general and Annie in particular, and finished by turning furiously upon his host.

"You said the whole thing could be settled, damn you! And all you do is to go on baiting me! You know as well as I do that I can't go to the police. However that sort of thing turns out, the mud sticks—you never get clear of it."

"And you couldn't trust your sister in the witness-box—could you?" Gregory Porlock's voice was sympathetic. "A nervous type. And she won't touch the money—will she?"

Into a stricken silence Masterman's voice came only just above a whisper.

"Who said so?"

Gregory Porlock laughed.

"Her fur coat. If she was handling the money she'd have bought herself a new one." He let something like a groan go by and resumed briskly. "That being that, we'd better get down to brass tacks. There really isn't any need to get in a flap. Neither of the two witnesses to that will are going to think anything about it unless someone puts it into their heads. Mrs. Wells has been away with a married daughter, and the cook at No. 17 has left and gone back to the north where she came from. Annie has devoted relations in Canada who have been begging her to join them for years. If she were to go out to them with her passage paid and a little something in her stocking foot, I have a feeling that her conscience would simmer down. Change of air, you know—change of scene—new interests—reunion with a loving family—I don't suppose she'd ever think about that will again. Of course you wouldn't appear in the matter at all. There wouldn't be the slightest connection. She hasn't asked for anything, and she won't know where the money comes from. An unknown benefactor supplies a long-felt want and no questions asked. I will see that her passage is taken and that she avails herself of it."

Geoffrey Masterman set his teeth and said,

"How much?"

"A thousand pounds."

CHAPTER 12

Mr. and Mrs. Tote and Moira Lane arrived in time for tea, Miss Lane very tall and elegant, with brilliant eyes, a flashing smile, and considerable charm.

Mrs. Tote presented as great a contrast as it was possible to imagine. A very expensive fur coat having been shed, there appeared a wispy little woman rather like a mouse, with scant grey hair twisted up into a straggly knot behind. Do her hair any other way than she had done it ever since she grew up, Mrs. Tote would not. She brushed it neatly, and she put in plenty of pins. It wasn't her fault if the fur turban which went with the coat was so heavy that it dragged the hair down. She hadn't wanted the fur turban. She would have liked a nice neat matron's hat in one of those light felts like she used to get when they had their business in Clapham, before Albert made all that money. The turban made her head ache, like a lot of the things that had happened since they got rich. She would have been glad to take it off like that Miss Lane had done with hers, pulling it off careless, and her hair all shining waves underneath. She liked to see a girl with a nice head of hair, and fair hair paid for dressing. Nice to be able just to pull off your hat like that and feel sure that you were all right underneath. But of course not suitable at her age, and the hairpins dropping out like they always did all the way down in the car.

Moira Lane's clear, light voice broke into Mrs. Tote's reflections. Gregory Porlock had just said, "Where's your young man?" and Moira was saying, "He won't be a moment—he's just putting the car away. Really angel of you to let me bring him, Greg, because if you hadn't, I'd have had to come by train, and if there's one thing that brings my sordid stony-broke state home to me more than another, it is having to travel third-class on this revolting line and grapple with my luggage at the change, whereas if I can float from door to door in somebody's car I get the heavenly illusion of being not only solvent but more or less in the class of the idle rich. So when I ran into Justin last night and found he was positively dying to meet you—well, it all did seem too good to be wasted, didn't it?"

Gregory Porlock put a friendly hand on her shoulder.

"That's all right, my dear. But—dying to meet me—why?"

Moira laughed.

"Well, to be quite accurate, it's the Martin Oakleys he's dying to meet. Sorry if it's a disappointment, but it's all the same thing, isn't it—Martin and you being the world's buddies and all that."

"Why does he want to meet Martin Oakley?"

She gave a slight impatient frown.

"Oh, some schoolgirl cousin umpteen times removed has just taken a job there—secretary to his wife or something. Justin says he's practically her guardian, so he wants to meet them. Amusing when you know Justin. I'm just wondering how ravishingly pretty she would have to be to make him come over responsible."

Gregory Porlock laughed.

"Well, you'll be able to see for yourself in an hour or two, because the Oakleys are dining here and I told them to bring her along."

He moved away from her to make himself charming to Mrs. Tote.

Miss Masterman poured out tea with an exhausted air. There were very good scones and home-made cakes, but the only one who did any justice to them was Mrs. Tote. One of the things she didn't like about being fashionable was the miserable sort of tea people gave you in London—little wafery curls of bread and butter, and the sort of sandwich that wouldn't keep a butterfly alive. She didn't care whether she ever had another late dinner, but she did like a good sit-down tea. And here was Mr. Porlock giving her a little table to herself and helping her to honey with her buttered scone.

When Justin Leigh came in he kept her company. Having missed lunch, he was hungry enough to deal appreciatively with the excellent tea provided by his host.

"Your cousin's coming to dinner," said Moira Lane.

"No—I don't eat tea. It's no use waving buns at me as if I was something in a zoo. What's her name?"

"Dorinda Brown."

Moira's elegant eyebrows rose.

"Bread-and-butter miss?"

Justin looked vague.

"I don't know that you would call her that."

She laughed.

"Why haven't I ever met her? You've been keeping her up your sleeve. I'm no good at shocks. You'd better break it to me—what is she really like?"

Justin smiled suddenly.

"Nice," he said, and reached for another bun.

When tea was over the party melted. The Mastermans disappeared. Moira took Justin off to play snooker. Mrs. Tote went up to her room.

It was perhaps half an hour later that her husband joined her there, and the first minute she set eyes on him she knew that there was something wrong. A regular state—that's what he had put himself into, and now she would have to soothe him down, and as likely as not he'd be upset the whole evening and not get his sleep at night. He was getting stouter, Albert was, and it didn't do him any good getting worked up, not with his short neck and getting so red in the face. He quite banged the door behind him as he came in, and began right away, saying he wouldn't stand it, not for nobody nor nothing.

"Now, Albert—"

"Don't you 'Now, Albert' me, Mother, for I'm not in the mood to stand it! I've had all I'm going to stand from anyone, and don't you forget it! And there's others that had better not forget it neither!"

Dear, dear, Albert *was* put about and no mistake! Mrs. Tote really couldn't remember to have seen him so upset about anything since Allie ran off to marry Jimmy Wilson whose father had the next-door shop to theirs in the old Clapham days. And of course Allie could have looked a good deal higher, with all the money Albert had made in the war. But there it was—you're only young once, and when you're young money doesn't seem to matter the way it does when you haven't got anything else. She remembered Allie standing up and saying all that to her father.

"Jimmy's good and he's steady. He's got a job, and I'm going to marry him. We don't want your money—we can make enough to keep ourselves. We'd like to be friends, but if you won't you won't, and we're getting married anyhow."

Well, of course, Albert was terribly put about. And obstinate—more like a mule than a man. Allie and Jimmy thought he'd come round, but she never really thought so herself. Not even when the baby was born—though how he could go on calling her Mother the way he did and never think that if it hadn't been for Allie he'd never have had any call to start doing it.

She came back to Albert fairly shouting out that he wouldn't stand it, and prepared to be firm.

"Now then, what's it all about?"

She didn't say "Father," because she never said it now—not since Allie went and he wouldn't have her name mentioned. You can't be a father if you haven't got a child. She said,

"You'd better tell me what's the matter, and not go walking up and down like that—there's no sense in it."

Red in the face and breathing short, Albert began to use language. He was still walking up and down, with an angry flounce when he had to turn where the washstand brought him up on one side of the room and the wardrobe on the other. Mrs. Tote put up with it for as long as she felt she could. She didn't approve of language, but if you didn't let a man swear when he was angry he might do worse. So she waited until she thought he must have got rid of the worst of it before she said with surprising firmness,

"Now, Albert, that's quite enough. You come here and tell me what it's all about. Carrying on like that—you ought to be ashamed."

He came, angry and glaring, to drop down on the couch beside her. The rage wasn't out of him, but he had a foreboding of what he would feel like when it had gone—cold—empty—afraid. He had to talk to someone. Emily was his wife. A good wife, but too fond of her own way. Obstinate. But she didn't talk—not about his affairs. It wasn't every man that could say that about his wife. He stared at her and said in a choked sort of way,

"It's blackmail. That's what it is—blackmail—"

Mrs. Tote came straight to the point.

"Who's blackmailing you?"

"That damned fellow Porlock."

"And what have you been doing to get yourself blackmailed?"

His eyes avoided her—looked at the pink and purple flowers on the chintz cover of the couch.

"Women don't understand business—it's a business matter."

Emily Tote went on looking at him. He'd got himself into a mess—that's what he'd done. You can't get rich all that quick and keep honest—she'd known that all along. Terribly easy to go over the edge in business when your mind was taken up with getting rich. She looked steadily at Albert, and thanked God that Allie was out of it. She said,

"You'd better tell me."

"He's blackmailing me. Oh, it's all wrapped up as clever as you please, but it doesn't take me in. Come to him by a side wind—that's what he says. Him saying he'll fix it up for me—as if I didn't know what that meant! I may have been a fool, but I'm not such a fool as not to be able to see right through Mr. Gregory Porlock. General agent, my foot! Blackmail—that's his business, I tell you—blackmail! But I'll be even with him!" Mr. Tote had recourse to language again. "I'll show him whether he can blackmail me! If he gets a knife in him some dark night he'll only have himself to blame!"

He had been shouting. Mrs. Tote leaned forward and tapped him on the knee.

"Be quiet," she said. "That's foolish talk. Do you want everyone in the house to hear you? You get a hold of yourself, Albert, and tell me what it's all about. What have you done?"

He said in a sullen voice,

"No more than hundreds of others."

"What was it?"

He threw her a fleeting look, sitting up there in the sofa corner with her skinny hands held together in her lap and her eyes looking at him. A little bit of a thing, Emily, but set in her ways. You could put her into a fur coat that cost a thousand, but you couldn't make her look like a rich man's wife. But she wouldn't talk—Emily wouldn't talk. He'd got to tell someone. He said,

"It wasn't anything to start with, only the use of the yard so a lorry could be run in and be handy when it was wanted."

"Wanted for what?"

"What had that got to do with me? Then they wanted the hire of my lorry as well, and I said I wasn't letting it out for any Tom, Dick or Harry to drive. And they said I'd be paid for what it was worth three or four times over."

Emily Tote said, "Who is *they?*"

"Sam Black, if you want to know. Well, by that time I was in it enough to get into trouble, but not enough for it to be worth while. I said to Sam, 'I'm not playing about with this any more. It's not worth my while.' And he said, 'It might be.' And to cut a long story short, it was."

"Black market?" said Emily Tote.

He threw himself back in his corner.

"Money going begging—that's what it was."

She sat up very straight in the blue flannel dressing-gown which it was no use trying to make her change for a silk one. That was Emily all over. She sat there, and she said as cool as a cucumber,

"Five pounds to a lorry-driver to get out and have a cup of cocoa or a glass of beer, and a dozen barrels of sugar, or it may be butter, gone before he comes back. Was that the game?"

His jaw dropped.

"Why, Mother!"

"Do you think I don't read the papers? It's all been there in black and white for anyone to see. And some of the ones they caught got stiff sentences, didn't they?"

Mr. Tote's ruddy colour had faded.

"That was in the war," he said.

"And what you did—wasn't that in the war?"

"Don't talk like that! It isn't going to come out, I tell you. Who's going to bother about what happened three or four years ago? If I pay up, it will be only because I don't want any unpleasantness."

Mrs. Tote was still looking at him.

"You didn't make all that money out of a few odd barrels."

He actually laughed.

"Of course I didn't! That was only the beginning. I got into it in a big way. Why, if I was to tell you some of the hauls we made, you wouldn't believe me. Organizing ability—that's what they said I had. One of the planners—that was me. There's a funny thing about money, you know—once you start making it, it fair runs away with you and makes itself. When we started with that twopenny-halfpenny business in Clapham, I lay you never thought you'd be a rich man's wife."

Deep inside herself Emily Tote answered with the words which she would never allow to pass her lips—"I never thought I'd be married to a thief."

She said aloud, "I wouldn't say too much about that. You've only told me half. What does Mr. Porlock know, and what is he going to do?"

The blood rushed back into his face, swelling the veins, purpling the skin.

"He's got dates and places, curse him! There was a lot of petrol from an aerodrome—he's got that. And a biggish haul of butter from the docks. Two or three other big jobs. Says there are witnesses that can swear to me. But I don't believe him. It's three years ago—who's going to take any notice of people swearing to where you were, and to what you said and did as long ago as that? If I pay, it will be because it doesn't do you any good in business to have things said. And if I pay, I know damn well whose pocket the money'll go into! Mr. Blackmailer Porlock—that's who! And when I think about it, I tell you straight it makes me feel I'd rather swing for him!"

He was shouting again. Emily Tote said,

"Don't talk so foolish, Albert."

CHAPTER 13

Gregory Porlock came into the billiard-room shepherding the Mastermans.

"Well, now, here we are. And I'm going to carry Moira off. Just finished a game? Who won?"

Moira Lane laughed.

"Oh, I'm not in Justin's class—he's way up, practically out of sight."

"Ah, then he can take Masterman on, and Miss Masterman can see fair play. We'll come back presently."

He took her off to the study, a comfortable country room with book-lined walls, warmly coloured rugs, and deep brown leather chairs—a room that had been used and lived in. Granted that Gregory Porlock had taken the house furnished, he might be given the credit for his choice. He fitted the room too—fresh healthy skin, clear eyes, good country tweeds which had been worn in country weather. There was a tray of cocktails on the table, and he handed Moira one.

He said, "I've brought you here to ask you a question, you know."

"Have you?" Nothing could have been more friendly than her voice. She sipped from her glass. "Sounds intriguing. What is it?"

He met her laughing eyes and said quite gravely,

"What do you make of me, Moira? What sort of man would you say I was?"

She didn't look away, but she looked different. The smile was still in her eyes, but there was something else there too—something a little wary, a little on guard. She said in her pretty, light voice,

"A good fellow—a good friend—a charming host. Why?"

He nodded.

"Thank you, my dear. I think you meant that."

She was sitting on the arm of one of the big chairs, leaning against the back, every line of the long figure graceful and easy. She took another sip from her glass and said,

"Of course I did."

He went over to the fire and put a log of wood on it. When he turned round he had his charming smile again.

"Well, that being that, I can go on."

"Go on?"

"Oh, yes—that was just a preliminary. The fact is—let me take your glass—well, the fact is, I've got something for you, and I wanted to feel sure of my ground before I gave it to you."

"Something for me?" She laughed suddenly. "Greg, my sweet, how marvellous! Is it a present? Because I warn you I shall consider I've been lured here under false pretences if it isn't. It will be a sort of breach of promise, because you've quite definitely raised my hopes."

He laughed too.

"Have I? Then I shall have to do something about it. Or perhaps you will. We'll see. Meanwhile, here it is."

He took a small parcel wrapped in tissue paper from his pocket, laid it upon her knee, and went back to the hearth again. From a couple of yards away he watched her sit up straight and undo the wrappings. She had a laughing look, but at the first touch of the paper and what it held there was a faint instant check. Her hands stayed just as they were, measuring the weight of the parcel, feeling the shape of it through the thin paper.

Something moved under her fingers like the links of a chain, and she knew.

Gregory Porlock saw her colour go, quite suddenly, as the flame goes when you blow a candle out. One moment it was there, bright and vivid. The next it wasn't there any more. The bright, living thing had gone. Only her eyes stayed on him in a long searching look before she turned them to what the paper held.

She was unwrapping the paper now, letting it drop into the seat of the chair. What emerged was a bracelet—a band about an inch and a half wide, diamond trellis-work between two rows of fine brilliants, and, interrupting the trellis at distances of about three quarters of an inch, light panels of larger stones with a ruby at the centre of each. The rubies were very fine and of the true pigeon's blood colour. The workmanship was exquisite.

Moira Lane held the bracelet out on the palm of her hand. Her blood might have betrayed her, but her hand was steady.

"What is this?"

Those dancing eyes met hers. He might have been enjoying himself. Perhaps he was.

"Don't you know?" As there was no answer, he supplied one. "I think you do. But you know, you really ought to have been more careful. Of course there are so many ignorant people that one gets into the habit of expecting everyone to be ignorant. But you can't really count on it. Anyone in the trade might happen to know something about historic jewels. Even outside the trade there are people like myself to whom the subject is of interest."

"I don't know what you mean. In fact I don't know what you're talking about."

She really did look blank. He said in an incredulous voice,

"My dear girl, you don't mean to say you didn't know what you were taking!"

A frown crept across the blankness.

"It's a bracelet. The stones are very good. I suppose it's worth a lot of money. Is there anything else to know about it?"

"Well, well," said Gregory Porlock—"the True History of the Ruby Bracelet. Instruction for you. Opportunity to show off for me. You may have noticed that I do like showing off."

"Yes. What have you got to show?"

He laughed good-humouredly.

"Just a little specialized knowledge. That's another thing you may have noticed about me—I'm fond of odd bits of information—little blind-alley bits and pieces. And you know, sometimes—sometimes they come in useful."

"Do they?" Her voice was as steady as her hand had been, but the ring had gone out of it.

"Well, you shall judge for yourself. Anything about jewels—that has always fascinated me. Years ago— why it must be quite twenty—I picked up a shabby little book on an Edinburgh bookstall. It was called *Famous Jewels and their History, with a Particular Account of the Families of the Nobility and Gentry in whose Possession they are to be Found*. Not a well-written book, I am afraid, but containing some interesting facts. Do you know, for instance, that a good many of the French crown jewels were brought over to England during the Revolution and entrusted for safe keeping to the Marquess of Queensberry—the one who was known as Old Q? He is said to have buried them in the cellar of his town house, and all trace of them appears to have been lost. He kept the secret too well, and died with it undisclosed. A couple of London clubs now occupy the site, and somewhere under their foundations there may still be lying the jewels of the Queens of France—" He paused, and added briskly, "Or perhaps not. You never know, do you? Jewels are like riches—sometimes they take to themselves wings. But this is a digression. I mustn't let myself be carried away. It is Josephine's ruby bracelets with which we are concerned. You did know, I suppose, that this is one of a pair?"

She glanced down at the trellised diamonds and said, "How should I know?"

If it was meant for a question, there was no direct answer.

"Then I can continue to show off. My little book mentions these bracelets. Napoleon gave them to Josephine on rather a special occasion. Just turn to the inside of the clasp and you will see the N surmounted by the imperial crown."

There was no interest in face or manner as she turned the clasp. The crowned N looked at her from the pale gold.

Gregory Porlock had come over to stand beside her.

"Now turn it and you'll see the date at the other end of the clasp, rather faint but legible—Fri. 10, 1804."

She said, "What does it mean?"

"The tenth of Frimaire, eighteen hundred and four. That is, December the first, the date on which Josephine at last induced Napoleon to go through the religious ceremony of marriage with her. He cheated, because by deliberately omitting the presence of the parish priest he left a loophole of which he availed himself later on when he applied for a declaration of nullity. The bracelets were a wedding present. The imperial N is there because December the first was the eve of their coronation. Didn't you really know the story?"

She looked up with a startling anger in her eyes.

"What has it got to do with me?"

He went back to the fire.

"I can tell you that too. Josephine died in eighteen-fourteen. The bracelets are not specifically mentioned in her will. In fact they disappeared for about forty years, when the second Earl of Pemberley bought them in Paris as a wedding present for his bride. Where they had been in the interval does not transpire, but Lord Pemberley was, apparently, satisfied as to their history, and they have been handed down in the family ever since. The title is now extinct, but the widow of the last Earl survives. You are connected with her, I think, through your mother."

"So that is why I am supposed to know about the bracelets!"

He nodded.

"We are getting to the point. About ten years ago I had the pleasure of meeting Lady Pemberley at a charity ball—she was one of the patronesses. Imagine my interest when I saw that she was wearing the Josephine bracelets. I ventured to remark on them, and when she found that I knew their history she was kind enough to take them off and show me the initial and the date—the same on each. So you see, when I encountered the bracelet which you have in your hand—"

She broke in with a raised voice,

"What has this got to do with me?"

"I'm boring you? I've really almost done. A friend of mine who knows my hobby told me he had come across a bracelet of very beautiful workmanship. I went to see it, and of course recognized it at once. I needn't tell you the name of the shop, because of course you know it.

What you probably didn't know was that the proprietor knew perfectly well from whom he was buying the bracelet. You see, you figure quite a lot in the Society papers, and he recognized you. In point of fact, he would not have bought so valuable a piece of jewellery, from an unknown client. Knowing your family connections, he did not hesitate."

There was a long pause during which he watched an averted face—brows drawn together, lips pressed into a rigid line.

When he thought the silence had lasted long enough he broke it.

"I'm your friend, you know. There's no need to look like that."

The colour rushed back into her face. She swung round on him, eyes wide and glowing.

"Greg—"

His smile had never been more charming.

"That's better!"

"Greg—she gave it to me. I don't know what you've been thinking—"

He laughed.

"Well, I bought it. I won't tell you what I paid, because there's always a revolting difference between the buying and the selling price, and I don't want to rub it in. Anyhow, now it's my property there's nothing to stop my making a gesture and sending it back to Lady Pemberley, is there?"

"You can't do that! I naturally don't want her to know I sold it."

"Oh, naturally! Have you got the other one—or did you sell that too?"

"She only gave me one."

He shook his head.

"My dear girl, it won't do. You know, and I know.

And you know that I know. What's the good of keeping up this farce? If I were to go to Lady Pemberley and say that I had recognized her bracelet in a sale room, what do you suppose would happen? There would be a bit of a crash, wouldn't there? She wouldn't run you in—oh, no! We don't wash our dirty linen in public. But I think Miss Lane's name would come out of Lady Pemberley's will, and I shouldn't be surprised if it didn't get round the family that dear Moira had spilt rather a lot of ink on her copybook. In fact, in the language of melodrama, 'Social Ruin Looms.' "

Moira Lane got to her feet. She put the bracelet down on the corner of the writing-table and said rather quietly,

"What good would that do you?"

He could admire her, and he did. Courage appealed to him, and the breeding which set him at a distance. She wouldn't cry or make any appeal, she wouldn't break. He looked at her approvingly.

"That's where we really get down to brass tacks. And the answer is, it wouldn't do me any good at all. There's nothing in the world I want less than to hurt you. All I want is for us to stop playing comedies and get to business."

"What business?"

He came up to the table and gave her another cocktail.

"Better have a drink. You look played out. Now, Moira, listen! I could ruin you. But why should I want to? I don't. I admire you very much, and I like to think that we are friends. I'll go farther and tell you I'd like to have you as a partner."

Standing there, glass in hand, she looked at him with a little scorn. She finished her cocktail, put the glass back on the tray, and waited, her eyebrows delicately raised.

He stood perhaps a yard away, easy and smiling.

"I told you I was a collector of odd bits of information. When people know you like them they come your way, sometimes in a very surprising manner. But that sort of thing has to be very carefully checked. It doesn't do to slip up. Some of it—rather an important part—comes from the circles of which you are a privileged member. Exclusive circles, very intimately linked. It would be a great advantage to me to have what I might call a consultant who was in and out of those very exclusive circles."

The eyebrows rose a little higher still.

"You used the word partner just now. You are asking me to be your partner in a blackmailing business?"

He put up a deprecatory hand.

"Now, Moira—what's the good of talking like that? It may relieve your feelings, but I assure you it doesn't do anything at all to mine. They have acquired a complete resistance to sarcasm, so you are wasting your time. If, on the other hand, you did by any chance succeed in making me angry, the results might be unfortunate—" He paused and added, "For you. I think that my use of the word partner was not a very happy one. It implies responsibility, and you would have none. Consultant is a much more accurate description. All I should ever ask you to do would be to keep me straight as to facts, and to assist me with your personal specialized knowledge of the people concerned. To give you a simple illustration. Certain things admitted to be facts might in one case be extremely compromising, whereas in another no one would attach the slightest importance to them. That is where your personal contacts would come in. I needn't say that the whole thing would be completely confidential and sufficiently remunerative. As far as Josephine's bracelet is concerned, it is yours to do what you like with. If I might make a suggestion, it would be that you should find some opportunity of restoring it to Lady Pemberley. It would be better not to run any further risk. It is the future that matters now."

The last words set her blood storming. The future— and what a future! If she could have killed him then, she might have done it. Perhaps he guessed that. The sudden brilliance of her glance, the sudden scarlet in the cheeks which had been so pale, declared an inner fire. He could have no possible doubt as to its nature, but he gave her marks for self-control.

It was not until the flame had dropped from flaring-point that she let herself speak. When she did, it was any guest to any host.

"My dear Greg, you're too flattering. But I'm afraid I shouldn't be any good at business—I expect you have to be born that way. Too kind of you to let me have my bracelet back. You must let me know what you paid for it. I shouldn't like my cousin to know that I had sold her present. The fact is, I was in a frightful hole just then, and I simply had to have the money."

The bracelet was on her wrist as she spoke, withdrawn from the table and slipped over her left hand so swiftly and smoothly that Gregory Porlock would hardly have had time to intervene. In point of fact he made no move to do so, but laughed and said,

"Well, don't sell it again! It's a bit too dangerous. Someone else might recognize it next time—you never know." Then, as she turned to go, he came a step nearer, took her by the wrist, his big hand closing down over the diamond trellis, pressing it into her flesh. "I've got the receipted bill, you know. It describes the bracelet. You can have till Monday morning to make up your mind. Meanwhile we'll call a truce."

He let go of her, and she turned and went out of the room without a word.

She was half way up the stairs, when she heard the front door open and shut. The cold of the outer air came in and followed her, with the sound of Leonard Carroll's voice. The last of the house-party had arrived.

Without turning her head she went on past the door of Miss Masterman's room to her own. A short distance, a short time, from door to door, from the study to this small charming bedroom with its pale blue curtains drawn, its clean fresh chintzes with their flowery pattern picking up the colour of the curtains and blending it with purple and rose, its warm sparkling fire. But in that distance, in that time, Moira Lane had made up her mind what she was going to do.

CHAPTER 14

The Grange was an old house. The drawing-room, long and low, its four rather narrow windows curtained in a pale flowered brocade which toned charmingly with the ivory panelled walls, its chairs and couches repeating the same soft shades, preserved the formal delicacy of another day. Gregory Porlock, awaiting the arrival of his guests, considered, not for the first time, how much better the scene would have been suited by an older style of dress. For the women piled curls and spreading hoops, with knee-breeches and coloured coats for the men. He could have fancied himself very well in a prune velvet, with a touch of powder in the hair.

His mood was a buoyant one. He felt the exhilaration of a man who drives a difficult team over a dangerous course. If there were no difficulties, no dangers, there would be no pleasure in doing it. The hairsbreadth turn, the moment when everything was in the balance, the bending of nerve and will to curb, to guide, to master a straining team, gave adventure its zest and made every risk worth while. He was taking risks tonight. Linnet would always be a risk. Women at the best were incalculable—women with nerves, like the crazy compass in a magnetic storm. For all he knew, Linnet might even now be having hysterics and breaking it to Martin Oakley that she was a bigamist. Imagining the scene, he permitted himself to be amused. But he rather thought she would hold out a little longer. That opened up the possibility of her arriving for dinner only to faint into her soup-plate. He must see that she had a cocktail when she arrived. And he must be very, very nice to her. Linnet always responded to kindness. If the period of their marriage had not coincided with the lowest depths of his fortunes, she might have been adoring him still, but the sweetest temper may turn sour in a slum, and the whole business had become wretchedly sordid. He recalled it with distaste.

Dorinda Brown was another risk. She had not, of course, been intended to accompany the Oakleys tonight. It had amused him to invite her warmly, whilst taking steps to ensure that she would not be able to come. Just where the plan had slipped, and how, he didn't know, but he meant to find out. Dorinda should have had another engagement—not so pleasant, but one which would have admitted of no excuse. He didn't like his plans going wrong. They were always very carefully laid, and if they didn't come off, he made it his business to see that someone got into trouble. Apart from annoyance on this point, the fact that Dorinda would presently arrive in the wake of the Oakleys served to heighten the interest of the occasion.

He allowed himself some amused speculation as to what she would be like. Seven years is quite a time, and the seven years between fourteen and twenty-one are longer than is warranted by the mere months and years. He remembered a child with a rosy face, a thick bright plait, and round eyes. No, that would be earlier still. At fourteen the plait had gone, but the face was still rosy, and the eyes the eyes of a child. He had a sudden memory of them meeting his own in a long, grave stare. Mary had aggravated him into swearing at her, and Dorinda had walked in on them. She had opened the door and stood there looking at him with that shocked, solemn stare. Come to think of it, it was the last time he had seen her, and the question was, would she remember him, or would she not? In his own estimation he was not an easy person to forget. He rather flattered himself that no woman would ever quite forget the memories he had given her. But a child might forget—or might not. There was no counting on it. Suppose she remembered him. . . . He was of the opinion that it really didn't matter very much. A girl who had been brought up by Mary would certainly not be so ill-bred as to make a scene, and when all was said and done, she couldn't be sure. Reluctant as he was to admit the possibility that he might have a double, such things were not uncommon, and doubt once planted could be so fostered as to bring in a satisfactory crop. He felt a swelling confidence in his ability to deal with Dorinda Brown.

Linnet Oakley sat looking into her mirror with

frightened eyes. She was dressed, but she didn't know even now whether she meant to go or not. She had not been in the same mind about it for half an hour at a time all the day, or all the night, or all the day before, or all the night before that.

Sometimes she saw herself going—getting into the car, driving a little way, getting out again, going into the Grange, which was a strange house of which she could make no picture—and she felt she couldn't do it. She couldn't go into that house and meet Glen. She couldn't touch his hand. Perhaps he would take her in to dinner. . . . She couldn't, couldn't do it—not with Martin there—not with Martin looking on.

Sometimes she saw herself staying at home—saying she felt faint, saying she had a headache. But Glen would know it wasn't true. Martin would go without her, and how did she know what Glen would do or say? He might be angry. . . . The something inside her which never stopped shaking shook a little more at the thought of Glen's anger. And Martin would want to know why she had a headache, why she felt faint. He wouldn't be angry—Martin was never angry with her. He would be kind. And if he was kind, she wouldn't be able to help crying, and then, however hard she tried, she wouldn't be able to help telling him.

Something called out in her, "No—no—*no!*" She saw Martin turning her out. She saw herself in the street, in the dock, in prison—quite cast off, quite ruined, quite lost.

She stared into the glass and saw her own reflection in rose and silver. Hooper was a good maid. The fair hair had been made the most of, the delicate make-up had been applied with artistic discretion. It seemed impossible to believe that that pretty tinted image really belonged to the trembling, hunted creature she felt herself to be. In some very feminine way it gave her courage. The things that were frightening her so much didn't seem to have anything to do with that picture in the glass. It was the first time she had worn the dress. It was very becoming. The new lipstick was just right with it, and the nail polish. She pushed back the dressing-stool and stood up to get the full-length effect. The line was perfect.

Hooper put one drop of her own special scent on a tiny handkerchief and gave it to her. It was a new creation—faint, fresh, delicious. Then she remembered that it was called *Souviens tu?* She put out a hand to the dressing-table to steady herself. She couldn't go—she couldn't stay—

Martin Oakley came into the room, frowning.

"Damned nuisance having to go out! A nice quiet evening at home—that's what I feel like."

She managed a smile for him. The discreet Hooper had vanished.

"Do you like my dress?"

"It's the one I always do like, isn't it?"

"Silly! You've never seen it before. It's new."

"All right, let's have a look. Turn round!"

She did a graceful dancing turn and dropped into a curtsey.

"Do you really like it?"

She didn't need to ask—not when he looked at her like that. He put both arms round her and held her close. The terrible trembling was stilled. She could go with Martin. Martin would take care of her. She needn't be frightened any more. Martin wouldn't let anyone hurt her.

CHAPTER 15

Dorinda followed the Oakleys into the big old hall with its great beams, its deep roomy hearth, and jutting chimney-breast. A log fire burned between iron dogs. The old flag-stones under foot were softened by rugs, the sconces on the panelled walls now held electric candles. Otherwise she was seeing what any winter guest might have seen any time in the last three hundred years. The thought came to her as she slipped out of the fur coat which Mrs. Oakley had lent her. She would have liked to go up the staircase and follow the gallery which ran round three sides of the hall, but Mrs. Oakley was saying, "Oh, no—we have come such a little way."

The stair ran up on the left-hand side with bare polished treads as black as the old beams. She dropped her coat on a big carved chair and turned reluctantly to follow Mrs. Oakley's rose-and-silver to the drawing-room. It was a pretty dress, and it had probably cost the earth. She wondered whether Mrs. Oakley ever wore anything but pink. You'd think she'd get tired of it—just one pink thing after another. Why not blue for a change, or green—

She had got as far as that, when she saw Gregory Porlock coming to meet them. There was a scatter of people round the fire, but she really only saw him. Coming to meet them with an outstretched hand and a charming smile. It would have been plain to anyone that he was their host, and that he was Gregory Porlock. It was perfectly plain to Dorinda that he was Glen Porteous, Aunt Mary's husband—the Wicked Uncle.

She mightn't have been so sure if it hadn't been for the Rowbecker photograph. Seven years is a long gap, as Gregory himself had concluded. If it hadn't been for the photograph, she might not have taken so confident a leap, or landed with so much certainty upon the other side. As it was, she had no doubts at all. But Aunt Mary's training held. She heard Mrs. Oakley murmur her name, met Gregory's smiling eyes, and put her hand in his.

If she had remembered nothing else, she would have remembered that warm, strong clasp. She had always remembered it. It was one of the things she had loved, and afterwards hated. Her colour deepened, her eyes sent him a steady look, and he knew just as well as if she had spoken his name that she had recognized him. Well, it would be more amusing that way. He said,

"But we have met before—on the telephone. And do you know, I think I could have described you. You are just like your voice. Now tell me—am I at all like mine?"

"I think so."

There was something of the gravity of the child he remembered, something of her simplicity and directness. If she wouldn't make a scene, neither would she play a game with him. Really quite an entertaining situation.

And then she looked past him and saw Justin Leigh. Gregory Porlock did not doubt that the surprise was as complete as it was delightful. It was so delightful that she forgot everything else. She went to meet him with a bloom and radiance which couldn't possibly escape the experienced observer. He had to turn from their meeting to introduce the Oakleys to the Totes and Mastermans. How they were going to mix, he had no idea, and whilst his social sense, functioning quite automatically, would do its best with six people of whom at least two were hating him furiously and two more were badly frightened, the sense of humour which very seldom left him drew its own detached amusement from the scene.

When Leonard Carroll added himself and his crooked smile to the already ill-assorted group he contributed a touch of the bizarre. Watching him cross the floor, Gregory wondered, by no means for the first time, whether the impression of some slight physical deformity arose from fact or fancy. Was one shoulder really a little higher than the other, or did it only appear to be so because the left eyebrow tilted whilst that on the right was straight? Did the left foot halt in the least perceptible limp, or was it a mere affectation akin to a drawling speech? Carroll could drawl when he liked, just as he could find a pungent phrase for point-blank rudeness. For the rest, he had very fine brown hair and not too much of it, a face rather oddly lined for what appeared to be his years, and a physique at once slight and full of nervous energy. His bright sardonic eyes passed over the five elderly people to whom he was being introduced in a manner which made it perfectly clear that as far as he was concerned they were so much furniture, dwelt for a moment upon Linnet Oakley, and was done with her. Gregory, prompt in hospitality, hastened to alleviate the situation with cocktails.

Justin Leigh had been surprised at the feelings with which he watched Dorinda come into the room. To one part of them he was by now no stranger, but this strong proprietary sense rather took him aback. It was, of course, increased by the fact that she was wearing the dress which they had chosen together. It was a good dress, and she looked well in it. The small bright circlet of his mother's brooch caught the light. But it wasn't only that. He had to admit that even in garments which his taste deplored there always had been something about Dorinda. You couldn't help noticing it when you saw her in a crowd. It was partly the way she held her head, and partly the curious, unusual way in which nature had taken the trouble to match her eyes and hair. Unusual colouring, a good carriage, the look of a wise child—these were contributory. But there was something more—the something which would have given him the feeling that they belonged if he had met her a stranger in a bus, a shipwreck, a bazaar in Bombay, or the desert of Gobi. It was one of those things. You couldn't explain it, you couldn't get rid of it, and, most significant of all, you didn't want to.

Her "How did you get here, Justin?" made no attempt to conceal her pleasure. He had, for once, no desire to hide his own. He laughed and said,

"Moira Lane was coming down for the week-end. She rang up and asked if she could bring me."

Dorinda had been too well brought up to allow her smile to fade. She hoped it didn't look as stiff as it felt.

And then, unbelievably, Justin was saying,

"Don't be silly. I came down to see you—at least not you, the Oakleys—in my capacity as chaperon."

She said, "Oh!" That is the only way it can be written, but it was a sound in which a little spring of laughter bubbled up.

And on that Gregory Porlock intervened.

"Now he's going to be next to you at dinner, so you must come and meet everyone else. And you must have a cocktail."

The introductions which followed gave her a lot of impressions, as it were in layers. Mr. Tote, red and stout, with eyes like an angry pig. Mr. Masterman, who reminded her of an undertaker though she couldn't have said why. Mrs. Tote, small and wispy behind a lot of grey satin and diamonds, with her hair screwed up as if she was going to have a bath, and a general resemblance to a kind but anxious mouse. Dorinda wondered why anyone should put on so many diamonds when all they did was to glare and glitter on a skinny neck and make the face above it look about a hundred and fifty.

Miss Masterman hadn't any diamonds. She wore an old-fashioned black lace dress, quite long in the sleeves and almost high in the neck, where it was fastened by a small pearl brooch. Meeting the dark eyes, Dorinda felt the word "mourning" come into her mind—"She's in mourning." But it hadn't anything to do with the black lace dress. It was the look in the eyes—as if something had been lost and could never be found again.

She had only had time to decide that she disliked Mr. Carroll, when the door opened upon the latest guest. Moira Lane came in with a definite air of having just bought the earth. She wore a velvet picture dress of the colour of a damask rose, and her cheeks matched it. Her extremely beautiful arms were bare to the shoulder, and upon her left wrist she wore Josephine's diamond and ruby bracelet. After pausing for a moment on the threshold she passed swiftly and lightly to the group by the fire and held out that arched left wrist to Gregory Porlock.

"There, Greg darling! Doesn't it look nice?"

She turned from him to sweep the whole company with a brilliant glance and said in her lightest, clearest tones,

"It's a joyous reunion. I lost my lovely bracelet, and Greg has just got it back for me. Quite too marvellous of him! I must never, never lose it again, must I?"

On the last words her eyes came back to Gregory's face. If it expressed admiration, it was no more than he felt to be her due. In the most public manner possible she was challenging him to claim the bracelet. What he didn't do now he could certainly never do again. It was a most definite "Speak now, or forever hold your peace!"

As the door opened and the butler appeared to announce that dinner was served, Gregory smiled back at her and said,

"More careful another time, my dear—that's the motto."

CHAPTER 16

Gregory shepherded them.

"Mrs. Tote, shall we lead the way? No formality, I think. I am afraid our numbers don't balance, but at an oval table that doesn't matter so much, does it?"

As they crossed the hall, Justin felt a sharp pinch on the arm. Looking down, he saw Dorinda's hand withdrawn, her eyes imploring. He fell back a pace and let the rest go by.

"What is it?"

Almost without moving her lips she said,

"He's the Wicked Uncle."

"Who is?"

"Mr. Porlock."

"Nonsense!"

She gave an emphatic nod.

"He *is*."

And with that they were at the dining-room door.

When they were in their places Dorinda found herself looking across the length of the table at Gregory and Mrs. Tote. Between her and them on her right were Mr. Masterman, Mrs. Oakley, Mr. Tote, Miss

Masterman, Gregory; and on her left Justin, that odd-looking Leonard Carroll, Moira Lane, Martin Oakley, and Mrs. Tote.

Her eyes came back to Moira, laughing with Leonard Carroll. Quite honestly and doggedly she accepted her as something quite out of her own class—a beautiful magical creature dispensing smiles and wit with easy charm and perfect poise. She took her soup soberly, and had so far forgotten Gregory that when Justin said, "Did you mean that?" she had lost the thread and could only give him a blank look.

"What you said just now," he prompted. "It seems incredible."

"Sorry—I was thinking of something else. Of course I did."

"You can't be sure."

"Oh, but I am. Quite—quite—*quite* sure."

"Then we'd better talk about something else."

Dorinda looked again at Moira Lane. Leonard Carroll was leaning towards her with his crooked smile. A rapid cut and thrust flashed back and forth between them. She said quite low to Justin,

"How beautiful she is."

She wondered why he should be amused.

"Decorative creature," he said. "All the lights on to-night. I wonder why."

Something in Dorinda's mind said, "Oh, Justin, they're for you." Didn't he know? She thought he must. But perhaps you didn't when it was for you. . . . She wondered about that. When you were very, very fond of anyone, did it make you see clearly, or did it make a kind of mist in which you had to grope your way? She thought it might do both these things—not at the same time of course, but first one and then the other. Like with her and Justin—because sometimes she felt that she could see right into his mind and know just what he was thinking, like when he hated her blue dress, but other times she didn't know at all, like just now about Moira Lane.

She emerged from this train of thought to help herself to an entrée. Justin and Moira were talking across Leonard Carroll. No, he was talking too. They were laughing together. On her right Mr. Masterman was staring at his plate. Mrs. Oakley beyond him had turned to Mr. Tote, to whom she could be heard recounting some instance of Marty's unusual precocity and intelligence. The words, "And he was only three at the time," impinged upon Dorinda's ear. They must have impinged upon Mr. Tote's ear too, but he gave no sign that they had done so. He had taken a very large helping and was eating his way through it in an impervious manner.

Urged by social duty, Dorinda addressed Mr. Masterman's profile.

"I do hope it isn't going to snow—don't you?"

His full face was even less reassuring than his profile. He looked at Dorinda as if she wasn't there and said, "Why?"

"Messy—so perfectly horrid when it thaws. And never enough of it to do anything with."

She got the profile again. He had taken up a fork and begun upon the entrée, but with the same air of not noticing what it was. Which seemed a terrible waste, because it was frightfully good and very intriguing. Even in the middle of feeling how beautiful Moira was, and what a marvellous wife she would make for Justin, Dorinda couldn't help wondering what it was made of. The three on her left all laughed again. Justin sat turned away, making no attempt to include her. She couldn't guess how devoutly he was hoping that she had not heard the joke.

It was at this moment that Linnet Oakley, having finished her anecdote, found herself addressed by Gregory Porlock across Miss Masterman and Mr. Tote. Just what prompted him remains a matter for conjecture. On his right Mrs. Tote was engaged with her other neighbour, Martin Oakley. They appeared to be comparing notes upon the intelligence of infants as exemplified by Marty and her daughter Allie's child. Gregory had, perhaps, exhausted the flow of conversation which he had been perseveringly directing towards Miss Masterman, and to which she had remained completely unresponsive. He may have been provoked to malice, he may merely have felt that a diversion of some kind was a necessity. Be that as it may, he addressed Linnet by name.

"Mrs. Oakley, I hope you were successful in getting the luminous paint you wanted."

Her helpless, startled air was noticed then, and remembered later. Mr. Tote noticed it. Woman looked like a frightened rabbit—just about that much brain. Mr. Masterman on her other side would not, perhaps, have been roused to notice anything if it had not been for the fact that her left hand was on the table between them, and that when she started in that senseless way she very nearly had his champagne-glass over. On the other side of the table Mrs. Tote thought Mrs. Oakley very nervous, and Martin Oakley, watching her change colour, wondered whether she wasn't feeling well.

Linnet drew a fluttering breath and said, "Oh, yes," took another, and said,

"It was Miss Brown who got it."

"Without any trouble, I hope," said Gregory Porlock, to Dorinda this time. And the moment he said it

Dorinda was perfectly sure that he knew just what had happened at the De Luxe Stores. Their eyes met. Each said something to the other. Gregory's said, "You see— take care." Dorinda's said, "I know."

And she did. She would never be able to prove it, but she was quite, quite sure that he had pulled the strings which took her to the De Luxe Stores and took someone else there to put stolen goods in her pocket. Why? To get her away from the Oakleys, where she couldn't help meeting him and might be inconvenient enough to recognize a Wicked Uncle.

She came back to the conversation, to find that practically everyone round the table had entered it. Martin Oakley was saying,

"The stuff has been extraordinarily difficult to get, and we wanted it for Marty's clock. I was really grateful to you for the tip, Greg. I told my wife to get on with it, as Miss Brown was going up to town."

Dorinda sorted that out. Gregory Porlock had told Martin Oakley that the De Luxe had luminous paint, and Martin had told his wife. It all fitted in. As she got there, Mrs. Tote said,

"But, Mr. Porlock, whatever did *you* want with luminous paint?"

Leonard Carroll broke in with a laugh.

"Don't you know? I guessed at once. He goes creeping round with it in the dead of night looking for kind deeds to do by stealth. The perfect host—nothing escapes him. Comfort for the guest, and a twenty-four hour service—that's the way it goes."

Gregory laughed too. Mrs. Tote considered that "that Mr. Carroll" had had quite enough champagne. Something in the acting line, and a bit too free with his tongue. Some of the things he'd been saying to Miss Lane—well, really! And all she did was laugh, when what he wanted was a good setting-down. Give that sort an inch, and they'll have the whole bolt of cloth before you can turn your head.

Gregory was laughing too.

"I'm afraid I'm not quite as attentive as that. I wanted the paint for that beam which runs across as you go down a step into the cloakroom. I don't know why they built these old houses up and down like that— I suppose they didn't bother to get their levels. Anyhow it's a bit awkward for anyone who doesn't know his way. You can reach the switch without going down the step, but only just, and you clear the beam if you're not over six foot, but an extra tall guest is liable to brain himself, and anyone might come a cropper over the step. So I had the bright idea of painting the beam and the switch with luminous paint. By the way, I must apologize for the smell. It's had one coat, which I hope is dry, but it's got to have another, so we left the paint in the cupboard."

Mrs. Oakley said in rather a high voice,

"Marty loves his clock. Martin gave it another coat just before we came out. Marty says he loves to wake up in the night and see it looking at him. He says it's like a big eye. He has so much imagination."

Mr. Tote turned a cross red face.

"How can it look like an eye? It's only the hands that's painted! Funny sort of an eye!"

Linnet gave a flustered laugh.

"Oh, well—you see—Marty painted the whole face. He didn't know. And Nurse says it doesn't matter, because the hands can be painted black, and then she'll get quite near enough to the time by the position they're in without bothering about the numbers. And of course Marty doesn't care so long as it shines in the dark."

"So shines," proclaimed Mr. Carroll, "a good deed

in this naughty world. Much ado about nothing. Night's candles are burnt out. Let us eat, drink, and be merry. I could go on for hours like this if anyone would like me to."

"They wouldn't," said Moira.

"Then I'll tell you the latest, the very latest scandal—night's scandals being by no means all burnt out." He dropped his voice, and Justin turned back to Dorinda with the feeling that this was the most ill-assorted company he had ever been in, and that he wouldn't be sorry when the evening was over.

It was at this moment that it occurred to him to wonder why a man of Gregory Porlock's unquestionable social gifts should have assembled at his table people so incompatible as the Totes and Leonard Carroll, the Mastermans and Moira Lane, to mention only the extremer instances. To this "Why?" he had no reply, but it was to return and clamour for an answer before the night was out. For the moment he dismissed it and fell into easy, natural talk with Dorinda.

CHAPTER 17

You can bring a horse to water, but you cannot make him drink. Assembled in the drawing-room after dinner, Gregory Porlock's guests exemplified this proverb. As far as the Totes and the Mastermans were concerned, they might have been compared to a string of mules gazing blankly at a stream at which they had no intention of quenching their thirst.

Neither Mrs. Tote nor Miss Masterman played cards, but Gregory drove them with determination into other games. It is, of course, one way of breaking the ice, but it is not always a very successful way. Required to write down a list of things all beginning with the letter *M* which she would take to a desert island, under such headings as Food, Drink, Clothes, Livestock, and Miscellaneous, Miss Masterman gave up a perfectly blank sheet, while Mrs. Tote contributed Mice and Mustard. Mr. Carroll's list was witty, vulgar, and brief; Dorinda's rather painstaking; and Gregory's easily the longest. Mr. Tote declined to participate, and Mr. Masterman was found to be absent. Returning presently, he participated in the second round with a kind of gloomy efficiency, and came in second.

Uphill work as it had been, there was some slight thawing of the frost. When Moira suggested charades, no one except Mr. Tote absolutely refused to play. There was no doubt that the suggestion came from Moira. Everyone was to be clear about that, and that it was Leonard Carroll who violently objected to a charade, as he said that to drive totally incompetent amateurs through one scene would endanger his sanity, but that to attempt three would certainly wreck it, so he wasn't prepared to go beyond doing a proverb. Whereupon Moira cut in with an "All right, you pick up for one side, and Greg for the other." And Leonard Carroll put an arm round her shoulders and sang in his high, dry tenor, "You are my first, my only choice!" To which she replied with a short laugh, "You'll have to take your share, darling. You can't land Greg with all the rest."

Gregory at once picked Martin Oakley, thus making it practically certain that Linnet would fall into the other camp.

In the end the party to go out under Leonard Carroll consisted of Mrs. Oakley, Moira, Mr. Masterman, and

Mrs. Tote, while Gregory remained in the drawing-room with Miss Masterman, Dorinda, Martin Oakley, and Justin Leigh, Mr. Tote continuing to sit in a large armchair and smoke with an air of having nothing to do with the proceedings. His wife threw him rather an odd look as she left the room. There was apprehension in it, and something like reproof. It is all very well to be angry, but you needn't forget your manners, and Albert was old enough to know when he'd had as much drink as he could carry. A couple of cocktails, and all that champagne, and goodness knew how much port wine—no wonder he didn't feel like playing games. Well, no more did she, if it came to that. Games were for young people, and a pretty sight to see them enjoying themselves. They'd always had a Christmas party for Allie. Pretty as a picture she'd look with her fair hair floating.

It was just as the party reached the hall that the butler crossed it on his way to fetch the coffee-tray. He came back with it in a moment, a thin, narrow-shouldered man with a face which reminded Mrs. Tote of a monkey. Something about the way the eyes were set and the way his cheeks fell in. It was the first time she had noticed him. She did so now with plea-surable recollections of taking Allie to the Zoo and seeing the chimpanzees have their tea.

One of the drawbacks to games of the charade type is that half the company is consigned to a long, dull wait, whilst the other half has all the amusement of dressing up and quarrelling over what they are going to act. Leonard Carroll made it perfectly clear that he was going to have the star part, and that the others were only there to do what they were told. He was going to be the devil. Moira was to be a nun—"Go and get a sheet and two towels." Mr. Masterman was to wear a long black cloak—"There's one hanging up in the lobby." Mrs. Tote a mackintosh and the largest man's hat she could lay hands on. Mrs. Oakley could stay as she was. If she liked to take some of the flowers off the dinner-table and make herself a wreath she could. "And remember, everything's going to depend on the timing, so if anyone doesn't do what he's told, off to hell he goes in my burning claws! Oh, and we'll have to do it out here."

He opened the drawing-room door abruptly and addressed the group inside.

"We're doing it out here. Auditorium round the fire, nice and warm. Masterman will let you know when we're ready."

Inside the drawing-room Miss Masterman and Mr. Tote sat silent and the others talked. Dorinda found herself admiring the Uncle's flow of bonhomie. It really was quite easy to be amused and to join in. Perhaps the fact that Justin had come over to sit on the arm of her chair made it easier than it would have been if he had been out in the hall with Moira Lane. But of course Mr. Carroll wouldn't want him there. He admired Moira himself.

Mr. Carroll was a fast worker. It was certainly not more than ten minutes before the door opened and Mr. Masterman beckoned to them with an arm shrouded in black drapery.

Coming out of the brightly lighted room, the hall seemed dark. The glow had gone from the fire. All the lights had been extinguished except a small reading-lamp. It stood on the stone mantelpiece, its tilted shade covered and prolonged by thick brown paper in such a manner as to throw one bright beam across the hall. It fell slantingly and made a pool of light between the foot of the stair and a massive oak table placed against its panelled side. All beyond this was shadowy, the stair itself, the space around it, the back of the hall—degrees of darkness receding into total gloom.

Masterman piloted them to the hearth, around which chairs had been assembled, placed on a slant to face the stairway and the back of the hall. A point on which everyone afterwards seemed uncertain was whether Mr. Tote had taken his place among the rest. No one could declare that he had, and no one was prepared to say that he had not.

From somewhere above their heads a high, floating voice said, "The curtain rises," and down the length of the stair came a movement of shadowy forms, becoming more distinct as they came nearer to the pool of light, entering it and passing out of it again into the deeper shade beyond. Masterman first, really an effective figure in his black cloak, always the most macabre of garments, and a bandage, white and ghastly, blinding one eye and blotting out half his face. After him Mrs. Tote, bent double over a crotched stick, her grey satin and diamonds hidden by an old stained waterproof, her head lost in a battered wide-brimmed hat. She passed out of the light, and Linnet Oakley took her place—a dazzle of rose and silver, flowers in her hair, flowers in her hands. She had been told to smile, but as she stepped into the lighted space she was suddenly afraid. Her lips parted, her eyes stared. She stood for a moment as if she was waiting for something to happen, and then with a visible shudder went on into the dark. The tall white nun who followed her was Moira Lane. She walked with eyes cast down and a string of beads between her hands. Then full in the beam of light, the eyelids lifted, the head turned, the eyes looked back over her shoulder.

She passed on. At the moment she came level with

the oak table something moved on the stair above her and the single light went out, leaving the hall quite black. Upon this blackness there appeared the luminous shape of a face, two jutting horns, two luminous thrusting hands. They were high up—they were lower—they came swooping down. Moira's scream rang in the rafters, and was followed by a horrid chuckling laugh.

She did not scream again when Len Carroll caught her about the shoulders and brought his crooked mouth down hard upon her own, but she very nearly made her thumb and forefinger meet in the flesh of his under arm.

When Mr. Masterman switched on all the lights the devil was back on the table from which he had swooped, a dark pullover hiding his shirt, and a daubed paper mask dangling from his hand. The horns were paper too. They stuck out jauntily above a face which for the moment really did look devilish. The audience clapped, and Gregory called out, "Bravo, my dear fellow! First-class! But we've guessed your proverb—'The devil takes the hindmost.'"

Leonard Carroll waved a hand whitened with paint and came down from the table in an agile leap.

"Your turn now," he said. "I must go and get this stuff off, or it will be all over the place." He came forward as he spoke.

Everyone was to be asked about how near he was to Gregory Porlock. The evidence on this point presents a good deal of confusion. There is general agreement that he joined the group by the fire, spoke to one or two people, was congratulated on the success of the charade, and then turned away and ran up the stairs, taking them two at a time. Where the evidence fails is on the point of any direct contact with Gregory. When he was asked why he didn't wash in the downstair cloakroom he had his answer ready—he had to get rid of the pullover and resume the dinner-jacket which he had left in his room.

Conversation broke out below. Dorinda looked across at Moira and saw her stand just where she had been when the lights went on, between the table and the hearth. She was taking off the two white face-towels which had bound brow and chin for the nun's head-dress. Her eyes were angry, her fingers moved with energy. She threw the towels down upon the table, stepped clear of the sheet which had formed her robe, and flung it after the towels in a bundle, hit or miss. It slid on the polished surface and fell in a heap to the floor, taking one of the towels with it. Moira's hands went to her hair. There was no mirror in the hall. She shook out her full crimson skirt and came over to Justin.

"How is my hair? I can't be bothered to go upstairs. Will it do?"

He nodded.

"Not a wave out of place."

"Oh, well, I was pretty careful. How did it go?"

"As Porlock said—a first-class show. We shan't do half so well. You have a magnificent scream. A pity we can't borrow you."

She laughed.

"Would you like to?" Then with a jerk in her voice, "Oh, Len was the star turn."

Gregory had gone over towards the stair. He stood a little clear of the group about the fire and raised his voice.

"Well, it's our turn now. I'm afraid we shan't be a patch on you. You were really all most awfully good. Will you go back into the drawing-room now and leave us to do the best we can—Mrs. Tote, Mrs. Oakley, Moira, Masterman. Carroll won't get that stuff off in a hurry—he'll have to join you later. I don't think we want to wait for him. The rest stay here."

He began to walk towards them, but before he had taken a couple of steps the lights went out again. Linnet Oakley gave a little startled scream. Mr. Masterman called out, "Who did that?" There was a general stir of movement. Someone knocked over a chair. And right on that there was something between a cough and a groan, and the sound of a heavy fall.

Justin Leigh reached for Dorinda and pushed her back against the wall. If he groped his way along it he would come to the front door. He had no idea where the other light switches were, but in every civilized house there is at least one which you can turn on as you come in from outside. Disregarding the confusion of voices behind him, he made his way past a door which he didn't yet know to be that of the study, and arrived. Reckoning from the groan, it might have been three quarters of a minute before he found a switch and the light came on in the candles all round the hall.

The scene rushed into view—everyone fixed in the sudden, startling light—everyone fixed finally and distinctly in Justin's thought. The sketch he was to make an hour or two later shows everyone's position. In the open drawing-room door on the left, Mr. Tote staring in on what had been darkness but had suddenly changed to most revealing light. Coming down the stairs, but only three steps from the top, Leonard Carroll, one hand on the baluster, one foot poised for the next descent. Round the hearth, Dorinda where he had pushed her against the wall, Masterman, Mrs. Tote, Miss Masterman, and on the far side Martin Oakley. Between these people and the foot of the stair, two women and a man—Moira Lane, Gregory Porlock, and Linnet Oakley.

He lay face downwards on the floor between them, one arm flung out, the other doubled beneath him. Between his shoulder blades something caught the light— a burnished handle like a hilt, the handle of a dagger.

Everyone in the hall was looking at it. Having looked, Justin's eyes went to the panelling above the hearth. Between the sconces hung a trophy of arms— crossed flintlocks; a sword with an ivory handle; a sword in a tarnished velvet scabbard; a couple of long, fine rapiers; half a dozen daggers. He looked for a break in the pattern and found it. There was a gap in the inner ring—there was a dagger short. After the briefest glance his eyes went back to that burnished hilt between Gregory Porlock's shoulders.

No one had spoken. No one moved. No one seemed to breathe, until Linnet Oakley screamed. She screamed, took two steps forward, and went down on her knees, calling out, "Oh, Glen! He's dead! Glen's dead—he's dead! Oh, Glen—Glen—*Glen!*"

It was like a stone dashed into a reflection. The picture broke. Everyone moved, drew breath, exclaimed. Mr. Tote came out of the drawing-room. Mr. Carroll came down the stairs. Moira took a backward step, and then another, and another, all very slowly and stiffly, as if the body inside her damask dress had been changed from flesh and blood to something heavy, hard, and cold. She went on going back until she struck against a chair and stood in front of it, quite still, quite motionless, her face one even pallor, her eyes still fixed upon the spot where Gregory Porlock lay.

Martin Oakley went to his wife. She wept hysterically and cast herself into his arms, sobbing. "It's Glen—and somebody's killed him! He's dead—he's dead—he's *dead!*"

CHAPTER 18

In an emergency some one person usually takes command. In this instance it was Justin Leigh. He came quickly down the hall, knelt by the body, clasped the outflung wrist for a long minute, and then got up and walked to the bell on the left of the hearth, breast-high under a row of switches. Standing there and waiting there for the answer to his summons, he looked briefly about him. Switches by the front door—the light hadn't been turned off from there. Switches here, on the left as you faced the hearth, fifteen feet or so in a direct line from where Gregory had been stabbed—anyone round the fire could have reached them. Switches by the service door opening from the back of the hall where the panelled casing of the stairway gave place to a recess—certainly anyone could have opened that door with very little chance of being seen and have reached for the lights. The door to the billiard-room was also in the recess, at right angles to the service door—but the switches couldn't have been reached from there without coming out into the hall, with the strong probability of being seen by someone near the fire.

As his mind registered these things, the service door opened and the butler came in. Justin went a step or two to meet him, saw his face change, and said,

"Mr. Porlock has been stabbed. He is dead. Will you ring up the police and ask them to come as quickly as they can. Tell them nothing will be touched. Come back as soon as you have got through."

The man hesitated, seemed about to speak, and

thought better of it. As he turned and went out by the way he had come and Justin went back to the body, Leonard Carroll came to a stand beside him and said quite low, out of the side of his mouth,

"Taking quite a lot on yourself, aren't you? What about pulling out that knife and giving the poor devil a chance?"

Justin shook his head.

"No use—he's dead."

"You seem very sure."

"I was through the war."

Carroll said, with something that just stopped short of being a laugh,

"Well, that lands us in for a game of Hunt the Murderer! I wonder who did it. Whoever it was can reassure himself with the thought that the painstaking local constabulary will probably obliterate any clues he may have left." He did laugh then, and added, "Now I do wonder who hated Gregory enough to take a chance like this."

Justin made no reply. He was looking at the group of people any one of whom might be the answer to Leonard Carroll's question. Mrs. Tote was sitting in a small ornamental Sheraton chair. The waterproof she had worn for the charade lay along at her feet with a horrid resemblance to a second body, but she was still wearing the hat, an old-fashioned wideawake, now tipped well to one side. Her small features were sternly set. Perhaps the grey satin of her dress and the glitter of her diamonds contributed to her pallor. She sat without moving, stiffly upright, her hands in a rigid clasp, the large bediamonded rings still and unwinking. Miss Masterman had remained standing, but not upright. She had hold of the back of a chair and was bent forward over her straining hands. She wore no rings, and every knuckle stood up white. As he looked Justin saw her brother come over to her. He said something, and when she made no reply fell back again to the edge of the hearth, where he bent down to put a log on the fire. Linnet Oakley lay sobbing in a long armchair, Dorinda on one side of her, Martin Oakley on the other. The pink and white carnations which she had taken from the dinner-table to make a wreath had for the most part fallen. There was one on the arm of the chair, and one on her lap. A bud and a leaf hung down against her neck like a pendant earring. Her face was hidden against her husband's shoulder. He looked across at Justin now, and said in a deep, harsh voice,

"I've got to get my wife out of this—she's ill."

Justin crossed the space between them. He dropped his voice.

"I'm sorry, but I'm afraid you'll have to wait until the police come."

Their eyes met, Martin's dark with anger.

"And who's going to make me?"

Justin said, "Your own common sense, I should think."

"What do you mean by that?"

"What do you suppose? Anyone who gets out is going to attract a good deal more attention than it's worth."

There was a moment of extreme tension. There was something as well as anger. Justin remembered that the Wicked Uncle's name was Glen—Glen Porteous. Mrs. Oakley had cried out that Glen was dead. Nine people had heard her say it, as well as Martin Oakley. If he held his tongue, the others couldn't and wouldn't. Mrs. Oakley, who had met Gregory Porlock tonight as a stranger, would certainly have to explain to the police why she had flung herself down weeping by his body and called him Glen. As he went back to his post he saw one of her pink carnations. The heavy bloom had broken off. It lay between Gregory's left shoulder and the thick curly hair.

Mr. Tote had gone over to stand beside his wife. Not a muscle of her face moved. The small greyish eyes stared steadily down at her own hands.

Leonard Carroll said sharply,

"What we all want is a drink."

He was still where he had been, a yard or two from the body, staring at it. There was a curious white mark on the back—a round pale smudge, with the knife driven home in the centre of it.

It came to Justin with horror that the smudge was luminous paint.

CHAPTER 19

That   Saturday   night
brought very little sleep to the Grange. With dreadful suddenness it had ceased to be a private dwelling. Justin, whose mother had been a devoted bee-keeper, could not help being reminded of the moments when she used to remove part of the outer covering and watch through a sheet of glass the private activities of the hive. Cross the line which divides the law-abiding from the law-breaker, and all cherished rights of privacy are gone. The police surgeon, the photographer, the fingerprint man, Sergeant, Inspector, Chief Constable—each and every one of them comes and takes a look through just such a pane of glass and watches to see who shrinks from the observing eye. Murder, which used to be one of the most private things on earth, is now attended by

a vast deal of ceremony and publicity, and whilst an efficient constabulary attended to its rights, Inspector Hughes sat in the study taking statements.

It was late before Martin Oakley was permitted to take his wife and her secretary back to the Mill House, and later still before those who remained could separate and go to bed if not to sleep.

At ten o'clock on the Sunday morning Detective Sergeant Frank Abbott rang up Miss Maud Silver at her flat in Montague Mansions.

"Miss Silver speaking."

"This is Frank. I'm afraid I shan't be able to come to tea. A bloke has got himself stabbed in Surrey, and as everyone who can possibly have done it hails from London and the corpse was London too, they've thrown the job at us, and the Chief and I are off. What's the odds you crop up as we go along?"

Miss Silver gave her characteristic cough.

"That, my dear Frank, is hardly likely."

She heard him heave an exaggerated sigh.

"I wish it were. Never a dull moment when you're about. Uplift a speciality—morals strictly attended to."

"My dear Frank!"

"I'm afraid it's a case of 'Never the time, and the place, and the loved one all together.' I must fly."

Later on in the morning Justin rang up Dorinda.

"Are you all right?"

"Oh, yes."

"Get any sleep?"

"Well—"

"I don't suppose anyone did much. How is Mrs. Oakley?"

"Very upset."

"I'd come up and see you, but I hear the job's been turned over to Scotland Yard. They may walk in at any moment now, so I think I'd better be here. They'll want to see everyone of course."

There was a pause. Then Dorinda said,

"Horrid for you—but, oh, it does make such a difference your being in it too!"

He said firmly, "Neither of us is in it," and rang off.

Actually, Chief Detective Inspector Lamb and Sergeant Abbott did not reach the Grange until a little after two o'clock, having meanwhile conferred with Inspector Hughes, gone through the statements which he had obtained, and partaken of a mediocre lunch at the local inn.

Admitted by the butler, Lamb stared hard at him before letting him take his coat and hat. Coming in out of the grey afternoon light, the hall seemed middling dark. The man threw open the first door on the right and stood aside to let them pass into the study. The Chief Inspector walked as far as the writing-table and, turning, called him.

"Come in and shut the door! You're the butler?"

"Yes, sir."

The light from three windows showed a middle-aged man with a slight forward stoop, thinning hair, brown eyes, and rather hollow cheeks.

Lamb said sharply, "Pearson! I thought so!"

The butler did not speak, only lifted his eyes with a deprecatory expression and stood there waiting.

Frank Abbott looked from one to the other and waited too.

Very deliberately the Chief Inspector pulled up a chair to the table and sat down. He was in the habit of judging the furniture in a house by the way in which any given chair stood up to his weight. Since this one received him without a protesting creak, it was approved. Perhaps he judged men by the manner in which they sustained his formidable stare. If so, Pearson would not come off so badly. He stood there, meek, elderly, and silent, but not very much discomposed. The stare continued.

"Pearson! My word! I didn't expect to see you here, and I don't suppose you thought of seeing me."

"No, sir."

"You're butler here?"

"Yes, sir."

"What's the game?" Lamb shifted his gaze to Sergeant Abbott, who had been an interested spectator. "This is Mr. Ernest Pearson of the Blake Detective Agency. Used to be in the Force—invalided out." He turned back again. "Come along, man—out with it! What are you doing here?"

"Well—"

Lamb gave the table a sudden bang with his fist.

"What's the good of hemming and hawing? This is murder. You don't need me to tell you that any private game you may have had will just have to go to the wall. Why are you here?"

The mild brown eyes were still deprecatory, but not alarmed.

"I know that, sir. I was just thinking how I could put it. The fact is, it's a bit delicate. Mr. Blake sent me down here to watch Mr. Porlock."

"Divorce?"

"Oh, no, sir—" he hesitated, and then came out with it—"blackmail."

Frank Abbott's eyebrows rose. The Chief Inspector allowed himself to whistle.

A faint shade of melancholy triumph invaded Pearson's manner as he repeated the word.

"Blackmail—that was Mr. Porlock's business. One of our clients was in a terrible state over it—something he'd got on her, she wouldn't tell us what. So Mr. Blake, he sent me here to see if I couldn't get something that would scare Mr. Porlock off."

"Blackmailing the blackmailer—eh?"

"Oh, no, sir."

Lamb gave a short laugh.

"What else? But that's not my pigeon. You say Porlock was a blackmailer. Have you any evidence of that?"

Pearson diffused a certain modest pride.

"Only what I've heard with my own ears."

Frank Abbott had drawn a chair up to the far side of the table. His overcoat removed, he was seen to be elegantly attired—grey suit, grey socks, a blue and grey tie, a blue and grey handkerchief just showing above the line of the pocket. As always, his very fair hair was slicked back and mirror-smooth, his light eyes cool and observant, his manner cool and detached. Lamb jerked a "Notes, Frank," over his shoulder, and the long, pale hand began to move busily above a writing-pad.

Lamb leaned forward, a hand on either knee, his body vigorous in spite of the flesh it carried, his florid face expressionless under the thatch of strong dark hair just beginning to thin away from the crown. He looked at Pearson and repeated his words.

"What you heard with your own ears? Do you mean that he was blackmailing any of these people in the house?"

The shade of triumph deepened.

"Most of them, I should say."

"If that's the case, you'd better pull up a chair and we'll get down to it."

Quietly and deferentially Mr. Ernest Pearson fetched himself a chair. When he was seated, hands folded, feet nearly together, he coughed and observed that it was a little hard to know where to begin.

Frank Abbott leaned across the table to lay a list of names before his Chief. It was received with a grunt and a nod. Lamb read from it the names of Mr. and Mrs. Tote.

"Know anything about them?"

"Oh, yes. Him and Mr. Porlock had very high words in this room after tea yesterday. By leaving the door unlatched after attending to the fire I was enabled to overhear part of what passed between them. A butler has great advantages in the line of overhearing conversations, if I may say so. What with taking in drinks, and fetching out trays, and attending to fires, he can pretty nearly always have an excuse for being close to a door, and with a centrally heated house no draught is felt if the door should be left on the jar."

Frank Abbott's hand covered his lips for a moment. Mr. Pearson's meek ingenuity had threatened him with a smile. Lamb's face remained a frowning blank. He said,

"You overheard a conversation between Porlock and Mr. Tote?"

The mild brown eyes met his without a tremor.

"Part of it, sir. Mr. Porlock was saying things to Mr. Tote that made him very angry—Mr. Tote, if you take my meaning."

"What sort of things?"

"Well, you couldn't call it anything else except blackmail—you really couldn't. Mr. Tote, he used the word himself—fairly shouted it out. And then there was one of the maids come through the hall and I was bound to move away. I crossed over to the morning-room on the other side of the hall, and when I got back Mr. Porlock, he was saying, 'Well, there's two can swear to time and place, and you know as well as I do that if the police begin to look into it there'd be plenty more.' "

"What were they talking about?"

"Black market, sir. Mr. Porlock, he put it to him straight when he tried to explain it away. 'You can tell that to Scotland Yard,' he said. 'I suppose you think they'll believe you,' he said. 'And if they don't, you can always try the Marines!' he said, and he laughed hearty. Very fond of a joke, Mr. Porlock was."

"And did Mr. Tote laugh too?"

"Oh, no, sir—he cursed and swore something shocking. And Mr. Porlock said, 'Come, come, Tote—you've made a pot of money, and if you won't spare a thousand to shut these men's mouths you don't deserve to keep it.' And Mr. Tote said, 'Shut their mouths, my foot! It's your mouth wants shutting, and if you don't look out you'll get it shut so that it'll stay that way! I'm not a man to be blackmailed!' And Mr. Porlock laughs very pleasant and says, 'Black market or blackmail— you pay your money and you take your choice.' "

Lamb's frown deepened.

"You say Mr. Tote was threatening him?"

"He used the words I've said, and his manner was very threatening too, sir."

"Hear any more?"

"No, sir. Mr. Tote got up—using very violent language, he was. So I went back and attended to the hall fire until he came out, which he did almost at once, and off up the stairs, as red as a turkey cock."

Without moving his position Lamb said,

"That's Tote. Who else?"

Mr. Pearson hesitated slightly.

"Well, sir, Mr. Porlock came out of the study and went into the drawing-room. But he didn't stay there. He came out again with Miss Masterman and her brother and took them off to the billiard-room, so I went to lay the table for dinner. That's the dining-room, sir, on the other side of that wall behind you, and where those book-shelves are there's a door going through. You can see it on the other side, but of course it can't be used because of the shelves. Still, you know how it is—voices carry through a door the way they wouldn't if it was a wall. And presently I could hear that Mr. Porlock was in the study again, and one of the ladies with him, so I went up close—polishing my silver in case of anyone coming in."

"Well?"

Ernest Pearson looked mournful and shook his head.

"Not very satisfactory, I'm afraid, except that it was Miss Lane he'd got with him, and there was something about a bracelet, and I heard her say, 'I shouldn't like my cousin to know,' and something about being in a frightful hole and having to have the money. I don't find a lady's voice quite so easy to follow—not so resonant, if you take me. Now Mr. Porlock, he had what I should call a ring in his voice—I could hear him all right. I don't know what you'll make of it, but this is what he said—'Well, don't sell it again. It's a bit too dangerous—someone else might recognize it next time.' And then he said, 'I've got the receipted bill, you know. It describes the bracelet. You can have till Monday morning to make up your mind. Meanwhile we'll call a truce.' And I couldn't help noticing when she came down to dinner that Miss Lane was wearing a very valuable diamond and ruby bracelet."

Lamb grunted.

"You said you didn't know what I'd make of all this. What do you make of it yourself?"

"Well, sir, with one thing and another, it did come into my mind to wonder about Miss Lane selling the bracelet—whether she had the right to, as you might say. I certainly got the impression that Mr. Porlock thought he'd got something he could use against her. But it didn't look to me as if it was money he wanted, because if he bought that bracelet he must have paid a lot of money for it. It looked to me as if there was something he wanted Miss Lane to do, and she didn't want to, so he was giving her time to think it over. She's a lady that goes about a lot—very well connected, as you might say. A high-class blackmailer like Mr. Porlock—well, there are ways a lady like Miss Lane could be a lot of use to him."

Lamb's grunt may have meant that he agreed. On the other hand it may just have been a grunt.

Frank Abbott's pencil travelled, and his thoughts too. What a case! What a pity to have to hang even a Tote for removing a blackmailer from the body politic. Perhaps it wasn't Tote. He hoped quite dispassionately that it wasn't the lady who might or might not have stolen a diamond and ruby bracelet. But perhaps there were others. . . . He turned his attention to Pearson, who was at that moment producing Mr. Leonard Carroll like a rabbit out of a hat.

"*The* Leonard Carroll!" he exclaimed.

Lamb turned the frown his way.

"Know him?"

"Society entertainer. Clever—sophisticated—very much the rage at the moment. I don't know him personally. If I did I should probably dislike him quite a lot."

The Chief Inspector enquired darkly,

"One of these crooners?"

"Oh, no, sir. There's always one bright spot, isn't there? It is nice to reflect that whatever else he has done, he has never crooned."

"Well, what *has* he done?" growled Lamb.

"Perhaps Pearson is going to tell us, sir."

Ernest Pearson had plenty to tell. Mr. Carroll had arrived later than any of the other guests. He had gone straight into the study, and circumstances being favourable, there had been some very satisfactory listening-in. "Everyone being upstairs dressing for dinner, as you might say. Which of course Mr. Carroll would count on, for there wasn't any keeping his voice down. Not exactly loud, if you know what I mean, but very carrying."

"What did he say?"

"It's more what didn't he say, sir—or what both of them didn't say. Mr. Carroll, he started in hammer and tongs. 'What's all this about Tauscher? I don't know the man from Adam. Who is he—what is he? You're a damned blackmailer, and I've come down here to tell you so!' And Mr. Porlock says, 'You've come down here to save your neck.'"

The Chief Inspector whistled.

"His neck—eh? What had he been up to—murder?"

Pearson shook his head.

"Worse, if you'll excuse my saying so. Because there's murders you can understand how a man came to do them. I wouldn't like you to think I was excusing them, but you can see how they got there. But meeting enemy agents on the sly when you were supposed to be out with a concert party entertaining the troops, and giving things away that might mean hundreds of lives—well, that's the sort of thing that nobody can understand except those that have demeaned themselves to do it." A dull flush coloured his cheekbones as he spoke. "I'd a boy out there myself in 'forty-five, and I've got my feelings."

Lamb said, "That's all right. What did you hear?"

"Well, it was a bit here and a bit there. Seems there's

a man called Tauscher that Mr. Porlock got his information from, and according to Mr. P. this is what it
amounted to. Tauscher says he had a brother who was
a Nazi agent. When this brother died—he got bumped
off towards the end of the war—this Tauscher opened
up a box of papers his brother had left with him. That's
Mr. Porlock's story, if you understand, and I'm not saying how much of it's true. All I say is, he put it to Mr.
Carroll that Tauscher had left notes of their meetings
which incriminated him up to the hilt, and what did he
propose to do about it? Mr. Carroll, he uses most awful
language and says it's all a lie, and Mr. Porlock laughs
and says of course he knows his own business best, and
if that's the way he feels, then it don't matter about
Tauscher going ahead and turning his brother's papers
over to our people out there—it being his idea to show
what a good German he is by doing so. I thought Mr.
Carroll was going to have a fit—I really did, sir. And
anything like the language—well, you know what you
come across in the way of business, but I give you my
word it was enough to curl your hair. Mr. Porlock, he
just laughed very pleasantly and said, 'We won't say
another word about it, my dear fellow.' And Mr. Carroll says, fit to kill, 'How much do you want, damn
you?' "

Sergeant Abbott, having written this down, looked
across at his Chief and observed,

"Quite a party—"

He received no reply. Lamb's frown had become fe-
rocious. His eyes, which that irreverent young man was
in the habit of comparing to bullseyes, were definitely
bulging. He said on a deep growling note,

"Is that the lot?"

Pearson sustained both growl and frown with an air
of conscious virtue just perceptibly tinged with regret.

"In the matter of Mr. Masterman, I was quite unable to hear as much as I should have wished."

"Masterman?" Lamb's voice threatened to rise. His colour had deepened to a rich plum.

"Oh, yes, sir. Mr. Porlock took him off into the study before tea, and what with having my duties and other guests arriving, the hall was really not available as, if I may put it that way, an observation post. I was thrown back upon the dining-room, where the conditions for listening are not at all what I should describe as satisfactory. The parlourmaid came in once or twice about the silver, and altogether the only things I can swear to are that there was a quarrel going on, that Mr. Masterman used the word blackmail, and that there was some mention of a missing will. But I happened to be in the hall when Mr. Masterman came out of the study, and the way he looked—well, what it reminded me of was a Channel crossing on a rough day. The wife and I used to be very partial to one of those day trips to Boulogne before the war. Very good sailors, both of us, but you know how it is with a choppy sea—the way most people look. Well, I couldn't compare Mr. Masterman with nothing else."

"Look here, Pearson, you're not making this up?"

"Me, sir?"

"Because you'd better be careful. You're not on what I should call very firm ground, you know. Let's see— you say in your statement to Inspector Hughes that you were in the servants' hall having supper at the time of the murder—" He picked up a paper from the table in front of him and read: " 'I had fetched out the coffee-tray from the drawing-room about a quarter of an hour or twenty minutes earlier. I did not go through to the front of the house again till the bell rang. During this time I was in the company of the cook, the parlourmaid, and the head-housemaid.' Anything to add to that?"

"No, sir."

"Sure you didn't go through to the hall between taking out the coffee tray and answering the bell after the murder had happened?"

"Quite sure." Mr. Pearson's tone was one of reasonable protest. "The Blake Agency gives good service, sir. The clients' interests are our study, but it wouldn't run to murder—now *really,* sir!"

Lamb said grimly, "I suppose it wouldn't."

CHAPTER 20

Some time later, Pearson having departed with instructions to ask Mr. Justin Leigh if he would come and speak to the Chief Inspector, Sergeant Abbott said,

"Plenty of suspects, sir."

If he had thought this the moment to provoke a reprimand, he might have added, *"Embarras de richesse."* Quotations from foreign languages being so many red rags to the official bull, he judged it better to abstain. There would, for one thing, hardly be time for the Chief to do himself justice on the kindling theme of Police College pups and wind in the head engendered by overeducation. Frank Abbott knew most of it by heart, and would have been sorry if the salt had lost its savour. As it was, he got a grunt and a "Just about beats the band!"

Taking this as encouragement, Frank proceeded.

"If Pearson is to be believed—it all seems to turn on that, doesn't it?"

Lamb grunted.

"There's nothing against Pearson. He'd a good character in the force. Had a bad accident and was invalided out. He got better after a year or two and went to Blake's. It's a respectable agency."

Frank balanced his pencil thoughtfully.

"If Porlock was a blackmailer, almost anyone may have bumped him off. Seems a pity anyone should be hanged for it."

"Now," said Lamb, "none of that! The law's the law, and duty's duty. Murder's no way to set things right. Don't you let me hear you talk like that! There's no reason why Pearson shouldn't be telling the truth, and I expect he is. He hasn't got any axe to grind that I can see. So if we take what he says, Porlock was blackmailing Tote and Carroll for certain, and both of them for pretty serious offences. Masterman and Miss Lane are only probables. There may be others. We'll see if Mr. Leigh can tell us anything. By what Pearson says, he was giving the orders after it happened. The man who keeps his head is the man who is likely to have noticed things. It's no good saying I wish we could have been here before they moved everything. The locals have done a pretty good job with photographs and all, but it's a handicap all the same. Photographs and fingerprints are all very well, but they don't give you the feel of a place and the people. We come into it a matter of eighteen hours after it's happened and everyone's had time to tighten up and think what they're going to say. If you can get there before they've got their balance you're going to get something a good deal nearer the truth—especially from the women. And I don't mean that just for the guilty parties. It's astonishing what a lot of people have got something they'd like to hide or dress up a bit different for the police. Why, I remember thirty years ago there was a woman carried on as guilty as you please, telling lies as quick as shelling peas, and all it came to in the end—she wore a wig and she didn't want her husband to find out. Well, here's Mr. Leigh."

He introduced himself and Frank with solid dignity.

"Detective Inspector Lamb of Scotland Yard, and Sergeant Abbott. Sit down, Mr. Leigh. I hope you will be able to help us. I've got your statement here, and I'd like to ask you a few questions. Now, how well did you know Mr. Porlock?"

Justin had been thinking that these two were interesting examples of the old-style policeman and the new. Lamb the product of village school, secondary education, and the wide, unsurpassable university of experience. Solid as English earth and English beef, that's what he looked. The countryman's burr on his tongue, the countryman's balanced shrewdness in his eye. Just so the bargaining farmer balancing prices against pigs and heifers. These were larger matters, but the shrewdness and the competence were the same. Abbott might be any young man in his own club—public school—Police College—clothes that looked as if they came from Savile Row—noticeably well-kept hands. He wondered if he would ever fill the old man's boots. He didn't look as if he would, but you never could tell. The impression passed in a flash. He said,

"I didn't know Mr. Porlock at all. I never met him until yesterday when I arrived here with Miss Lane in time for tea."

Lamb nodded.

"Miss Lane brought you—then you know her?"

"I know her very well. Perhaps I'd better explain. Mrs. Oakley's secretary, Dorinda Brown, is my cousin. She has only just gone to the job, and as she is quite young and I'm her only relation, I thought I would like to meet the Oakleys. I was trying to find out something about them, and to meet someone who knew them. Porlock's name was mentioned as being a near neighbour of theirs in the country, and very friendly with Martin Oakley."

"Who mentioned it?"

"It was Miss Lane. So when she said she was coming down here for the week-end and she could easily ring up and suggest bringing me, I rather jumped at it."

"Miss Lane knew Mr. Porlock well?"

"I don't know how well she knew him. They seemed to be on very friendly terms. She told me he loved entertaining and practically kept open house. He was certainly a most genial host."

"How did he strike you, Mr. Leigh?"

Justin considered.

"Well, he was what I've just said, a genial host. A lot of social charm—all that sort of thing. And enjoying himself. That's what struck me more than anything else. It was an ill-assorted, uphill party, and it must have been hard work, but I'd swear he was enjoying himself."

Lamb focussed the stare upon him.

"Just what do you mean by ill-assorted, Mr. Leigh?"

Justin's charming smile appeared.

"You won't ask me that after you've met them."

Lamb grunted and let it go.

"Anyone appear to be out of sorts—nervous—out of temper?"

"Well, of course I don't know what Mr. Tote's like as a rule, but I suppose you could say he was put out." He laughed a little. "That's putting it mildly. He didn't talk, he didn't join in any of the games. He looked as if he was in a foul temper, and just sat."

"Eat his dinner?"

Justin couldn't help laughing.

"Everything he could get hold of. Porlock has a marvellous cook."

"Anyone else seem put out?"

"Well, as I said, I don't know these people. Masterman may go about looking like a death's head all the time—he was certainly spreading gloom last night. The sister looks as if she hadn't smiled for years."

"Mr. Leigh, I'd like to ask you something, but of course you don't need to answer if you don't care to. It's not anything personal. I'd just like to know how Mr. Gregory Porlock struck you. You said he had a lot of what you'd call charm. What I'd like to know is just this—would you have said he was straight?"

Well—would he? He wondered what he would have thought if he hadn't known what he did. Very difficult to divest yourself of knowledge and decide what your mental processes would have been without it. Once Dorinda had said "He's the Wicked Uncle," he couldn't go back and judge the man as Gregory Porlock. And was he going to tell the Chief Inspector about the Wicked Uncle? He thought not. Dorinda would almost certainly do so—the art of practising a concealment was one to which she would never attain. There was something reposeful in the thought. He decided that she might be left to deal with the Wicked Uncle in her own ingenuous manner. Meanwhile there was no reason why he shouldn't say what he thought. With no more than what seemed quite an ordinary pause for consideration he replied,

"No, I don't think I would."

After a moment or two, during which he appeared to be digesting this answer, Lamb returned to the charge.

"I'd like to ask you something in confidence. These people who were here last night—they were all strangers to you except Miss Lane?"

Justin nodded. "And my cousin, Dorinda Brown." He wondered what was coming.

"They say lookers-on see most of the game. You'll understand this isn't to be talked of, but what I'd like to know is this—would it surprise you to hear that some of these people were being blackmailed?"

"By Porlock?"

"You've got it."

"Well then—no."

Lamb leaned forward.

"Which would you pick on, Mr. Leigh, if you had to make a guess?"

Justin frowned.

"I don't think I care about guessing in a murder case."

Lamb gave a slow, ponderous nod.

"I'll put it another way. We have evidence that two of the party were being blackmailed. You've mentioned two of the party being out of sorts—Mr. Tote and Mr. Masterman. What about the others? Any sign of relations being strained?—with Mr. Porlock I mean. What about Mr. Carroll?"

Justin said, "Carroll is an actor." The words were no sooner out than he regretted them. He said quickly, "I shouldn't have said that. I don't like the fellow, but there was nothing to make me say what I did."

Another of those slow nods.

"That's all right, Mr. Leigh."

The questions went on. Everything that had been said or done came under the microscope. Presently it was,

"Did you happen to notice that Miss Lane was wearing a bracelet—could you describe it?"

He could, and did.

"A kind of diamond trellis—panels set with rubies."

"Valuable?"

"Extremely, I should think."

"Ever seen it before?"

"No. As a matter of fact, Miss Lane came into the drawing-room before dinner and showed it to us. She said it had been lost, and Porlock had got it back for her. She seemed very grateful."

"Will you tell me as nearly as possible what was said?"

When he had done so the questions began again. The evening was gone through down to the time of the murder.

"I'd like you to come out into the hall and show me just where you were and what you did."

Justin had the feeling that he would presently be doing it in his sleep. Abbott timing him, he did just what he had done the night before in the dark, finishing up at the front door with his hand on the light switch.

"And then?" This was Lamb, solid and observant, from the hearth.

"I came down to where Porlock was lying. You've got all that in my statement."

Lamb gave an affirmative grunt.

"And then you rang the bell and told Pearson to send for the police. Now we'll go back to the study."

When they had got there he had another question.

"You knelt down by the body?"

"Yes. I felt for his pulse to see if he was dead."

"He was lying on his face with the handle of the dagger sticking out between his shoulder blades?"

"Yes."

"Notice anything else—anything peculiar?"

"There was a white patch all round the dagger."

"Know what it was?"

"I thought it was luminous paint—they'd been using it in the charade."

"Did you think it could have come there by accident?"

"Not possibly."

"How did you think it had come there?"

"I thought the murderer had marked him with the paint so as to be sure of getting the right spot in the dark."

"Now, Mr. Leigh—two questions. Who knew that there was luminous paint in the house, and how soon did they know it?"

"I can't answer that. It was certainly mentioned at dinner."

"Will you tell me just what was said?"

Justin told him. Lamb went on.

"Then there were two lots of the stuff. The Oakleys had some to paint a clock, and Porlock had some to paint the beam in the cloakroom—the pot being in the cupboard there, where anyone could have got at it."

"There was plenty of the stuff about. Carroll had it all over his hands for the charade, and a luminous mask and horns. Miss Lane was dressed up as a nun with a couple of towels and a sheet. Carroll jumped down on her from that table against the stairs. She must have been fairly daubed with the paint. As soon as the lights went on she got out of the stuff she was wearing and threw it on the table. Carroll left his mask there. Anyone could have picked up enough paint to put that mark on Porlock's back. We were all standing fairly close together round the hearth after the charade was over. Anyone could have done it."

"And no one noticed it, Mr. Leigh. At least no one admits to having noticed it. Anyone could have done it, and anyone could have taken the dagger, but nobody seems to have noticed that it was missing. I don't mean to say that there's anything peculiar about that in a strange house. That's what strikes me—that it was a strange house. They all say that in their statements except Miss Lane. She was the only one who had ever been here before, and she couldn't have known about the luminous paint till the middle of dinner. Yet the crime was very carefully planned. The person who planned it was bold, ingenious, quick-witted. He used what was to hand—the dagger, the luminous paint, the charade. It was Miss Lane who proposed the charade, I think?"

"That was really quite an unwarrantable suggestion." Justin had stiffened a little. He said quietly, "Of all the guests Miss Lane was on the best terms with Porlock."

Lamb's face was stolid.

"I'm not making suggestions, Mr. Leigh, I'm stating facts. That's what I'm here for—to collect facts. Now here's a matter of fact about which you can help us. I want to know just where everybody was when you turned on the light. You'd have a good view of them all, looking down the hall like that. Could you make me a rough sketch, do you think?"

"Yes. As a matter of fact I've made one."

He produced a sheet of paper and pushed it over the table.

Frank Abbott got up and came round to look over Lamb's shoulder. The two of them studied the plan for some time. At last Lamb said,

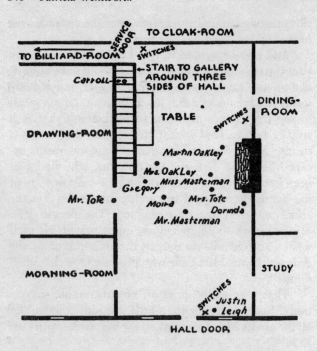

LEIGH'S SKETCH: POSITION OF GUESTS AT TIME
OF GREGORY PORLOCK'S DEATH

"The two women were nearest to him, one on either side. Miss Lane between you and the body. Mrs. Oakley on the far side. Was Mrs. Oakley facing you?"

"Yes. She was facing towards the body."

"How far off?"

Justin hesitated.

"Five or six feet."

"And Miss Lane?"

"About the same distance. She had her back to me."

"But you could see Mrs. Oakley's face. How did she look?"

"Shocked—horrified."

"And then she went down on her knees by the body, calling him Glen, and saying that someone had killed him?"

"Yes."

CHAPTER 21

The Chief Inspector continued to interview Mr. Porlock's guests. He may have got tired of asking the same questions over and over again, but his manner did not vary. Some of the interviews were very short. Some may have seemed intolerably long to the persons concerned.

Mr. Masterman came out of his interview with something of the complexion already noticed by Ernest Pearson. On his way to his own room a bedroom door opened and his sister called to him.

"Geoffrey—I want to speak to you."

He said, "Then you can't," and went on.

But before he could reach his room, let alone slam himself in, she was beside him, a hand on his arm. He could feel the tense, bony strength of it through the stuff of his sleeve. She said in an almost soundless whisper,

"If I can't speak to you, I'll go down and speak to them. Would you rather I did that?"

He turned and looked at her. Women are capable of any folly if you push them too far. He judged her capable of this. He said with cold self-command,

"I'm not talking over anything in this house. If you'd like to put on your coat and hat, we can go out."

She left him without a word, and without a word came back again, the old fur coat caught round her, the shabby black felt hat pulled on. They went downstairs together, out by the front door, and through the garden to the wide green expanse of the croquet lawn. The surface was not what it had been in the days before the war when the Miss Pomeroys had given croquet parties to their elderly friends, but it had one inalienable merit, if you kept to the middle of the grass, no one could possibly hear what you said, since no one could approach within earshot without being seen.

It was not until they had reached this vantage-point that Masterman broke the silence.

"What did you want to say to me? I think we had better walk up and down. It will look more natural."

She was clutching her coat in the same nervous grip with which she had held his arm. Without looking at him she said,

"What did those men say to you? What did you tell them? What did they want to know?"

He gave a slight shrug.

"The usual things—how long I'd known Porlock— whether this was our first visit—what sort of terms we were on. Then all about yesterday evening—the conversation at dinner—"

"What part of it?"

He threw her a sideways glance.

"If you're too sharp you'll cut yourself. If you want to know, he was asking about the luminous paint. Porlock had been marked with it. You must have seen the white smudge round the dagger. The police naturally want to know who put it there, and the first step is to find out who could have put it there. Unfortunately, anyone could have done it—except perhaps Tote—I don't know about him. It's funny no one can say for certain whether Tote came out into the hall to watch the charade. It was so dark he could have been there without anyone noticing him."

She said rather breathlessly,

"He wasn't there when you turned the lights on."

"After the charade? No. But then he wouldn't have been if he was going to stab Porlock. He could have put the mark on him in the dark, slipped out through the service door, and waited there. No one would have noticed if that door had been ajar. Then when the charade was over and the lights were on again he had only to go on waiting until Porlock moved clear of the rest of us, as he did, and then turn off the lights—there's a set of switches by the service door. It wouldn't take him any time to reach Porlock, stab him, and get back to the drawing-room doorway, where he was when the lights came on."

She checked in her mechanical walk.

"Is that what happened?"

"My dear girl, how do I know? It could have happened that way."

She drew a choking breath.

"Geoffrey—"

"Yes?"

"It wasn't you—"

He gave a short laugh.

"Really, Agnes!"

"It wasn't—"

He laughed again.

"No, my dear, it wasn't. I don't mind saying that there were moments when I could have killed him with pleasure. But I didn't do it. Somebody saved me the trouble. The nuisance is, there's been some eavesdropping—the lantern-jawed butler, I imagine. And that

Scotland Yard Inspector seems to have got the idea that Porlock might have been blackmailing me."

Agnes Masterman's dry lips parted on two words.

"He was."

"You'd better not say that to the Inspector." His tone hardened. "Do you hear—you're to hold your tongue! There's no real evidence—I'm practically sure of that. Something about a missing will—not very much to go on there! He said part of my conversation with Porlock had been overheard. He said the word blackmail had been overheard, and something about a missing will. You've got to hold your tongue. Do you hear, Agnes? Whatever he asks you, you just stick to it that Porlock's a business acquaintance of mine and you don't know anything about my business. You never met him before. He was very friendly. You stick to that, and it will be quite all right." The short, dry sentences jerked themselves to a halt.

Agnes Masterman drew a long, desperate breath. She had always been afraid of Geoffrey, always lacked the courage to face him. But she had to find it now. Or never. At that prospect of drifting on through the nightmare world which he had made for her she did find something. Words which she had rehearsed over and over through interminable hours of sleepless nights and locked away in her aching heart through interminable days now came hurrying from her lips in a torrent of shaking speech.

"Geoffrey, I can't go on like this—indeed I can't. You must tell me what you did with Cousin Mabel's will. You found it, and you took it away. She told me you had taken it away. After I'd got her quiet she told me she had got it out and was looking at it, and you came in and took it away. She was dreadfully, dreadfully frightened—I oughtn't to have left her alone. Geoffrey, you've got to tell me—did you go back and frighten her again or—or anything?"

Geoffrey Masterman said, "My dear Agnes, what morbid ideas you have! Why on earth should I go back? I had the will. If Cousin Mabel hadn't died in her sleep during the night, I should doubtless have seen her again, and I should probably have given her back the will—with some good advice. As it was, there was no need—nature intervened. If you are asking me whether I assisted nature—one may hold views on the iniquity of old ladies leaving their money away from their own flesh and blood without being a murderer, you know."

She had stopped walking. Everything in her seemed to be concentrated in the look she bent upon his face.

"Geoffrey, will you swear you didn't go back—didn't frighten her—touch her?"

He said, "I will if you like. What's the good of swearing? Let's stick to plain facts. I didn't go back."

He could see that she believed him—perhaps better than if he had made any protestations. He was aware of her relaxing, letting go. Her breast lifted in a long sigh, and then another. He put a hand on her arm and said,

"We'd better walk. It looks odd our standing here talking."

They had gone a little way before she said in a different voice, more alive, more natural,

"What was in the will? You'd better tell me."

He laughed.

"Oh, you come off all right! You get your fifty thousand all the same—'To my dear cousin Agnes Masterman who has always been very kind to me!' "

He gave that angry laugh again. "But I only get a beggarly five thousand, and no 'dear' in front of my name, while a solid forty-five thousand goes down the drain in charity! Do you expect me to lie down under that?"

The colour sprang into her cheeks. Just for a moment you could see what she would look like if she were happy. Her eyes brightened and her voice rang.

"But, Geoffrey—why didn't you tell me? We can put the whole thing right. You can have the money—I don't want it. You can take the fifty thousand and let me have what she was leaving you. You've only got to go to the solicitors and say you've found this later will. You can say it was hidden in her biscuit-box—and that's absolutely true, because that's where she did hide it, poor old thing. There won't be any risk about it at all, and we'll get rid of this nightmare which is killing me. It is, Geoffrey—it is!"

Her voice throbbed with passion though she kept it low. Her very walk had changed. It was she who had quickened the pace.

He looked at her with surprise.

"My dear Agnes—how vehement! If you really want to give forty-five thousand pounds away in charity, I don't suppose I shall interfere. I'd no idea you had such an expensive conscience. I advise you to bridle it. Anyhow I haven't got the will in my pocket, and Trower and Wakefield don't live over the way, so I think the whole matter can wait until we get home. Meanwhile you'll please to remember that if there's any trouble over this Porlock business, any encouragement of the blackmail idea, I shan't be in a position to produce that will. So if you want it produced you've got to put up a pretty good show for Scotland Yard."

CHAPTER 22

Mr. Carroll came into the study with a jaunty air. The cold blue eyes of Sergeant Abbott took him in from head to foot. Their owner decided that the fellow was putting on an act. Might mean nothing—putting on acts being more or less second nature to an actor. Might mean something to hide—according to Pearson, quite a lot. He sustained a slightly insolent return stare with equanimity and took up his pencil.

Mr. Carroll's act, which permitted a derogatory glance at the Sergeant, tumbled over itself with bright helpfulness towards the Chief Inspector.

"You'll understand I don't know any of these people except Miss Lane—I've met her of course. But anything I can do to be of any help—"

"I take it you knew Mr. Porlock?"

Mr. Carroll's crooked eyebrow rose.

"As a matter of fact, hardly at all. I'd met him once or twice in houses where I've had a professional engagement, so when he offered me one for this week-end—"

"You were here professionally?"

The eyebrow twitched, the whole crooked side of the face twitched in a crooked smile.

"My dear man, have you seen the rest of the house party? Wild horses wouldn't have got me anywhere near them if I hadn't been paid for it! And I don't mind telling you I was going to put it to Porlock that I'd expect a bonus." He settled himself back in his chair with a gesture which dismissed the Totes and Mastermans to some appropriate limbo, and said, "Well, go ahead—

ask me all the questions you want to. I'm quite at your disposal, but not, I'm afraid, very useful. You see, I'd gone upstairs to wash after the charade—I was all smothered in paint—so I wasn't on the scene when Porlock was knifed."

"So I understand. This is Mr. Leigh's sketch of the hall, showing everyone's position when the lights came on after the murder." He passed the paper across. "Will you take a look at it and tell me whether it corresponds with what you remember?"

Leonard Carroll looked, nodded, passed it back again, all between a couple of breaths.

"That's O.K. by me. I was about the third step down. Tote coming out of the drawing-room. At least—" one side of his lip lifted a trifle—"I suppose that's what it was meant to look like. And Moira Lane and Mrs. Oakley one on either side of Porlock. All very arresting and dramatic—especially when Mrs. Oakley went down on her knees and began to scream 'Glen—Glen! Someone's killed Glen!' I suppose you can't tell me why she called him Glen, can you? As his name was Gregory, and his friends all called him Greg, one couldn't help wondering, could one? Especially as I understand he had only met the lady once, a couple of days before. In which case her emotion seemed a little excessive, and one wondered how she came by quite a different Christian name."

Lamb said, "Quite so. Now, Mr. Carroll—about your own movements. I have your statement here." He lifted a paper from the blotting-pad. "I see you say that when the lights came on after the charade was over you were standing on that oak table in the hall, with Miss Lane just below. You were wearing a paper mask covered with luminous paint. You took it off and dropped it on the table. You then came forward, received the congratulations of your audience, and made your way upstairs to get the paint off your hands. Why did you go upstairs? The cloakroom was nearer, wasn't it?"

"I'd left my dinner-jacket in my room. I was wearing a pull-over."

"How long were you away?"

"I don't know—a few minutes."

"You got the paint off your hands very quickly."

Carroll gave his crooked smile.

"I'm a professional. You have to be quick between turns."

"I see."

"I wish I could be of more use. But there it is—I was well out of the way. I had just got to the top of the stairs, when the lights went out."

"Could you see the hearth? There are switches there on the left—could you see who was nearest to them?"

"Afraid not. I'd just come to the corner. As soon as I got there the lights went out."

Lamb leaned forward.

"Mr. Carroll, there are four sets of switches. The hall lights can be turned on or off from any of the four."

"I'm afraid I don't know anything about that."

"Yet you arranged that the lights should be turned off for your charade and then turned on again."

Carroll shrugged.

"Sorry—my mistake. I knew about the switches by the hearth of course. Masterman was in charge of the lighting for the charade—any other switches didn't come into it."

Lamb resumed.

"There are four sets of switches—one at the front door, one on the left-hand side of the hearth, one by the service door at the back of the hall, and one at the top of the stairs. Mr. Leigh turned the lights on at the front door after Mr. Porlock had been stabbed. There are his fingerprints on the switch. I think we may take it as certain that the lights were not turned off from there. That leaves the three other switches. You say Mr. Masterman used the switch by the hearth to turn the lights on after the charade?"

"Yes."

"Well, that accounts for his fingerprints on that switch. If anyone else had touched it after he did, his prints would have been spoiled."

"Perhaps he touched it again himself."

"Just so. But there are two other switches that might have been used—the one by the service door, and the one at the top of the stairs."

Leonard Carroll laughed.

"So handy for me! Sorry to disappoint you, but I didn't even know that the switch was there. If I had known, and had wanted to stick a knife into Porlock— incidentally depriving myself of quite a handsome fee— how do you suppose I managed it? I should have had to fly down and back again, to reach him and be where Leigh saw me when the lights came on. I'm afraid it couldn't be done."

Lamb showed a stolid face.

"Oh, I think it could. In theory, Mr. Carroll—of course just in theory. A slide down the banisters would be almost as quick as flying. And Mr. Porlock would be quite handy when you got down—very handy indeed, with his back towards you, and the best place to strike marked out in luminous paint. As to getting back—if you went up two steps at a time as you did before, I should say it could be done whilst Mr. Leigh was feeling his way to the front door."

Leonard Carroll had turned an ugly colour. The Chief Inspector would have described it as tallowy.

Sweat glistened on his temples, his eyes shifted. It was a moment before he said,

"Is this a joke?"

Lamb said, "I don't joke on duty, Mr. Carroll. You said it couldn't be done, and I was showing you that it could. I don't say it *was* done, but it could have been—just as a matter of theory."

Frank Abbott saw a curious thing. The hand on Carroll's knee didn't close. It stiffened—he got the impression that it would have clenched if a very strong effort had not held it open. When he looked higher than the hand he saw evidence of a similar restraint—in the muscles of the throat and face. If angry blood had an urge to rise, it was being frozen. If angry words leapt to the tongue, they were halted there.

Lamb's gaze dwelt upon these phenomena with bovine calm. Frank Abbott's glance flicked over him and came back to his notes. There was scarcely a pause before the Chief Inspector went on.

"You see, Mr. Carroll, I am bound to consider the possibilities of the case. The idea that it was physically impossible for you to stab Mr. Porlock is one which you really mustn't ask me to accept. Whether you had any motive for wishing him out of the way is another matter. You say you only knew him slightly."

The hand that hadn't been allowed to clench had relaxed.

"Well, you know, you can hardly say I knew him at all—a couple of casual meetings in somebody else's house, and a professional engagement—" He shrugged.

"Meaning you didn't know him well enough to quarrel with?"

No one could say that Carroll wasn't quick. He burst out laughing.

"Well, I wouldn't go as far as that. You can always

quarrel if you're feeling quarrelsome, whether it's the first time you meet a man or not. But it would hardly go the length of murder—would it?"

Lamb's mental comment was that Mr. Carroll was as slippery as an eel. Quick in the uptake too—and that's what he was looking for. It was someone uncommon quick and clever who had murdered Gregory Porlock. He said in his measured voice,

"That's as may be. You had a quarrel with Mr. Porlock in this room not long before dinner, didn't you?"

"I had a talk with him, and a couple of drinks."

"You asked him, 'What's all this about Tauscher?' and you called Mr. Porlock a damned blackmailer and said you'd come down here to tell him so. And he said, 'You've come down here to save your neck.' "

If the first shock of danger had brought the sweat to Mr. Carroll's face and stopped his tongue, he was now over the worst of it and very much in command of his faculties. He said,

"What's all this rubbish?"

Lamb looked at him with gravity.

"Your conversation was overheard."

He took that without a tremor.

"Then whoever overheard it was a damned bad listener. Porlock asked me if I knew a man called Tauscher, and I said I didn't know him from Adam."

"There's a good deal more to it than that, Mr. Carroll. I understand that this man was an enemy agent, and that Mr. Porlock was suggesting that you had met him when you were out with a concert party entertaining the troops at a time when the war was still going on, and that you supplied him with information likely to be of use to the Nazis. . . . No, no, no—wait a minute—wait a minute, if you please! It's not me that's putting out these suggestions. I'm only telling you that Mr. Porlock was overheard putting them out—and I suppose you would agree that there would be the makings of a quarrel in that."

There was another of those twists, for Mr. Carroll laughed.

"I'm afraid your eavesdropper was a bit handicapped by being on the other side of the door! A pity he didn't come in and join us! Then he'd have got the matter straight! Porlock told me this man Tauscher was an enemy agent. Said he was knocking about in Belgium about the time I was there, and asked me if I'd met him. I wasn't best pleased—I thought it was an offensive thing to say. I let Porlock see I didn't like it—I mean—well, who would? I'd never seen the fellow in my life, and on the top of telling me he's an enemy agent he asks me if I know him. I don't mind owning I lost my temper. But you don't murder a man because he's been a bit tactless. I mean—well, do you?"

CHAPTER 23

Lamb sat back and said, "Well—"

Frank Abbott transferred his gaze from the door which had recently closed upon Leonard Carroll to his Chief's face. It was a cool and sarcastic gaze. It conveyed an opinion of Mr. Carroll which would hardly have pleased him.

"Well, sir?"

"I'm asking you."

There was nothing in this to minister to a junior officer's self-esteem. Schoolboys do not get wind in the head when the schoolmaster asks them a question. All this, and more, was not only a well-established fact, but was even now conveyed by the Chief Inspector's air and manner. Frank became deferential.

"They're all full of reasons why someone else should have done it. Masterman was very ingenious about the possibility of Tote's having slipped across the hall in the dark and waited behind the service door. Carroll had a few kind words for Tote too. And both he and Masterman, and Tote himself, simply tumble over themselves to underline the fact that Mrs. Oakley went down on her knees by the body and addressed it as Glen."

Lamb grunted.

"Yes—we'll have to go into that. Let me see—we haven't seen Miss Lane or Miss Masterman. Mrs. Tote is negligible. If she'd seen her husband in the hall she wouldn't say so, and she didn't want to say anything about anyone else. I think we can count her out. I'd say it was one of those three men, if it weren't for the complication about Mrs. Oakley. There might be something there that would give Oakley a motive, so I'm keeping an open mind. But taking the three in the house—Carroll's clever enough and quick enough, and by Pearson's account he'd motive enough. Masterman had his fingerprints on the switch by the hearth and a very good reason for having them there. We don't know much about a motive, but it looks as if he might have had one. The Yard can get on with looking up his record. Then there's Tote—now, what did you make of Tote?"

Frank lifted his eyebrows.

"If the murderer had to be clever and quick, you'd hardly say that Tote would fill the picture. On the other hand, if Tote was quite as thick in the head as he seems, how did he make so much money?"

Lamb nodded.

"There's two answers to that, you know. The first is,

he didn't make it, he stole it. And the other is that he's not such a fool as he looks."

Frank thought the Chief was in good form. He said, "I don't think so much of the first reason. That Black Market racket had brains behind it. If a man was stupid, they might use him as a tool, but they wouldn't let him get away with anything big—why should they? Tote, I gather, is fairly rolling, and if that's the case, I doubt his stupidity. A little man would make a little profit. If Tote got away with the big stuff, the second answer is right—he's not such a fool as he looks."

Lamb sat there looking blank. He drummed with his fingers on the blotting-pad.

"He would have had to mark Porlock with the luminous paint, and he would have had to get to one of those switches. There was just a muddle of prints on the one by the service door, and the same on the door itself. It's more or less what you'd expect. But the one at the top of the stairs had been wiped clean."

"That looks like Carroll."

Lamb nodded.

"Or Tote. He could have got up there if he'd gone through the service door and up the back stair—though I don't know why he should."

Frank shook his head.

"Doesn't seem likely. He's not the build for sliding the banisters or running down stairs. You know, sir, I don't see how anyone could have run down or up those stairs without being heard. You can't walk silently on bare oak."

"Not unless you're in your stocking feet. If Carroll slid the banisters and ran back up the stairs he could slip off his pumps and leave them handy to get back into. Tote could have carried his down in his hand—fat men are often extraordinarily light on their feet. I don't think there's much in that. But I don't know why he should have bothered to go upstairs to turn off the lights, when it would have been a whole lot simpler to have done it downstairs from the service door."

"Well, that's Masterman's theory—he could have followed the others out of the drawing-room when they went out to watch the charade and got across the dark hall to wait behind the service door, and he could have put the mark on Porlock as he followed him into the hall. That would give him the switch by the service door to play with, and the luminous paint on Porlock's back to guide him when the lights were out again. It's all quite possible in theory, and not as much evidence as you could balance on the point of a needle."

The door was opened in a tentative sort of way. Pearson made his appearance with a tray. Something about his manner suggested that he was, for the moment, a butler and not a detective. The tray supported a tea-pot, milk-jug and sugar-basin of a Queen Anne pattern, two cups and saucers, a covered dish, a dark fruit cake, and a plate of sandwiches. There was an agreeable smell of muffins, or perhaps buttered toast.

Pearson shut the door behind him dexterously and set down the tray.

"I thought you'd be ready for some tea, sir. Anchovy toast under the cover, and the sandwiches are egg and Gentleman's Relish." Then, reverting to the private detective, "If I may offer a word, sir, there's something I think you ought to know."

"What is it?" Lamb recalled his eye from the covered dish. "Well, speak up, man!"

Pearson looked deferential.

"In the matter of Mrs. Oakley's maid—"

"What about her?" He jerked round upon Frank Abbott, who had picked up the tea-pot. "Pour out your own wash if you want to. If I have a cup of tea I like a bit of body in it. Brew it well, stand it well, sugar it well—that's what my old Granny used to say, and she made the best cup of tea I ever tasted." He turned back again. "What's this about Mrs. Oakley's maid?"

"Hooper, sir—Miss Hooper. Nothing, sir, except that she was in Mr. Porlock's pay."

Lamb sat up square, hands on knees.

"Oh, she was, was she? What makes you think so?"

Pearson looked more deprecating than ever. Quite irrationally, Frank was reminded of an earwig coming out from under a stone—or didn't earwigs come out from under stones? He didn't know, but that was what Pearson reminded him of. He was saying,

"Oh, I don't think, sir—I know. In this sort of house the telephones are very convenient for listening in, and a butler is most commodiously placed with an extension in the pantry all to hand and private, as you might say. If I happened to know that Mr. Porlock was telephoning, I'd only to go into my pantry and shut the door. Or, in this case, if Miss Hooper rang him up—which she did, only not of course under that name—I'd only to put the call through to Mr. Porlock and make believe to hang up myself. With a little care the click can be induced or avoided, to suit the occasion."

Frank Abbott put three drops of milk in his straw-coloured tea. Lamb grunted.

"How did you find out that it is this Hooper woman, if she didn't give her name?"

Pearson evinced a modest pride.

"The young lady at the telephone exchange was able to give me the subscriber's number. The name Miss Hooper gave was Robinson. I soon discovered that there was no one by that name at the Mill House. From the substance of the conversations it was quite clear that someone of the nature of a personal maid was speaking."

"What had she got to say?"

"Well, the first time was last Tuesday. She said her name was Miss Robinson, and I put her through to Mr. Porlock. Tuesday evening it was. He says, 'Anything to report?' and she tells him, 'Not very much. They've arrived, but Miss Cole, the governess, she's gone back to town, and the old nurse is there again.' Mr. Porlock says he's not interested in old nurses—what about the new secretary? And the maid sniffs and says Mrs. Oakley's all out to spoil her, sending her up to London to get herself an evening dress. And Mr. Porlock says, 'When?' The maid says, 'Tomorrow,' and Mr. Porlock takes her up sharp. 'Now listen,' he says—'this is very particular.' And he tells her Mr. Oakley wants some luminous paint to dodge up a clock for the little boy, and she's to get Mrs. Oakley to send Miss Brown— that's the secretary—to the Luxe Stores between twelve and one o'clock, because they've got some there. 'Now don't forget, and don't make a mess of it,' he says. 'She's to go to the Luxe Stores between twelve and one.' And he asks her what Miss Brown will be wearing, and she tells him she's only got the one coat, a light brown tweed, and shabby at that. So he asks about her hat, and her shoes, and her handbag, all very particular. He says with a sort of a laugh, 'Do her hair and eyes still match?' and the maid sniffs and says she hasn't taken that much notice. Then he says, 'Is there anything else?' and she says, 'Something funny's happened.' And he says, 'What?' and she tells him. It seems Mrs. Oakley went through from her bedroom to the boudoir before dinner—there's a door going through. Hooper hears Mrs. Oakley call out as if she was hurt. She goes to see what's the matter, and she finds her with a crumpled-up photo in her hand, staring at it. Mrs. Oakley, she sits down sudden as if she's going to faint, and Hooper picks the photo up. 'Well?' says Mr. Porlock, and the maid says, 'Do you want me to tell you who it was?' A very nasty sort of way she says it. And Mr. Porlock says, 'You can tell me the photographer's name.' She says, 'Rowbecker & Son, Norwood,' and Mr. Porlock whistles and rings off. A minute or two later he rings up a London number—here it is, sir—and talks to someone he calls Maisie. He tells her, 'It's for between twelve and one tomorrow. Look out for a long tweed coat, light-coloured and shabby,' and gives her the rest of the description he's got from the maid, and finishes up with, 'Her hair and eyes used to be a perfect match. I expect they are still—golden brown and very attractive. Get on with it!' That was all that time, sir."

"There were other times?"

"Yes, sir. Miss Hooper rang up next day about half past seven—said she couldn't ring before, she had to wait till Mrs. Oakley went to her bath. She says Mr. Oakley and Miss Brown was back, and Mr. Porlock swore. And then laughs and says, 'What's the odds?' and rang off."

"That all?"

"No, sir. She rang up yesterday afternoon and said Mrs. Oakley had been very upset ever since Wednesday—'the day you came to see her.' And Mr. Porlock says, 'Is she coming tonight?' And the maid says she's in two minds about it, but she don't want Mr. Oakley to know there's anything wrong, and she thinks she'll come."

Lamb said, "H'm!" and then, "Thanks, Pearson."

When the door had shut again he turned to the tray, poured out a good stewed cup of tea, added milk and sugar with a liberal hand, and did full justice to the anchovy toast, the sandwiches, and the cake, the only contribution he made to the case from start to finish being a grunt and a "So he went to see her on Wednesday. Well, we'll be along as soon as we've finished our tea."

They were passing through the hall on their way to the front door, when Justin Leigh came up.

"If you can spare me just a moment—I'm arranging to do some of my work down here until after the inquest, but I shall have to run up to town and get the papers I want. I thought of going up first thing in the morning. I'll be back in time for lunch."

"That's all right, Mr. Leigh."

It appeared that Mr. Leigh hadn't finished.

"Miss Lane would like the lift both ways. I suppose there's no objection to that?"

The Chief Inspector didn't answer so quickly this time. When he spoke, it was to say,

"I haven't seen Miss Lane yet. She mayn't be very important, but I want to see her. Will you make yourself responsible for having her back here by two o'clock tomorrow?"

"I'll do my best."

Lamb walked on, then halted rather suddenly and looked back.

"What does she want to go up for?"

"Her cousin, Lady Pemberley, is an invalid. She wants to go up and see her. She's afraid all this may have been a shock. I've arranged to drop her there and pick her up again."

There was another slight pause. Then the Chief Inspector said,

"All right, Mr. Leigh. But I shall be wanting to see her not later than two o'clock."

CHAPTER 24

Martin Oakley met them with a flat refusal.

"My wife's ill—she can't see anyone."

"Have you a doctor's certificate, Mr. Oakley?"

"No, I haven't, and I don't need one. I know my wife a great deal better than any doctor. She's not fit to see anyone. Good heavens, man—a gentle, delicate woman has a man killed practically next door to her, and you expect her to be able to discuss it! Why, the shock was enough to kill her. And she's got nothing to say, any more than I have myself. We were all there, standing close together. Mr. Porlock had gone over towards the stairs. Then he began to come towards us again, and the lights went out. We heard a groan and a fall, and less than a minute after that the lights came on, and there was Porlock lying dead on the floor with a dagger in his back. That's all I know, and that's all my wife knows. She's very sensitive and tender-hearted. She went down on her knees to see if there was anything to be done, and when she found he was dead she became hysterical."

Lamb said, "So I understand."

They were in the study, among its incongruous chromium plating and scarlet velvet, registered by the Chief Inspector as 'gimcrackery.' He knew what an English gentleman's study ought to look like, and it wasn't anything like this. He said,

"How long have you known Mr. Porlock?"

"A couple of months."

"And Mrs. Oakley—how long has she known him?"

"She never met him until he paid a formal call on Wednesday last."

"Are you quite sure of that?"

"Of course I am—you can ask anyone you like. I'd met him in the way of business. She didn't so much as know him by sight."

"Then will you explain why she should have called him Glen?"

"She did nothing of the kind."

"Mr. Oakley, there were eight people present besides yourself and your wife. They all agree that Mrs. Oakley called out repeatedly, 'Oh, Glen! Glen's dead—he's dead! Oh, Glen—Glen—*Glen!*' "

"I should say they had made a mistake. How could she call him Glen? His name was Gregory. We were all calling him Greg. She was in the habit of hearing me speak of him as Greg. What she said was, 'Greg's dead! He's dead—dead—dead!' She was sobbing and crying, you understand, and I can't think why anyone should have thought she said Glen—it makes nonsense."

The Chief Inspector allowed a pause to follow this statement. When he thought it had lasted long enough he said,

"I should like to see Miss Dorinda Brown and Mrs. Oakley's maid. Perhaps I might begin with the maid."

Martin Oakley stiffened.

"The maid? She's only been with my wife a week. She wasn't there last night."

"I should like to see her, Mr. Oakley."

Hooper came into the room in a black dress with a small old-fashioned brooch at the neck. The faded hair might have been a wig, or the part-wig which is called a front. It had small, close curls fitting tightly on to the head. Under it one of those round bony foreheads, dull pale cheeks, and a tight mouth. She came up to the table and stood there with an air of professional respect.

"Your name is Hooper, and you are Mrs. Oakley's personal maid?"

The tight lips opened the smallest possible way.

"Yes, sir—Louisa Hooper."

"How long have you been with Mrs. Oakley?"

"It will be ten days. I came in on the Saturday. We came down here on the Tuesday."

She didn't look at him when she spoke. She kept her eyes down. The lids reminded Frank Abbott of those little hooded awnings which you see at the seaside, keeping out the light, hiding the windows.

Lamb's next question came rather quickly.

"How long had you known Mr. Porlock?"

"Mr. Porlock?"

He said sternly, "Come, come—we know you knew him. We know you were in the habit of telephoning to him. Your conversations were overheard. What's the good of wasting time? You were in his pay—I want to know why?"

The lids did not rise, the lips were tight. Then quite suddenly they produced a smile—not a nice smile.

"If a gentleman takes an interest in a lady, I don't see that it's any business of the police."

"Then you'd better do some thinking. When a gentleman's murdered everything to do with him is of interest to the police. Got that? Now—why did he pay you?"

The smile persisted.

"He took an interest in Mrs. Oakley."

"Whom he'd never seen till Wednesday last."

The lids came up with a jerk. The eyes behind them were cold, with a bright point of malice.

"Who says so?"

"Mr. Oakley does. If you know any different you'd better say so."

The lids came down again.

"He came to see her on Wednesday afternoon. I suppose a gentleman can come and call on a lady he's taken a fancy to?"

Lamb fixed her with his bulging stare.

"Now look here, Miss Hooper, it's no good your giving me that kind of stuff. I've told you your conversations with Mr. Porlock were overheard. You rang him up on Tuesday night and told him about Mrs. Oakley finding a crumpled-up photograph and being very much upset over it. You asked him if you should tell him whose photograph it was, and he said to give the photographer's name, which you did—Rowbecker & Son, Norwood. Now—whose photograph was it?"

"How should I know?"

"You knew all right when you were talking to Mr. Porlock."

She looked up again, not meeting the stare but, as it were, sliding past it.

"Well then, it was Mr. Porlock."

"Sure about that?"

She nodded.

"He takes a good photograph."

"Do you know where it came from?"

"The little boy must have got at it. It was in his toy-cupboard. Nurse was saying how spoilt he'd got whilst she was away. She said Miss Brown picked up a photograph from the nursery floor and took it away."

"What happened to the photograph?"

"Mrs. Oakley said it was spoilt, and she went over and dropped it in the fire."

"Mr. Porlock came to see her on Wednesday afternoon?"

"Yes."

"Where did she see him?"

"Upstairs in her sitting-room."

"And how much of their conversation did you over-hear?"

"I don't listen at doors."

"Is there a door you could have listened at—a door through to her bedroom?"

"I don't listen at doors."

"I'm asking you if there's a door through from her bedroom. I can ask Mrs. Oakley, you know."

"There's a door."

"And you don't listen at doors? Look here, Miss Hooper, I'm making no threats, and I'm making no promises—I'm just pointing out one or two facts. This is a murder case. It's a serious thing to obstruct the police in their inquiries. If you listened at that door and got any information that would help the police, it's your duty to tell them what it is. If you have any idea of trying to dispose of that information for your own profit, it would be a very serious offence—it would be blackmail. Blackmail is a very serious offence. You know best what your past record is—whether it will bear looking into. I don't want to have to look into it. Now then—how much of that conversation between Mrs. Oakley and Mr. Porlock did you hear?"

She stood there weighing her chances. Mr. Oakley would pay her to hold her tongue. Would he? Gregory Porlock was dead. Mrs. Oakley would pay her. Yes, and go and cry on Mr. Oakley's shoulder next minute and tell him all about it. Mr. Oakley was the sort that might turn nasty. She couldn't afford to have the police come ferreting round. Chances were all very well when you were young and larky. She'd got past taking them. Safety first—that's what you came to. It wasn't safe to get on the wrong side of the police. Better tell him what he wanted to know, and see what pickings she could get from Mrs. Oakley—quick, before it all came out. She'd be easy managed the way she was, crying herself silly one minute, and wanting her face done up so that Mr. Oakley wouldn't notice anything the next.

Lamb let her have her time.

"Well?" he said at last.

She gave a businesslike little nod.

"All right, sir."

"Good! You'd better have a chair."

She took one with composure, settled herself, folded her hands in her lap, lifted those cold eyes, and said,

"The door wasn't quite shut. I didn't do it, Mrs. Oakley did. She knew Mr. Porlock was coming, because he telephoned—I took the message. But she didn't have any idea who he was—she didn't know who she was going to see."

"Sure about that?"

"I don't say things unless I'm sure."

"Go on."

"I thought I'd like to hear what they said, because all he'd told me was, I was to go there as maid and tell him anything he wanted to know. He didn't tell me why, and I don't like working in the dark, so I thought I'd listen."

"Yes?"

"Well, the first I heard was him calling her by her Christian name. 'Well, Linnet,' he said, 'I thought it would be you, but I had to make sure.' Then he said to pull herself together. And she said, 'I thought you were dead,' and she called him Glen."

"Go on."

"Well, I can't remember it all, but she was crying and saying why did he let her think he was dead. And he said, 'I suppose you told Martin you were a widow?' and she said she thought she was."

"Do you mean—"

She nodded.

"It was as plain as plain—you couldn't miss it. They'd been married, and he'd gone off and left her, and nine months after she'd married Mr. Oakley. Mr. Porlock, he kept talking about bigamy, and saying she'd broken the law and he hadn't, and in the end he got her so she'd do anything he wanted. And what he wanted was for her to put Mr. Oakley's dispatch-case out on the study window-sill. Mr. Oakley was expected down by teatime. She was to put the case outside the window when he went to dress for dinner and leave the window unlatched, so that everything could be put back and no one any the wiser. And in the end that's what she agreed to."

"Did she do it?"

"I couldn't say, but if you want my opinion, she'd be too frightened not to. She's easy frightened, and he'd got the whip hand—talking about putting her in the dock for bigamy, and Mr. Oakley putting her out in the street. Well, in my opinion she wouldn't have dared not do what he told her."

"Now look here—did she tell Mr. Oakley?"

"She wouldn't do that—not if she'd any sense."

"Why do you put it that way?"

"Because that's the way Mr. Porlock put it—said he knew she couldn't hold her tongue, but if she went crying to Mr. Oakley about it she'd find herself in the dock for bigamy."

"So you don't think she told him?"

"No, I don't."

"They didn't have anything like the scene there'd

have been if he'd found out she wasn't really married to him?"

"No—nothing like that." She hesitated. "Not unless it was just before they started for the dinner party. He came in when she was dressing, and I left them there. She might have said something then, or in the car."

Lamb grunted.

"But you don't know whether she did?"

"No, I had to go downstairs."

When he had sent her away with instructions to say that the Chief Inspector would like to see Miss Brown, he turned to Frank Abbott and said in an expressionless voice,

"That gives Mr. Martin Oakley a pretty big motive."

"If she told him."

"We'll know more about that when we've seen her."

CHAPTER 25

Miss Masterman was writing a letter. It began, "Dear Mr. Trower—" and it ended, "Yours sincerely, Agnes Masterman." It was written in a firm, legible hand.

When she had signed her name she folded the sheet, put it in an envelope, and addressed it to Messrs. Trower and Wakefield, Solicitors. Then she put on her hat and the shabby fur coat and walked down the drive.

She came back in about twenty minutes. Mr. Masterman was knocking about the balls in the billiard-room. When he saw his sister come in, still in her outdoor things, he frowned and said,

"Where have you been?"

She came right up to the table before she answered

him. Watching her come, he felt a growing uneasiness. When she said, "To post a letter," the uneasiness became an absolute oppression. He wanted to ask her, "What letter?" but he held the words back. It wasn't any concern of his, but she wrote so few letters—none at all since old Mabel Ledbury died. Why should she write to anyone now?

They stood there, not more than a yard apart, with that uneasiness of his between them. He didn't like the way she was looking at him. There was something hard about it, as if she had made up her mind and didn't give a damn. He put down his cue and said,

"Hadn't you better take your things off? It's hot in here."

She didn't take any notice of that, just looked at him and said in quite an ordinary voice,

"I've written to Mr. Trower."

"You've—what?"

"I've written to Mr. Trower to say that we've found another will."

"Agnes—are you mad?"

"Oh, no. I told you I couldn't go on. I said it was hidden in her biscuit-box—there won't be any trouble about it. I told you I couldn't go on."

He said in a stunned voice, "You're mad."

Agnes Masterman shook her head.

"Oh, no," she said. "I thought I'd better tell you what I'd done. Now I'm going to take my things off."

Afterwards he was glad that Leonard Carroll chose this moment to drift into the room, obviously bored and wanting a game. Agnes walked out with the same detached air which she had worn throughout their brief encounter, and he had the satisfaction of beating young Carroll's head off. Much better than having a row with Agnes. No use having a row if the letter was posted.

They'd have to go through with it, but he would keep her to her offer about the fifty thousand. He'd be no worse off if he had it, and he'd be safe. If he had known how Agnes was going to carry on he would never have risked it at all. Women hadn't the nerve for a bold stroke, and that was a fact.

Whilst the game of billiards was going on Justin went up to the Mill House.

"Put your hat on and come out," he said.

Dorinda went away and came back again. They walked down the road towards the village in the late dusk of a damp, misty evening. Little curls of smoke came up out of the chimneys of the village houses to join the mist and thicken it. Here and there a lighted chink showed where a curtain had been drawn crookedly. There was a faint smell of rotted leaves— especially cabbage leaves—manure, and wood smoke.

Just short of the first house a lane went off between high hedgerows and overarching trees. Until they had turned into it neither of them had spoken. There was that feeling of there being too much to say, and an odd sense of being too much out in the open to say it. Here in the lane they were shut in—alone.

Justin spoke first.

"How are you getting on?"

She didn't answer the question, but said quickly,

"The police came—"

"Did they see Mrs. Oakley?"

"No—Mr. Oakley wouldn't let them. He said she wasn't well enough. They're coming back tomorrow. They saw the maid, and they saw me."

"You'd better tell me about it."

"They were very nice. I mean they didn't make me feel nervous or anything. The Chief Inspector asked all the questions, and the other one wrote down what I said. And—oh, Justin, the very first thing he asked me was how long had I known Mr. Porlock."

"What did you say?"

She had turned and was looking at him through the dusk. It was really almost dark here between the hedges and under the trees. He had sent her to put on a hat, but she had come down in her tweed coat bareheaded. The colour of the tweed was absorbed into all the other shades of brown and russet and auburn which belonged to drifted leaves, brown earth, and leafless boughs. Her hair had vanished too, melting into the shadow over-head. There remained visible just her face, robbed of its colour, almost of its features, like the faint first sketch of a face painted on a soft, dim background. The sunk lane gave an under-water quality to its own darkness. She seemed at once remote and near. He could touch her if he put out his hand, but at this moment it came to him to wonder whether he would reach her if he did.

The pause before she answered was momentary.

"I said I didn't know him at all when we went there last night. Justin, it doesn't seem as if it could be only last night—does it?" She caught her breath. "I'm sorry—it just came over me. Then I said when we came into the drawing-room I recognized him."

"Oh, you told them that?"

She said in a voice which was suddenly very young,

"I thought I must. And I thought if I was going to, then I had better do it at once."

"That's all right. Go on."

"Well, they asked a lot of questions. I told them his name was Glen Porteous when I knew him, and that he was Aunt Mary's husband. And they asked when she died, and I said four years ago. So then they wanted to know whether there had been a divorce, and I said yes, she divorced him about seven years ago after he went away the last time, and that I hadn't seen him since. They wanted to know whether I was sure that Gregory Porlock was Glen Porteous, and I said I was, and that he knew I had recognized him. He did, you know. You can always tell by the way anyone looks at you, and that was the way he looked at me. Well, after that they asked about the photograph I picked up off the nursery floor. I don't know who told them about it. I said it was the twin of the one Aunt Mary had and I recognized it at once. And then they went back to that horrid business at the De Luxe Stores. And do you know what I think, Justin? I think the Wicked Uncle cooked that up to get me out of my job with the Oakleys. You see, he couldn't count on my not recognizing him, and if he was going about being Gregory Porlock he wouldn't want a bit of his past turning up and saying, 'Oh, no—that's Glen Porteous, and my Aunt Mary had to divorce him because he was an out and out bad lot.' I mean, would he?"

"Probably not."

"They seemed to know about Miss Silver. The young one got a sort of twinkly look when I told them how she talked to the manager at that horrid Stores. He said something that sounded like 'She would!' and the Chief Inspector went rather stiff and said that Miss Silver was very much respected at Scotland Yard. Oh, Justin, I do wish she was here!"

"What makes you say that?"

She caught her breath.

"It's the Oakleys. Justin, I feel frightened about them. You know how she called out when she saw that he was dead? She called him Glen. She must have known him before he was Gregory Porlock. She wasn't supposed to know him at all. There's something frightening there. She does nothing but cry, and Mr. Oakley looks as if it was a funeral all the time. There's something they're both dreadfully afraid about. She's afraid to tell him what it is, and he's afraid to ask her. It's grim."

He said, "I don't like your being there."

"Oh, it isn't that. I can't help feeling sorry for them—even if—"

"What did you mean by that, Dorinda?"

She said almost inaudibly, "It frightens me."

The thought which frightened her hung between them in the dark. A desperate hand striking a desperate blow. Perhaps a woman's hand—perhaps a man's—

She said with a little gasp,

"He was the sort of person who gets himself murdered."

CHAPTER 26

"Will you see Miss Moira,
my lady?"

Lady Pemberley had breakfasted in bed. She was now reading the paper. She said,

"Miss Moira? She's very early. Yes, of course. Take the tray, and ask her to come up."

The paper she had been reading lay tilted to the light. A black headline showed—"Murder in a Country House. Guests Questioned." When the door opened and Moira Lane came in it was the second thing she saw. The first was Sibylla Pemberley's face, pale and rather austere under the thick iron-grey hair which she wore drawn back in a manner reminiscent of the eighteenth century. Everything in the room was very good and very plain—no fripperies, no bright colours; a dark

oil painting of the late Lord Pemberley over the mantelpiece; a jar of white camellia blooms on the shelf below;
a purple bedspread which Moira irreverently dubbed
the catafalque; a lace cap with purple ribbons; a fine
Shetland shawl covering a night-dress of tucked nun's
veiling. With all these Moira was quite familiar. They
made up the picture she expected. Her first glance was
for the look on Lady Pemberley's face, which told her
nothing, and her second for the newspaper, which told
her a good deal. To start with, it wasn't the sort of
paper Cousin Sibylla read. Headlines and pictures
weren't what you would call in her line. That meant
that Dawson had brought it up specially, and if she had,
it meant not only that the murder was in it, but that
Miss Moira Lane was mentioned.

"Amongst those present was Miss Moira Lane." Almost a daily occurrence in some paper or another. You
got to the point where you took it for granted. "Attractive Miss Moira Lane"—"Lord Blank and Miss Moira
Lane at Epsom"—"The Duke of Dash, Lady Asterisk,
and Miss Moira Lane on the moors"—"Miss Moira
Lane and Mr. Justin Leigh . . ." Not so good when it
was a murder story—"Miss Moira Lane at the Inquest
on Gregory Porlock."

She came up to the bed, touched a thin cheek with
her cold glowing one, and straightened up again.

"Good-morning, Cousin Sibylla."

"You're very early, Moira."

"I had the chance of a lift. Justin Leigh brought me
up. He's fetching papers from his office. We'll have to
get back by one or so. I suppose it's all in the papers?"

Delicate dark eyebrows lifted. There was no other
likeness between the young woman and the old one, but
those fine arched brows belonged to both. In Lady Pemberley they gave an effect of severity. The eyes beneath

them were grey, not blue like Moira's. Grey eyes can be most tender, and most severe. In Lady Pemberley's rather ascetic face they tended to be severe. She said,

"It is very unfortunate—very unpleasant."

Moira nodded. She sat down on the edge of the bed. "I'm going to tell you what happened."

The story did not go down at all well. The atmosphere became charged with all the things Lady Pemberley had said in the past. She didn't say them now, but there they were, quite as insistent as if she had. If you kept to your own set you did at least know by what rules they played the game. If you went outside it you were out of your own line of country and anything might happen. A man could leave his own set and amuse himself elsewhere, but it was folly for a woman to attempt it. These themes, with endless variations, had been so often sounded in Moira's ears that it needed no more than a single note to recall the whole. She went through to the end.

Lady Pemberley repeated her former remark.

"Very unfortunate—very unpleasant."

"Epitaph for Gregory Porlock," said Moira with a tang in her voice.

The eyebrows rose again.

"My dear—"

Moira was looking at her—a straight, dark look.

"Do you know, I meant that."

"My dear—"

Moira gave an abrupt nod. Her glowing colour had gone. She looked pale and hard in her grey tweeds.

"He was a devil."

"Moira—"

"He was a blackmailer." She stood up straight by the bed. "He was blackmailing me. I've come here to tell you why."

There was a brief silence. Lady Pemberley had become paler too. She said,

"You had better sit down."

Moira shook her head.

"I'd rather stand. Cousin Sibylla, you won't believe me—I suppose nobody would—but I'm not telling you about it because Gregory Porlock has been murdered. I was coming anyhow. I made up my mind that I would—after I got down there on Saturday—after he tried to blackmail me. I was coming up to tell you. You won't believe me of course."

"I haven't said so. Go on, please."

The dark blue eyes went on looking at her.

"A little while ago I was in a bad hole—money. I went down for a week-end with some people who played a bit too high for me. I had the most damnable luck. It put me in a hole."

"Yes?"

Moira set her teeth.

"I came to see you. You remember—it was the first week in November."

"Why didn't you tell me?"

"I was going to. Everything went wrong. The La-monts were here. You were vexed."

"I remember."

"Mrs. Lamont had made you vexed. She's always had a down on me."

"She is one of my oldest friends."

"She hates me like poison—she always has."

"You should not exaggerate, Moira."

"Let's say she doesn't love me."

"I don't think you have given her much reason to do so—have you? Your manner towards her is scarcely—"

"Oh, I expect I was as rude as the devil! Don't you

see, I wanted them to go, but they stayed, and stayed, and stayed. And then—" She broke off.

"And then, Moira?"

"You sent me to tell Dawson you wanted your jewel-case. You were talking about Molly Lamont's wedding, and you said you would like her to have a brooch you had worn at your own wedding. You wanted her to have it because Cousin Robert gave it to you and he was her godfather. I brought the case down, and you showed her the brooch, and then they went away. You went on showing me things."

"Yes, Moira?"

"There was a diamond and ruby bracelet. You began to say something about leaving it to me. Cousin Sophy Arnott was shown in, and you said, 'Oh, take these things back to Dawson, Moira.' And I said, 'Well, I'll say good-bye,' because I knew it wasn't any good— Cousin Sophy's a sticker.'"

She came to a standstill. It was not only difficult, it was impossible. But there were times when the impossible had to be done. This was one of them. Everything in her was stiff with effort. She went on.

"I took the things upstairs. Dawson wasn't there. I looked at the bracelet again. You said you were going to leave it to me. I was angry—you know I've got a foul temper. I don't think I'd have done it if I hadn't been angry."

Lady Pemberley's face was almost as white as the lace of her cap. She said,

"Why should you have been angry?"

"Mrs. Lamont staying on like that—I knew she'd been saying things. She hates me. I thought you kept her on purpose because I wanted to speak to you."

"But when she went you did not speak—"

"I was working up for it—and then Cousin Sophy

had to come in—I felt as if everything was against me. I took the bracelet."

There was silence for some time before Lady Pemberley said,

"What did you do with it?"

It was out now. There couldn't be anything worse. She drew in her breath.

"I meant to pawn it. I had to have the money at once. I meant to pawn it and tell you what I'd done. And then you got ill—I couldn't."

"You pawned it?"

Moira shook her head.

"I tried to. I got the wind up—the man asked questions—I should have had to leave my name and address and pay interest. I funked it. I went into Crossley's and sold it over the counter. They didn't ask any questions. It seems they knew me, though I didn't think of that at the time. I couldn't get at you—you were very ill."

She heard Lady Pemberley say,

"And you thought that if I died, the bracelet would be yours and nobody would know?"

It was true. She hadn't any answer to make. She made none.

After a while Lady Pemberley said,

"How does Mr. Porlock come into it?"

"He saw the bracelet. He recognized it. He said it was one of a pair, and that Napoleon gave them to Josephine. He knew they belonged to you. He bought the bracelet and tried to blackmail me. He wanted me to do jackal for him—scavenge for scandals, so that he could carry on his blackmailing business. I told him there was nothing doing. That was on Saturday evening. I made up my mind then to come up to town on Monday morning and tell you. Then after dinner somebody stabbed him."

"Do you know who did it?"

"No." She laughed suddenly. "I should have liked to do it myself! But you needn't be afraid—I didn't."

It is possible that Lady Pemberley had been afraid—it is possible that she now experienced relief. It was not in her character to admit to either. She put out a thin, ringless hand and rang the bell on her bedside table.

Dawson came in, elderly, sensible, a little prim. Lady Pemberley spoke to her at once.

"Oh, Dawson—my keys, and the large jewel-case. Miss Moira has one of the ruby and diamond bracelets, and she might just as well have the other. It is a pity to separate them. Get it out and let me have it."

Moira said nothing at all. It had not often happened to her to find herself without words. It happened now. She stood like a stone whilst Dawson set the jewel-case down on the dressing-table—whilst she unlocked it, lifted out trays, and came over to the bed to put the other bracelet into Lady Pemberley's waiting hand.

Dawson was a little cross because Miss Moira didn't speak. She thought she might have said something pretty and given her ladyship a kiss, instead of standing there for all the world like Lot's wife. She was locking up the jewel-case again, when Lady Pemberley spoke.

"Just remind me to alter the list of my jewellery, and to let Mr. Ramsay know about taking the bracelets out of my will. It will be much pleasanter to think of Miss Moira wearing them now. Thank you, Dawson, that will be all."

When the door had shut and they were alone again Moira lifted her eyes. She had the stolen bracelet in her hand. She took a step forward and laid it down on the purple coverlet.

"I can't take them, Cousin Sibylla."

Lady Pemberley said gently,

"But I want you to have them."

Something in Moira gave way. A kind of dizzy warmth swept over her. She sat on the edge of the bed and felt the tears run scalding down.

CHAPTER 27

When Justin Leigh walked into the hall of the Grange after putting his car away it was a quarter to one. They had made very good time on the way down. If he found Moira Lane unusually silent, he preferred it that way. He had plenty to think about.

He had hardly shut the front door behind him when to his surprise Dorinda came out of the study. She clutched him and pulled him back into the room.

"I want to talk to you—I thought you were never coming. It's quite dreadful. The police have only just gone, and Mr. Winter is washing his hands."

Justin shut the study door.

"Darling, you're gibbering. Who or what is Winter?"

Dorinda gazed at him with widened eyes.

"He's Mr. Porlock's solicitor. The Scotland Yard policeman got him down—he arrived about eleven o'-clock—"

He interrupted her.

"I wasn't really asking for a biography."

"Justin, it's too dreadful. They rang up and said would I come over, because he'd brought down Mr. Porlock's will. Only of course it isn't Mr. Porlock—it's Uncle Glen, and he's left everything to me."

Justin whistled. Then he said,

"Not really!"

Dorinda nodded.

"Frightful—isn't it?"

Justin looked at her curiously.

"What makes you say that?"

She had turned quite pale.

"Justin, I can't take it. He usedn't to have any money. I'm sure he made it some wicked way."

"Blackmail, my dear—just a little simple, innocent blackmail."

"Oh, how—" She hesitated for a word, and came out with a childish *'beastly!'* "I'm glad I said at once I didn't want it."

"You said that?"

"Yes, I did—to the policemen, and to Mr. Winter. I said I couldn't imagine why he'd thought of leaving it to me. And Mr. Winter said—he's a little grey man, very respectable, and industrious like an ant, only of course ants aren't grey, but you know what I mean—he twiddled his pince-nez, and he said his client had informed him that he had no relatives, but that he would like to benefit a niece of his late wife's—said he had lost touch with her, but he remembered her as a pleasant little girl. I suppose I ought to feel grateful, but when I think how he did his best to get me put in prison for shoplifting—well, I can't. He did, you know. The big policeman said so."

Justin was looking serious.

"What are you going to do?"

She said, "I don't know. I had to wait and see you. Mr. Winter says it will make everything a lot easier if he and I prove the will—we're executors. If I don't, the money will just go to the Crown, and there doesn't seem to be any point about that. He says it will be better to prove it, and then, if he's taken money from people, I can give it back. That bit isn't what he said—it's what I thought of myself. And then if there was anything over I could give it to something—for children perhaps. So I thought it would be better to let him get on with the will."

"Had he much to leave? What does it amount to?"

"He isn't sure. He knows there's about five thousand pounds—he doesn't know whether there's anything more or not. Justin—they want me to come here."

"Why?"

"They say it would be easier. You see, I'm one of the executors. In a way, it's my house. There's no one here to give any orders. Mr. Winter would like me to be here because, he says, we are responsible for the house and furniture—Uncle Glen had it on a year's lease. And the police say it would make it easier for them."

Justin said quickly,

"These people in the house—they're a queer crowd, and one of them's a murderer. I don't want you here."

"I don't particularly want to come, but of course I see their point."

"What did you say?"

"I said I wouldn't come here unless I could have Miss Silver."

"Miss Silver?"

"I told you last night I wished she was here. If you were here, and she was here, I wouldn't mind being here too."

"What about Mrs. Oakley?"

"That's the extraordinary thing. The police came up and saw her after breakfast. She made me stay in the room. She's dreadfully unhappy and dreadfully frightened. I can't tell you about it, but if I was here I might be able to help a little. I mean, there might be things amongst Uncle Glen's papers—that's what she's afraid of. And you see, if I'm an executor I should have the right to go through them with Mr. Winter and, I suppose, the police. And of course I would do my best for her, poor thing. She hasn't any brains, but she does love her husband and Marty, and she's sick with fright at the idea of losing them."

Justin looked at her straight and said,

"Did she kill Porlock?"

Dorinda's eyes became quite round.

"Oh—she wouldn't!"

He said, "I don't know about that."

CHAPTER 28

Miss Maud Silver arrived at tea-time in the black cloth coat, the elderly fur tippet, and the black felt hat with its purple starfish in front and its niggle of purple and black ruching behind. Having partaken of what she described as a most refreshing cup of tea, she was conducted to her room, where she removed her outer garments and had a conversation with Dorinda.

"It's very good of you to come."

Miss Silver smiled.

"It is certainly more suitable that I should be here with you than that you should be here alone. . . . My room is next to yours? That is nice, very nice indeed. And now, Miss Brown, tell me just what happened on Saturday night."

When Dorinda had finished Miss Silver coughed and said, "Very clear, very succinct." She looked at the watch she wore pinned on the left-hand side of her bodice. "And now I think I will go down. Sergeant Abbott said he would be here by five o'clock, and it is just on the hour."

Sergeant Abbott was punctual. He rang the front door bell as they came down the stairs, greeted Miss Silver a good deal more like a nephew than a policeman, and carried her off to the study, leaving Dorinda conscious for the first time that he was not only a very personable young man but quite human.

Inside the study he was less like a policeman than ever. He put an affectionate arm round Miss Silver as he guided her to a comfortable chair, after which he took an informal seat on the arm of another.

"It's a good thing you rang me up," he said. "The Chief was hopping mad at first, but I've got him soothed. The fact is, there are just about half a dozen people up to their necks in this case—and when I say up to their necks I mean up to their necks. And any blighted one of them could have knifed Gregory Porlock—and had every reason to."

Miss Silver said, "Dear me!" She had brought down a flowery chintz knitting-bag, the gift of her niece Ethel. She opened it now and took out a half-made infant's vest in the pale pink wool which she had bought on the occasion of her visit to the De Luxe Stores. The four needles clicked. The vest revolved without detracting in any way from the attention with which she was regarding Frank.

He nodded.

"As you say—'Dear me!' it is. One might almost call it the theme song. I take it you know more or less what happened on Saturday night?"

"Miss Brown has given me a commendably clear account."

"Would you like to read the statements first? They won't take you very long. The Chief let me bring them after blowing off the customary steam."

Miss Silver laid down her knitting and perused the

typewritten sheets in a silence which he did not attempt to interrupt. When she looked up from the last word he had another sheaf to offer her.

"These are my notes of the various interviews. There's quite a lot of information in them."

She read these too.

"It all fits very well into the framework given me by Miss Brown."

"Yes, she's got a head on her shoulders, and in spite of being the late unlamented's sole legatee she is one of the few people who isn't a suspect. Now for the ones who are. I've tabulated them for you, and you'll see how nice and simple it all is. Here we go."

He handed her some more of his neat typing and leaned over her shoulder to read aloud, with occasional excursions in the nature of comment or explanation.

"I. Leonard Carroll. Cabaret artist. Clever, slick, thoroughly unreliable."

Miss Silver coughed gently.

"I have met him."

"In fact you have him taped! Well, he had a very compelling motive. Porlock was blackmailing him. Their conversation was overheard by Pearson—you know about him. He was here to try and get something on Porlock because Porlock was blackmailing a client of his firm. The Chief knows him, and says he's all right. He was doing all the listening at doors he could, and as he said himself, a butler really has excellent opportunities. Well, Pearson heard Porlock talking to Carroll. He told him he had evidence that he had given information to the enemy when he was out at the front with a concert-party in 'forty-five. Carroll went right off the deep end—very much rattled, very abusive. You've had that—it's in my notes. An hour or two later Porlock is knifed. Now if you look at this plan of the hall you can see where everyone was when Justin Leigh turned on the lights. It's his plan, and nobody disputes it. Gregory Porlock's body was lying with the feet a couple of yards from the newel-post at the bottom of the stairs. He had gone over there from the group about the hearth, and just before the lights went out he had turned round and was coming back. That is to say, at the time he was stabbed he was facing the hearth and had his back to the staircase and the drawing-room door. If you look at the plan you will see that Carroll was on the stairs, third step from the top, and Tote was in the drawing-room doorway. Now, taking Carroll as the murderer, the theory is that on his way up to wash after impersonating the devil in his charade he left a spot of luminous paint on Porlock's back as he passed, and subsequently turned out the hall lights from the top of the stairs. He then slid down the banisters, stabbed Porlock right in the middle of the bright spot, and got back upstairs a couple of steps at a time. It could have been done. There were no fingerprints on the dagger. He may have worn a glove, or he may have taken a moment to wipe it clean."

Miss Silver gave her slight cough.

"What about the switch?"

"Wiped clean. And that's one of the most damning bits of evidence against Carroll. A switch like that ought to have been a perfect smother of everybody's fingerprints. It was as clean as a whistle. Why should anyone have wiped it? Well, there's only one answer to that, and only one person who had a motive for doing it—the person who turned out the lights. If it was Carroll—and I don't see that anyone else was in a position to reach that switch—then Carroll is the murderer. So much for him. Now we come to Tote. Porlock was blackmailing him over activities on the black market.

One of our leading operators. He was by all accounts very angry. Now, as you will have gathered, Tote wasn't one of the party who went out to play the charade. He stayed behind in the drawing-room with Porlock, Miss Masterman, Justin Leigh, and Dorinda Brown. What we don't know is whether he went on staying behind after the others came out to do audience in the dark hall. He says he did. Nobody else says anything at all. Gregory Porlock was last out of the room. He was the only person who would know for certain whether Tote followed him. He could have followed him. He could have marked him with the luminous paint. Everyone in the party knew the pot was standing handy in the cloakroom. And he could have crossed the hall without being seen and lurked behind the service door until the charade was over and everyone was moving about. Then he would only have needed to open the door a very little way in order to put out the lights. Of course there's no proof that he did anything of the sort—that switch has an absolute crisscross of fingerprints. And when Leigh turned on the lights from over by the outer door, Tote was in the open drawing-room doorway, apparently about to emerge into the hall. Look at the plan."

Miss Silver coughed and said,

"Very interesting."

Frank Abbott went on.

"But Tote could have done it. At the service door he was in a position to see the luminous mark on Porlock's back. That is to say, he was slightly behind him, the door being at the back of the hall in prolongation of the line of the stair. Like Carroll he could have worn a glove, or he could have wiped the dagger. After that he had only to reach the drawing-room door, open it, and turn round so as to look as if he was coming out. He could have done it on his head."

"My dear Frank!" Miss Silver's tone reproved the slang.

He threw her a kiss.

"We're getting along nicely—two murderers in about three minutes. Here comes a third. Shakespearean, isn't it? First, Second, and Third Murderers. Enter the rather saturnine Mr. Masterman, a gloomy cove who looks the part to a T, which murderers generally don't. Porlock was probably blackmailing him too. Our chief eavesdropper, Pearson, only got away with an intriguing fragment about a missing will, but I should say there was something in it. We've been busy on the telephone, and it transpires that Masterman and his sister came in for a packet about three months ago from an old cousin who boarded with them. Nothing extraordinary about that, but the death was sudden, and there was apparently some local talk, reinforced by the fact that, whereas Masterman has been spending in a big way, the sister has gone about looking like death and wearing out shabby old clothes. They were, I gather, tolerably hard up until they came in for fifty thousand apiece under the old cousin's will. Connecting this with what Pearson overheard, it looks as if Cousin Mabel might have made a second will and been tidied out of the way—or perhaps only the will. Now, to consider Masterman as Third Murderer. I don't think there's much doubt that Porlock was blackmailing him. He was in the charade, with ample opportunity for picking up a spot of luminous paint—probably on a handkerchief. He had every opportunity of marking Porlock, easy access to the switch by the hearth, and no need to wipe off his prints, since he was known to have turned on the lights there at the close of the charade. Say he put them out again as soon as he saw Porlock turn back from the foot of the stairs. He had only to cross the hall until he was behind him, strike him down, and get over to the other side of the hearth. All quite easy—and, as you are about to observe, unsupported by a single shred of evidence."

Miss Silver coughed, and said thoughtfully,

"That is not what I was about to say. But pray go on."

He gave her a sharp glance. It met with no response. He did as he was told.

"Now for Miss Lane. She was undoubtedly being blackmailed, and she is a very fine, upstanding, handsome young woman who wouldn't take at all kindly to it. Pearson only heard something enigmatic about a bracelet. If she was being blackmailed about that she pulled a fast one on the late Gregory—see description of her bounding into the drawing-room and displaying a very handsome bracelet and telling everyone how marvellous Greg had been to get it back for her after she had lost it. Well, he didn't contradict her, but we've come across the bill for the bracelet. He paid a pretty price for it. It wasn't true, what Pearson heard him tell her, that the bracelet was fully described in the bill—it wasn't. But we got on to the jeweller, and he said it was sold to him in November by Miss Moira Lane. Gives you something to think about, doesn't it? But on the whole, I don't know about Moira. I don't see how she could have turned out the lights without upsetting Masterman's fingerprints, for one thing."

Miss Silver coughed.

"A woman could raise or depress a switch without touching more than a very small portion of the surface, and if it were done with the fingernail, there would be no print."

Frank sat up with a jerk.

"You've got it! Anyone could have done it with a fingernail! What a dolt I am! I never thought about it. I've been trying to see how anyone except Masterman could have handled that switch, and there's the answer, right under my nose!" He spread out a hand and frowned at five well kept nails, then suddenly relaxed. "It was under the Chief's nose too—but perhaps we won't rub that in. Well, Moira Lane could have done it, and so—and a great deal more likely—could Martin Oakley."

Miss Silver fixed him with an intelligent eye.

"The statements you have given me to read do not include one from Mrs. Oakley."

"No, I kept that back. We saw Martin Oakley and her maid yesterday, but we didn't see her until this morning."

"Her maid? Had she anything to say?"

There was a sparkle of malice in his eyes.

"Only that Mrs. Oakley committed bigamy when she married Oakley—the first husband being Glen Porteous alias Gregory Porlock."

"Dear me!"

Frank produced another of his typewritten sheets.

"She listened to a conversation between her mistress and Porlock on Wednesday afternoon. You'd better read my notes."

When she had done so she looked up gravely and said,

"So he was blackmailing her too."

"Undoubtedly. She doesn't admit it—she doesn't admit anything. She just cries and says, 'Please don't tell Martin.' I wish you could have been there, because you would probably have known whether she was putting on an act. She's one of those little fluffy women—brain apparently left out. I say apparently, because the Chief says he's met that sort before, and you can't always tell. He swears they have an instinct for putting on a scene. I expect you would have been able to tell whether it was genuine or not. And it's important, because everything turns on whether she told Martin Oakley that Glen Porteous had turned up and was blackmailing her. If she did, he had all the motive any jury could want. If she didn't, he hadn't any motive at all. Porlock was his friend and they were doing business together. He simply hadn't got a motive—if Mrs. Oakley held her tongue. She says she did. Martin Oakley says she did, but then of course he would. I may say that he put up a most convincing show—dumb-founded astonishment, resentment, anger, and, at the end something as near a breakdown as you'd get in a man of his type. If he was putting it on he's an uncommon good actor. As far as the physical side of it goes, he could have turned off the lights, and he could have stabbed Porlock just as any one of the group round the hearth could have done. And that brings us to Mrs. Oakley."

"Yes?"

Frank nodded.

"She certainly had a motive, and she had the same opportunity as everyone else. She was right beside the body when the lights went on. Everyone says she looked dazed. She went down on her knees beside him and began to scream out his name, calling him Glen and saying, 'They've killed him!' Whether she had the brains to plan the murder—and it must have been carefully planned—is another matter. You wouldn't say she had. The Chief isn't sure—I think he's rather impressed by the strength of the motive. He says it's surprising what a woman will do if she's faced with the loss of her husband and her child."

Miss Silver had picked up her knitting. The needles clicked. She said,

"Women do not readily use a knife—not in this country, not unless it is a weapon snatched up in the heat of a quarrel. This was a premeditated blow, the dagger carefully selected. I will not say that no woman would be capable of such a deed, but I do say that only a very unusual woman would choose such a way of extricating herself from an unfortunate situation. The woman you and Miss Brown have described would be far more likely to weep upon her husband's shoulder and leave the matter in his hands. Of course I have not seen Mrs. Oakley, and the Chief Inspector has. I have a great respect for his opinion and can agree with his conclusions, but human nature can be very unexpected."

Frank Abbott laughed.

"He loves it when you agree with him. It doesn't happen very often, does it? Well, that's the field. Pearson wasn't on the spot, and, as he took pains to explain, devotion to a client's interests would hardly take him as far as murder. As for the others, Miss Masterman is a possible, and so, I suppose, is Mrs. Tote, but the Chief doesn't think either of them likely. Justin Leigh had no motive, and Dorinda Brown—well, she's sole legatee, but it's practically certain that she couldn't possibly have known the terms of the will. So there we are— Carroll, Tote, Masterman, Oakley and Mrs. Oakley, Moira Lane—"

There was a brief silence. The infant's vest revolved. The colour really was extremely pretty. Miss Silver appeared to be concentrating her attention upon the clicking needles. Presently, whilst continuing to knit, she raised her eyes and said briskly,

"Was there a fire in the hall?"

"Yes, I believe so."

"Then how much light did it give? As I passed just now I observed that there was a good wood fire. Such a fire would throw out a considerable amount of light. It would affect the question of whether Mr. Tote could have made his way across the hall without being observed and—"

Frank Abbott interrupted.

"Yes, I know—you think of everything, don't you? I ought to have told you that the fire had been dowsed."

"By whom?"

"By Masterman, under Carroll's orders. Carroll couldn't do with the firelight for his charade. He wanted the hall to be dark, with the single lamp on the mantelpiece arranged to be as much like a spotlight as possible. They put a cone of brown paper on it and tilted it so that the light fell in a pool just where it caught his people one by one as they came down off the bottom step and turned at the newel. Leigh says it was very effective. They came down the stairs and passed through the light and out of it into the dark back of the hall. Masterman was in charge of the lighting. Carroll told him to dowse the fire. He was also first in the procession, and when he had done his part he worked round the edge of the hall and came back to the hearth, ready to turn on the lights when the show was over. I say that Tote could have crossed the hall without being noticed, because nobody noticed Masterman work his way back from the service door to the hearth. Of course they were all watching the charade then, but I say Tote could have done it. Everyone would have been moving, and no one would have been thinking about him."

Miss Silver continued to knit. She said,

"Quite so. There is now a very important point which I wish to raise. Mr. Porlock's back was marked with luminous paint. How large was this patch?"

"About three inches by four. It was an irregular patch, not a circle. There is no doubt at all about its purpose."

"No," said Miss Silver. "Very shocking indeed. But the luminous paint must have been conveyed in some manner which would prevent its spilling and marking not only the victim but the murderer. You yourself suggested a handkerchief. I am inclined to agree. Has any such handkerchief been found?"

"No."

"If the fire was dowsed, the handkerchief could not have been burned. Did anyone leave the hall before the local Inspector arrived?"

"No. Leigh kept everyone there. He's an able chap—he wouldn't let anyone leave the hall. But I'm afraid that when Hughes arrived his ideas of a search were a bit perfunctory. He put the women in a room by themselves whilst he sent for a female searcher, and he had the men searched for bloodstains and paint-marks. There were no bloodstains, either on the men or on the women—there wasn't any external bleeding. Carroll had smears of luminous paint, and so had Moira Lane and Masterman. It just proves nothing at all. Carroll was smothered with the stuff in his part as the devil, and the charade ended with his embracing Miss Lane. Carroll threw down his luminous mask upon the hall table, and Miss Lane threw her things there too. She was wearing a red velvet dress under her robe, and there was a mark on her left sleeve—rather a wet one. Masterman had a smear on his right cuff. He could have got it stabbing Gregory Porlock, but apparently he didn't. Moira Lane says he pointed out the mark on her sleeve. She says he brushed up against her, and then exclaimed and said, 'You're all over paint. I've got some of it on my cuff. Hadn't you better wipe it off?' That was before Hughes arrived."

"My dear Frank!"

"Yes—I know. It's just what he might have done if he had noticed a smear which would have to be accounted for. On the other hand, he did brush up against her, and she had got a large wet patch on her sleeve. It wouldn't be any good putting that smear on his cuff to a jury—now, would it?"

"I suppose not—unless there was other evidence in support. Was there anyone else who was marked with the paint?"

"No, there wasn't. I think Hughes was quite thorough about that. What hadn't occurred to him was the question as to how the paint had been carried. I think he was all out for Carroll as the murderer, and he took it for granted that the luminous mark on Porlock's back had been made by a paint-smeared hand. Carroll's hands were all over paint, and he had gone upstairs to wash them. Nice simple line of explanation—perfectly satisfactory to Hughes, so he never looked below what you might call the surface of the men's handkerchiefs. I don't think the paint could have been hidden if it had been on one of those flimsy squares of muslin that women drop about all over the place—it would have come through."

Miss Silver coughed gently.

"My dear boy, not muslin—cambric, or linen."

An almost colourless eyebrow jerked.

"Call them anything you like—paint would show through. But a man's handkerchief could be carefully folded up to hide a paint-stain. Hughes just looked blank when I asked him if he'd had all the handkerchiefs spread out. He hadn't. You expect a man to have a handkerchief—you take it for granted. At least you don't, but Hughes did. Which gives the murderer the best part of twenty-four hours to get rid of the evidence. By the time I'd thought about a handkerchief and put Hughes on to going through the house with a tooth-comb there naturally wasn't anything left for him to find."

Miss Silver put away her knitting and got up.

"I should like to go into the hall, but before we do so, will you tell me what results have been obtained in the way of fingerprints?"

"I think I told you about the four sets of switches. The one at the top of the stairs had been wiped clean. The one by the service door was just a mess. The one by the hearth had Masterman's prints, and the one by the hall door Justin Leigh's—both quite innocently accounted for. The dagger had been wiped clean—there were no prints there—" He stopped beneath a searching gaze.

"Were no other prints found?"

The eyebrow jerked again.

"What other prints were there to take? Most of these people were staying in the house. The others had been dining, moving about in the hall. Their prints would be all over the place, and they wouldn't prove a thing."

Miss Silver coughed, picked up Justin Leigh's plan, and led the way into the hall.

It was empty. The electric candles shed a soft light upon the stone flags and the two long Persian runners which crossed them. But Miss Silver was not looking at the floor. She walked over to the hearth and stood there, her eyes lifted to the trophy of arms above the stone mantelshelf. Hanging there on the broad chimney-breast, it had the air of some military decoration pinned to a rough grey coat, for the chimney-breast like the ledge was of stone, breaking the panelled wall. There were old flintlocks, four cumbersome pistols, and a ring of daggers. The bottom dagger was missing. Miss Silver stood looking at the place where it had been.

After a little while she turned round and looked in the direction of the stairs. Then she turned her head, glanced towards the switches on the left-hand side of the hearth, and back again at the staircase. At the sound of approaching voices she went back into the study. When she had seated herself and taken up her knitting again she enquired,

"How tall are you, Frank?"

He looked surprised.

"Five-foot-eleven."

"Mr. Masterman would be a little taller?"

He said, "Yes. Oakley and Masterman are both taller—about six foot. I should give Justin Leigh another inch. Moira Lane must be all of five-foot-nine—Dorinda Brown not quite so tall. Mrs. Oakley is about your height. Tote not more than five-foot-seven."

She said, "I was extremely pleased to observe that there was dust upon the mantelshelf—quite a considerable amount. It seemed almost too much to hope for, but the hall does not really look as if it had been dusted."

Frank Abbott laughed.

"I don't suppose it has. Pearson had the sense to leave everything until we came, and I told him to go on leaving it until I said—well, I'm afraid I quite forgot to say."

Miss Silver smiled.

"A truly fortunate circumstance."

He was sitting astride one of the upright chairs with his arms folded on the back.

"Now, what are you getting at?"

She was knitting rapidly.

"I hope that it may be possible to recover finger-prints which may prove of great importance. I should like you to ring up and ask to have someone sent out at once. Will you do so?"

He looked at her sharply.

"Blind?"

She smiled. Miss Silver's smile had an extraordinary charm. It had before now captured hearts and converted the sceptic. Frank Abbott's heart had been captured long ago. A young man not much given to enthusiasms, he undoubtedly had one for his "revered preceptress." He had also a very complete confidence in her judgment. When, therefore, she said primly, "I do not think there is any time to be lost," he got up, went over to the table, and picked up the telephone receiver.

When the ensuing short conversation had been closed by a definitive click he came back to his place and said,

"All right, ma'am. Do I get anything explained to me, or do I just wait for the explosion?"

This time she did not smile. She looked across the busy needles and the pale pink wool and said,

"I shall be very happy to explain. But before I do so, perhaps you will go into the hall and measure the distance from the ground to where the handle of the missing dagger would have been."

"Oh—so that's it? All right."

He went out and came back again.

"Six foot or thereabouts. I take it fractions don't matter."

"No. I believe you see my point. The stone ledge which crosses the chimney breast and serves as a mantelshelf is, I should say, twelve to fourteen inches lower. It is perhaps fourteen inches deep. It has occurred to me that scarcely anyone would reach across such a ledge to remove an object hanging just above it without putting a hand upon the ledge. Of course—as you are about to say—anyone staying in the house might have rested a hand upon that shelf without having any connection with the murder. But if the prints of a suspect were found, their position and direction might prove valuable corroborative evidence."

He nodded.

"Have you got anything else up your sleeve?"

The smile came out again.

"I think so. All the suspects are known to have been present in the hall at the time that Gregory Porlock was stabbed, with the exception of Mr. Tote, who may have been in the drawing-room or waiting behind the service-door, and Mr. Carroll, who had gone upstairs to wash and was found to be on the third step from the top of the stairs when the lights came on after the murder. If we are accepting it as an axiom—and I think we must—that it was the murderer who had turned out the lights, Mr. Carroll, if it was he, could only have done so by using the switches at the top of the stairs. And the probabilities are that Mr. Tote, if it was he, would have used the switches at the back of the hall by the service door. These probabilities appear to be so strong as almost to constitute a certainty. For everybody else there was only one set of switches which was both accessible and, owing to the shifting of the group round the fire, not too much exposed to observation. I refer to the switches on the left of the hearth. Now, my dear Frank, pray consider. Leaving Mr. Carroll and Mr. Tote on one side for the moment, let us suppose that the murderer is one of that group round the fire. He has his plan all ready. He has put his mark on Gregory Porlock's back so as to make sure of finding a vital place in the dark. He turns out the lights. Now remember that Mr. Porlock, who had gone over in the direction of the staircase, had already turned and was coming back. That is to say, he was facing the murderer, and the bright spot of luminous paint on his back was therefore not visible. What would the murderer do? I think he would cross the hall as quickly as he could with a hand stretched out in front of him till he came up against the staircase. This would bring him behind his victim, and at no great distance. The luminous patch would be right in front of him as he turned, and he would only have to step forward and strike."

"You think we might get a print of the murderer's hand on the panelled side of the staircase?"

"Or on the balustrade. I am not clear as to the height reached by the stair at a point immediately opposite the switches."

Frank Abbott said thoughtfully,

"It's worth trying for. But if he was wearing gloves, it's a wash-out."

Miss Silver gave her gentle cough.

"I think it very improbable that he would have been wearing gloves. By the way, I assume that no glove has been found."

"No."

"It would almost certainly have been marked with paint. I do not believe that the murderer wore a glove. He would have so short a time to dispose of it. It would be much simpler and safer to wipe the hilt of the dagger. To return to a possible print on the side of the staircase. It would, I think, be likely to be a left-hand print, since the right hand would either be holding the dagger or ready to take hold of it without an instant of delay."

The cold blue eyes held a spark of admiration. Frank Abbott said,

"Any more aces?"

"My dear Frank!"

"I should like to know. You know what the Chief is like when you pull a fast one."

"My *dear* Frank!"

His eyes teased as well as admired.

"Come—as man to man, is that all?"

Miss Silver was indulgent to the young. She smiled benignly, gave her slight cough, and said,

"For the moment."

CHAPTER 29

The evening which ensued was a curious one. If the house party had seemed strangely incompatible whilst still held together by the rich and genial personality of Gregory Porlock, there were, now that he was dead, no longer any points of contact between its various members. If the original bond had been fear, it had been camouflaged by all that social sense could suggest. To vary the metaphor—if the current ran cold below, there had been a certain glitter on the surface. There was now nothing but a collection of frightened and uncomfortable people constrained to one another's company and dreadfully conscious that the shadow which lay across them was to deepen before it lifted, and that for one of them it would most probably never lift at all.

A little, as it were, on the edge of all this gloom, Justin could approve the manner in which Dorinda played a new and difficult part. She was the hostess, but there should be no stressing of the fact. She carried it quietly and simply—a young girl called to take some older person's place. She showed a charming consideration to

Miss Masterman, with her dark, drawn face, and to Mrs. Tote, more like a mouse than ever—a very unhappy mouse which had been crying its eyes out.

Miss Masterman had no response to make. She was now entirely given up to waiting for a reply to the letter which she had sent. All her intelligence, all her emotions, her whole consciousness, waited ardently for the moment when she would be free from the burden which she had carried for these intolerable months. Alone amongst those present she was not primarily concerned with Gregory Porlock and the manner of his death. There was not really room in her mind for anything except the release for which she waited.

Miss Silver was probably the only person who enjoyed her dinner. She appreciated good food, and even a murder in the house could not obscure the superlative excellence of Mrs. Rodger's cooking. When they adjourned to the drawing-room she produced her knitting. The pale pink infant's vest now approaching completion awoke a faint spark of interest in Mrs. Tote. Before she knew where she was she was telling this comfortingly dowdy little person all about Allie and Allie's baby, and how she hoped there would be another. "Not too soon, because I don't hold with that, but it doesn't do to put off too long either, because if it comes to years between like you get nowadays, where's the company for the children? Every one of them's an only child, as you may say, and when all's said and done, what a child wants is company, and not a lot of grownups keeping it on the strain. A child wants other children to tumble about with and fight and make up with. I only had the one myself—at least only the one that lived, but I know what children ought to have."

Miss Silver agreeing, they became quite cozy over a knitting-stitch.

Miss Masterman took up the paper. She did not read it, but if you hold up a newspaper, people leave you alone, and all she wanted was to be left alone.

Moira Lane turned from the fire, looked for a moment at Dorinda, and said,

"Come and talk to me." Then she laughed. "For God's sake let's be human! I don't think you did it, and I hope you don't think I did, but if you do you might as well say so. Let's get into the other settee and stop being polite and inhibited. Who do you think did do it? I don't mind saying, whoever the murderer was, he did an uncommonly good job. Greg was poison. If he's your uncle, you probably know as much about that as I do."

Dorinda looked into the blue dancing eyes. The dance was a defiant one. She thought about Morgiana dancing in front of the Captain of the Forty Thieves and plunging a dagger up to the hilt in his breast. A feeling of horror came over her. It showed in her voice as she said,

"Not my uncle—my aunt's husband."

Moira's laugh rang out.

"Who cares what he was? He was poison! And you're just choked up with inhibitions. You'd be a lot more comfortable without them. What were you thinking about just now when you looked as if you'd caught me red-handed?"

Something gave way. Dorinda said,

"Morgiana and the Captain of the Forty Thieves— out of the *Arabian Nights*, where she stabs him."

Moira was lighting a cigarette. Her hand was as steady as a rock. The flame of the match caught the paper and crept in along the brown shreds of tobacco. She threw the match into the fire and drew at the cigarette until the whole tip glowed red. Then, and not till then, she turned an interested gaze upon Dorinda.

"Do you know, I believe you're clever, because I can just see myself doing that. She danced, didn't she? Well, you could work yourself up like that—couldn't you? Of course you'd have to hate the man to start with, but however much I hated anyone, I couldn't stick a knife into him in cold blood—could you? It gives me pins and needles to think of it. But you might be able to work yourself up to it with some good whirling music and the sort of dance that gets faster and faster and faster—" She broke off, rather pale.

Dorinda said quickly, "You said I was clever. I'm going to tell you you're stupid. It's idiotic to talk like that, and you ought to have the sense to know it without being told."

Moira blew out a little cloud of smoke. Her delicate eyebrows rose.

"Going to tell the police?" Her voice was lazy.

Dorinda said, "Don't be silly!" as sharply as if they had both been schoolgirls.

"It might interest them," said the lazy voice.

"I shouldn't think so."

Moira laughed.

"Do you know, I like you."

"Thank you!"

"You needn't be sarcastic—I meant it. I oughtn't to, because I suppose you're my hated rival. Justin's in love with you, isn't he?"

"Oh, *no!*"

Dorinda hadn't blushed. She had turned rather pale. The gold-brown eyes looked at Moira with inescapable candour.

"Oh, *no—he isn't!*"

Moira seemed amused.

"Did he tell you so?"

Dorinda held her head up.

"He is my cousin, and he has been very good to me. I am very fond of him, and I hope he is fond of me."

Moira said, "Go on hoping!" Then she laughed. "Didn't anyone ever tell you that you ought to tell the truth—unless you can put up a really convincing lie? Which you can't. I can, but I'm not going to. I could have done with Justin myself, but I shan't get him. I might have done if it hadn't been for you." She blew out another little cloud of smoke. "I don't mean to say that I'm in off the deep end, so you needn't lock your door in case I creep in in the middle of the night with another of those daggers. But I could have done with Justin, and I've an idea that he could have done with me if there hadn't been any Dorinda Brown. So what a good thing I like you, isn't it?"

Dorinda looked troubled.

"Moira—"

"Yes?"

"We don't know each other at all—and we're talking like this. I think I know why."

"All right—why?"

Dorinda struck her hands together.

"It's because it's all too horrid really. We've got to get something else into it—something to make us forget how horrid it is. Making it all seem like nonsense is one way. That's why you said that idiotic thing about coming into my room with a dagger. And talking about Justin is another. It makes it all—" She hesitated for a moment and came out with, "fantastic. It's like turning it into a play—it stops it being real and—frightening."

Moira looked at her. Then she said drily,

"Quite a bright child, aren't you? In other words we dramatize this sort of thing in order to keep the upper hand of it. So awkward if it took charge and started in to dramatize us!"

Coffee was served in the drawing-room. Pearson having announced that fact to Justin Leigh, the men came wandering in. Miss Silver, to whose prompting the announcement had been due, watched them attentively. Mr. Carroll had drunk quite a lot at dinner. Left to himself, he would probably have drunk a good deal more, hence her hint to Pearson as the ladies crossed the hall. As a gentlewoman, she deplored any degree of intemperance. As a detective, she had no objection to his drinking enough to loosen his tongue, but no possible end would be served by his drinking himself into a stupor in the dining-room. She had wondered to what extent he would be amenable to social pressure, and was relieved when he entered the drawing-room a little flushed and with that crooked look rather more noticeable, but with no other sign that his glass had been filled about twice as often as anyone else's.

When Mr. Masterman and Justin Leigh came in, she reflected upon the contrast they presented—a contrast all the more marked because the same superficial description could have been applied to either. They were both tall, dark men, but there it ended. Mr. Leigh carried an air of distinction. By common consent, no one had dressed for dinner. Miss Silver congratulated herself upon this. The black and white of a man's formal evening dress tends to level out those evidences of individual taste which sometimes afford an invaluable clue to character. Mr. Leigh's grey suit was not only very well cut, but it appeared so completely right as to be almost part of himself. Mr. Masterman had not the same power of relegating his clothes to the background. They gave Miss Silver the impression of being too new, and of their having cost more than he had been accustomed to spend. This may have been because Mr. Masterman himself might have been encountered without surprise in places where his clothes would immediately have attracted attention—such places, for instance, as behind the counter of a bank or in any City office. There was, in fact, a sense of discrepancy.

Mr. Tote's suit had probably cost as much as it is possible for a suit to cost, because one of the main objects in Mr. Tote's life at this time was to buy where the buying was dearest, a process which he described as "getting the best." His figure had, unfortunately, proved very unresponsive. It is more than possible that the tailor may have lost heart. He would certainly have done so if he could have foreseen that Mr. Tote would violate the sartorial decencies and insult that discreet dark suiting with a bright green tie lavishly patterned in yellow horseshoes.

Mr. Carroll was in brown. Not quite the right shade of brown. Miss Silver considered that it was a little too marked to be in really good taste. Quite a bizarre shade. And the orange tie, the orange handkerchief—not at all suitable.

She herself was wearing her last summer's dress dyed prune, with the black velvet coatee which she always brought down to a country house in the winter. Central heating there might be, but sometimes quite unreliable. She had a gold chain about her neck, and wore a brooch of Irish bog-oak in the form of a rose with a large pale pearl in the middle of it.

With that nice sense of propriety which enabled him to play his butler's part with so much decorum, Pearson had set the coffee-tray in front of Miss Brown, having first placed a small table there to receive it. Dorinda, her colour deepening, took up the heavy coffee-pot and began to look from one to the other, waiting to ask about milk and sugar, but with the feeling that the stiff silence which had fallen was harder to break in upon than any buzz of conversation. Mrs. Tote had stopped talking about Allie and the baby as soon as her husband came in. She did not talk about anything else, because none of the other things which filled her thoughts were the kind of things you can talk about in a drawing-room full of strangers. You can't say, "Perhaps my husband is a murderer," or even, "Perhaps the police think so." Yet the minute she stopped talking about Allie the cold darkness of these thoughts rushed in and quenched the light. She sat in the dark and trembled. Perhaps she wasn't the only one—

Justin had his own ideas about that. He had come to Dorinda's rescue and solved her problem by handing round the milk and sugar in the wake of Mr. Masterman, who took the cups. When everyone was served except Miss Masterman, who refused coffee with a monosyllable and remained behind her newspaper screen, he came back to put down milk-jug and sugar-basin and take the place which the two girls had left between them on the settee. The silence had, if anything stiffened. Dorinda had the feeling that if anyone were to speak something might break.

It was Miss Silver who said, "What delicious coffee!" She looked round as if she were collecting votes. "Really delicious, is it not?"

Nobody answered her.

Mr. Masterman stood with his back to the fire, his coffee-cup upon the mantelshelf. Mr. Tote had taken an armchair and the *Times*. Mr. Carroll hovered, cup in hand, rather like an insect looking for a place to settle. He was on the outskirts of the group when he broke into strident laughter.

"Delicious coffee! Delicious company! And, hell—what a delicious evening in front of us!"

Moira threw him a cool glance.

"Going to make a fool of yourself to brighten things up? Quite an idea!"

His small bright eyes held hers for a moment. There was so hot a spark of malice in them that it startled her. If she had been another sort of woman she might have been afraid. As it was, everything in her sat up and took notice. "He's got something. What has he got? What is he going to do?" Her lips curled in a sarcastic smile.

Leonard Carroll's left shoulder, which always looked a little higher than the right, gave a quick jerk and he was off. He laughed again in the same edgy manner.

"All right—I'm an entertainer, aren't I? And now I'm going to entertain you. Ladies and gentlemen, I am about to present an entirely unrehearsed and original act entitled 'Whodunit?' Breathless excitement—thrills guaranteed. A nice pat on the back from the police for the person who spots the murderer."

Justin Leigh made an abrupt movement. He appeared to be about to get to his feet. Before he could do so he encountered Miss Silver's eye, warning, threatening, and commanding, as in Mr. Wordsworth's pen-portrait of the perfect woman. Its effect, which was immediate, was to make him lean back again and hold his tongue.

Everyone, with the possible exception of Miss Masterman, was now looking at Leonard Carroll. He had dropped his showman's manner and proceeded in an easy confidential tone.

"We're all thinking about Greg, so why not talk about him? You can't get rid of a corpse by ignoring it—well, I mean, can you? Let's have the whole thing out and clear the air. There's only one person who ought to mind. The murderer isn't going to like it, naturally. And naturally no one's going to say they don't like it after that. And now—'Ring up the Curtain!' " He threw back his head and sang the phrase with which the curtain rises upon *Pagliacci*, then dropped to a low narrative tone. "Act II, Scene I. The murder has taken place, the lights have just been switched on, the hall is full of people. Leonard Carroll is on the third step from the top of the stairs looking down on them." His voice went deep into the dark places where things crawl. "He is looking down on all the others, and he has a damned good view."

A bright, crooked glance zig-zagged from one to the other of the group which faced him. This group was, in point of fact, a half circle fanning out from where Mr. Masterman leaned against the mantelpiece. Leonard Carroll stood in the open side of the half circle and let his malicious glance run to and fro, flicking over the hands with which Miss Masterman held up her newspaper screen, over the congested face of Mr. Tote, who had dropped the *Times* across his knees, over Miss Silver and her knitting, over Mrs. Tote with her reddened eyelids, past Mr. Masterman's frown, to where Justin Leigh was leaning back with an abstracted air between a girl who had flushed and a girl who was pale.

Dorinda looked sideways and saw that Justin was angry. When he looked like that it meant that he was very angry indeed. It meant that he was holding himself in. The foolish, useless wish came into her mind that the evening might be over and everyone safe in bed. And all this just a dream to wake up from next day, and say, "How silly!" and say, "It doesn't matter how silly it is, as long as it isn't true."

Leonard Carroll's flickering glance came home again. He repeated his last words in a meditative tone.

"A damned good view. Leigh was so very quick, wasn't he? He may have been a thought too quick for someone. It's just possible—well, isn't it? And Leonard Carroll on that third step from the top of the stairs would have such a damned good view. If there was anything to see, he could hardly have missed it—well, could he?"

Mr. Tote lifted his heavy bulk, flinging round in the padded chair to fix small angry eyes upon Carroll's face. It was a look which might have given some men pause.

"What's all this hinting? Why don't you come and sit down and behave yourself? If you've got anything to say, why don't you say it and have done? And if you haven't, what's the good of hinting that you have?"

Carroll laughed.

"Oh, you mustn't be too hard on my poor entertainment. A little mystery—a little conjecture—a sprinkle of what you call hints—I'm afraid we can't do without them. For instance, take your own case. I'm not saying what I saw, or what I didn't see, but—now who was it was telling me you threw a pretty dart? . . . Oh, yes—it was your wife."

Mr. Tote's neck became quite alarmingly red.

"What's that to you?"

Carroll's lips twisted in a smile.

"To me? Oh, nothing. To Gregory Porlock perhaps a great deal. That dagger could have been thrown—well, I mean, couldn't it? And I'm still not saying what I saw or didn't see from my balcony stall."

"Look here—" Mr. Tote's voice choked with fury on the second word.

Miss Silver glanced brightly across her clicking needles and said,

"Dear me—how extremely interesting! Such an original entertainment! But quite impersonal of course—is it not, Mr. Carroll?"

He returned her look with one of light contempt. It changed to sparkling malice as he shifted it to Geoffrey Masterman.

"How very fortunate to have a balcony stall—isn't it? So pleasantly removed from the struggling herd in the pit. You know, that light really did come on a bit sooner than it was meant to—just a bit sooner. Just a bit too soon for somebody." His glance moved on, touching Dorinda, passing Justin, settling on Moira Lane. "Odd how you see things when the lights come on suddenly like that. Extraordinarily sharp and clear. Pitch dark one minute, and then biff—everything hits you in the eye. Quite an odd experience, and—yes, that's the word—unforgettable. Quite, quite unforgettable." He walked over to the tray and set down his coffee-cup. "And now, as you are all so pressing, I will entertain you upon the piano. Our lamented Gregory having engaged me for that purpose, I imagine that I shall have a claim upon his estate for my fee."

There certainly was a slight drag in his step as he walked over to the grand piano and opened it. The silence which had followed what might be called the first part of his entertainment persisted. Nobody moved, nobody spoke. More than one person must have been thinking furiously.

Carroll had a charming touch on the piano. A few chords came into the silence, followed by a light malicious voice in the words and the tune of an old nursery rhyme:

"Who killed Cock Robin?
I said the Sparrow,
With my bow and arrow,
I killed Cock Robin."

CHAPTER 30

Before ten o'clock the party had separated for the night. An evening of profound discomfort was now something to look back upon with feelings of interest, doubt, suspicion, uncertainty, fear, or derisive amusement. Whichever of these feelings predominated in Mr. and Mrs. Tote, Mr. Carroll, Mr. and Miss Masterman, Moira Lane, Dorinda, and Justin, there is no doubt that Miss Silver had been very much interested. She had been in her room for some twenty minutes, but she had not so much as unfastened her bog-oak brooch, when a light tap sounded on her door. Opening it, she beheld Pearson, with an air of meek mystery and a finger at his lips.

Emerging, Miss Silver looked the enquiry she forbore to speak, and was beckoned farther along the passage. They passed Dorinda's room on the right, and that occupied by Miss Masterman on the left, descended three of those unreasonable and quite dangerous steps so frequent in old houses, turned the corner, and came into an irregularly shaped room where an overhead light shone down upon bookshelves, a large globe on a mahogany stand, a battered upright piano, and what had obviously been a schoolroom table. Hovering midway between the butler and the fellow detective, Pearson hoped that Miss Silver didn't mind his disturbing her—"but I thought you ought to know."

"Certainly, Mr. Pearson. What is it?"

"You don't find it cold here?"

Since she had not removed that old and well-tried friend her black velvet coatee, Miss Silver was able to reply,

"Not in the least. Pray tell me what has happened."

It must be admitted that Pearson had been feeling a little out of it. Not that he wanted to be involved in a murder case—very far from it. But to be, as it were, unavoidably in the midst of one, and yet not to know what was going on was bound to put a strain on him. He had rather leapt at the first opportunity of relieving this strain. He was now hoping that his leap was not going to be considered precipitate. Like so many well-meaning people, he was given to doubts when they could no longer serve any useful purpose. Miss Silver was an unknown quantity. Her manner was gracious, but from a certain distance, and without quite knowing why, it daunted him. She saw his eyes shift like those of a nervous horse.

Quite unexpectedly she smiled. It was the smile with which in her distant governessing days it had been her wont to encourage a diffident or backward pupil. It encouraged Pearson to the point of speech.

"Seeing Mr. Carroll go into the study and shut the door, it came into my mind in what I might call rather a forcible manner that possibly it was his intention to use the telephone, and if such was the case, I thought it might be a good thing, as it were, if I was to—" He stuck, and Miss Silver helped him out.

"To listen in on the pantry extension?"

"Yes, Miss Silver. And when I heard the number—"

"You recognized it?"

"It was the Mill House number, and he asked straight away for Mrs. Oakley. Well, of course that was no go, because she never comes to the telephone, not if it was ever so. But he got Mr. Oakley, and directly he started in I could see he was going to be nasty. It's my opinion he'd had a good bit more to drink than he could carry, as I dare say you may have noticed yourself when he came into the drawing-room. Not to say drunk, he wasn't, but pretty far on with feeling he was cock of the walk, and not minding whether he got across anyone else or not."

Miss Silver coughed appreciatively.

"A very graphic description, Mr. Pearson."

"Well, I thought you must have noticed him, same as I did, the first minute he started talking to Mr. Oakley. 'That you, Oakley?' he said—very offhand, if you take my meaning. 'Not dragged you from your slumbers, I hope. Or perhaps you're not sleeping so much these nights. I shouldn't if I was you. But that's the advantage of single blessedness, one hasn't got these complications to cope with.' Mr. Oakley said very stiff, 'I don't know what you are talking about, but if you have anything to say, perhaps you'll say it.' "

Pearson broke off and looked in a deprecating manner at Miss Silver. "I don't know whether you happened to notice, but Mr. Carroll has got a way of laughing. Not at all what I should call the thing—more like what you might call a snigger, if you know what I mean."

Miss Silver knew exactly what he meant. She gathered that Carroll had sniggered at Mr. Oakley, and that Mr. Oakley's reactions had been exactly what might have been expected, whereupon Mr. Carroll had not only repeated the offence, but had said in what Pearson could only describe as a nasty voice, "Oh, well, I thought you might be interested. The looker-on sees most of the game, you know. That's what I've been telling the others. Of course I may have bored them, but I don't somehow think that I did. No—I'm almost sure I didn't. What a pity you and your wife weren't there. You'd have been deeply interested, because, you see, I really did have a very good view of the hall when the lights came on, and a particularly good view of your wife. But of course, 'Honi soit qui mal y pense.' "

Pearson's pronunciation of the famous Garter motto was patriotic in the extreme. It is safe to say that the country of its origin would have made very little of it. Miss Silver, herself addicted to a British pronunciation of the French tongue, understood him perfectly.

"Pray continue, Mr. Pearson."

"Well, there wasn't much more. Mr. Oakley said, 'Hold your tongue!' and Mr. Carroll said, 'Well, I've held it up to now, but that's not to say I shall go on holding it!' and he slammed down the receiver."

"Dear me!" said Miss Silver.

Pearson looked complacent.

"That's what I thought, madam. And it seemed to me that it would be a good thing to tell you—the Chief Inspector and Sergeant Abbott not being available, and not wishing to have it said that I kept anything back that might be useful to the police."

"You did perfectly right," said Miss Silver briskly. "How long ago did this conversation take place?"

"A matter of maybe five minutes or so. I had the locking-up to see to. By the time I got round to the front door Mr. Carroll was coming out of the study and going up to his room."

He was thanked and dismissed.

About five minutes later Sergeant Abbott was told that he was wanted on the telephone, an instrument very inconveniently situated in the narrow entrance-hall of the Ram, to which hostelry he had accompanied his Chief with misgivings already abundantly justified. The Ram had four bedrooms, and all the beds were lumpy and smelt of beer, the food exemplified every sin of omission and commission which a cook can perpetrate, the beer was bad, and the telephone was in the hall. He had to disentangle the receiver from somebody else's coat which reeked of shag.

Miss Silver's voice came incongruously to his ear. First her slight cough, and then a prim "Hullo!" He said,

"Frank speaking."

The primness persisted.

"I am extremely sorry to disturb you. I hope that you had not retired?"

"I'm putting it off as long as possible. I don't know what they've used in the mattress. It's not sharp enough for road-metal—I rather suspect mangelwurzels. I am covered with bucolic bruises."

Miss Silver's cough was hortatory.

"I am exceedingly uneasy."

She had slipped into her British French.

"What's up?"

"That very foolish young man Mr. Carroll is giving everyone to understand that he is in possession of some knowledge—evidence—I do not know what to call it. He pretends—" the word in French bears a more respectable meaning than in English—"he pretends to have seen something of an incriminating nature at the moment when the lights came on. I do not know if it is possible. He was certainly in occupation of a vantage-point—he may have seen something, or he may not. What troubles me is the possible consequence of this foolish boasting. It does not really signify whether there is any truth behind it. What does signify is that the murderer may believe that there is, and that he may act upon his belief. I am extremely uneasy."

There was a slight pause. After which Frank said,

"What do you want me to do?"

"It would relieve my mind very much to have you in the house. I feel sure that Miss Brown would offer no objection."

Sergeant Abbott said gravely,

"You know, this is bribery and corruption—Vi-springs instead of mangolds, and everything else to match. Well, I can put it up to the Chief—I don't suppose he'll mind. Will you hold on?"

Miss Silver held the line and meditated upon human nature—more particularly upon Mr. Carroll's nature. She found it a far from pleasant subject. Considering the motives which might have prompted him in his folly, she dealt with such qualities as a sense of inferiority to be compensated by aggression, jealousy of others more fortunately placed—in which connection she recalled her favourite Lord Tennyson's dictum, "Envy is the fume of little minds"—and, lastly and with great seriousness, the possibility that this cloud of words was in effect a smokescreen to cover his own guilt and blacken others with suspicion.

She was still occupied with these thoughts when Frank Abbott came back upon the line.

"All right—he hasn't any objection. Just murmured a few sweet nothings about mountains out of molehills, and suggested that I was after the fleshpots. Well, it won't take me more than five or six minutes. I'll be right along."

CHAPTER 31

It was to take longer than that. Not because of the distance, since the Grange lay on the outskirts of the village, with no more than a quarter of a mile between its pillared gateway and the creaking sign which displayed a gold ram, rather tarnished, on a green field a good deal the worse for wear. Frank Abbott, walking briskly, passed the corner where the church with its squat Saxon tower crouched behind a row of monumental yews so black and solid that they might have been a wall, except that they were darker than any masonry could be. A hundred yards down the lane was the entrance to the Grange. He had a flashlight in the pocket of his overcoat, but he preferred not to use it. He had been country-reared, and knew how quickly the eye accommodates itself—after a few moments of blindness the skyline becomes evident, hedgerows can be discerned.

The grey pillars which marked the gateway to the Grange caught some of the diffused light from a cloud-covered moon. He passed between them, the gate being open, and heard, a long way off up the drive, the sound of running footsteps. He heard them, but no sooner had he done so than they ceased. It was as quick as that. He was left with the certainty that he had heard someone running. He shifted his suit-case to his left hand, got hold of his torch, and proceeded up the drive. It was a long drive, leafless trees overhead and dead flat fields on either side. There was a sharp double bend like an *S*, with a pond catching the light in one curve, and a mass of what looked like old holly-bushes in the other.

It was when he was opposite the hollies that, standing still to listen, he heard a twig snap and saw something move. In a moment his hand swung up with the torch. The beam picked out a man's face—an arm thrown up to screen it. But not quite quickly enough. Frank Abbott called out "Oakley!" and Martin Oakley stood his ground.

"Who's that?"

There was something in his voice—something curious, desperate.

Frank said, "Abbott," and crossed the space between them.

"What's up?"

Something very odd here. The man was breathing as if he had been running for his life. It was all he could do to get enough of that hard-caught breath to speak with, and then it was only a single word—a name.

"Carroll—"

"What about him?"

"Dead—"

"Do you mean that?"

Martin Oakley had him by the arm. There was a frightful tension about his grip.

"He's dead—"

"Where?"

"Up by the house." He had his breath now. The words came pouring out. "I didn't do it—I swear I didn't! I came to see him, but he was dead when I got there. He rang up. I tell you he hinted the foulest things. What sort of mind has a man got to do a thing like that? I don't know if it was blackmail he was after."

Abbott had been holding the torch so that the beam slanted downwards. He turned it sharply now to let the light shine upon Martin Oakley's face. He blinked and threw up a hand. The tumbling words checked. Frank said,

"I wouldn't talk if I were you—unless you want to make a confession."

"I never touched him. Take that light away!" He stepped back out of its range, his hand still up to shield his face.

Abbott said dispassionately,

"Well, just bear in mind that anything you say is liable to be used in evidence against you."

"I tell you I never touched him!"

"All right. You'd better come along and show me where he is."

The drive wound back to skirt a piece of woodland. Frank Abbott thought the man who planned it had gone out of his way to make it as long as possible. Chesterton's "rolling English drunkard made the rolling English road," just slid into his mind and out again. Of course that was why he had heard Oakley when he began to run. He had been actually nearer the house then than for most of the rest of the way. Half the lanes in England were like that—you went away from the place you were going to, and then came back to it again.

They were coming back to it now. The drive came out on a gravel sweep—"That's where I heard him run. He must have been scared crazy to run on the gravel." He said aloud,

"Which way?" And Martin Oakley said, "Round here to the left."

There was a belt of shrubbery, not very thick—light leafless tracery of lilac and syringa, with a dense blackness here and there of holly and yew, a path threading it to come out upon a small paved court at the side of the house. Huddled on the paving stones, Leonard Carroll lying crookedly with the back of his head smashed in.

Martin Oakley said, "He's dead. I didn't touch him."

"Somebody did," said Frank Abbott coolly.

He stepped forward, felt the dead man's wrist, and found it warm. He stepped back again. Then he sent the beam of the torch travelling here and there. The flags lay damp and furred with moss. Where they met the wall of the house there was a withered growth of fern, the old fronds brown and broken, the new ones curled hard upon themselves like fossils, sheltering against the January frosts. There was no sign of a weapon. The beam slid up the walls and showed rows of casement windows closed and curtained. On the ground floor all the windows shut. No light anywhere to answer the wandering beam.

Abbott said sharply, "Who sleeps this side?"

"I've no idea."

"Then how did you come here?"

"I came to see him."

"But why here? What brought you here?"

Oakley fetched one of those hard breaths.

"My God, Abbott—you can't put it on me! I tell you I was coming to see him."

"What brought you here—round to the side of the house?"

"I came up to the front door. It was only just after ten when he telephoned. I made up my mind to see him, to find out what he meant. I came up to the front door. I thought I heard voices away over here on the left. The front of the house was all dark. I stepped back to listen. I thought I heard my own name. I came this way. My feet made a noise on the gravel. I suppose that's why I didn't hear any more. I had a torch. I did stop to listen once. I thought I heard someone. I called out, 'Carroll, is that you?' There wasn't any answer. I went on, and found him lying here the way he is now. I didn't touch him—I swear I didn't!"

"You didn't think of giving the alarm?"

"I only thought about getting away. I'm afraid I lost my head a bit. I'd come over to see him, and there he was—dead. My one idea was to get away. I started to run, but when I got on to the gravel I realized what a row I was making and stopped. I tried not to make any more noise. Then I bumped into you. That's the absolute truth."

Frank Abbott wondered. He said,

"We'd better go up to the house."

CHAPTER 32

The telephone had been busy. Martin Oakley had repeated his story to Chief Inspector Lamb, haled from the borderland of slumber to preside over another investigation and a new murder. Flashlight photographs were being taken of the moss-grown courtyard, and of Leonard Carroll lying there—positively his last appearance on any stage.

Lamb sat beneath the overhead light, his coarse, curly black hair a little rumpled. It was still thick and abundant except just on the crown, and showed only a few grey threads at the temples. Under this strong dark thatch his ruddy, weather-tanned face had no more expression than a piece of wood. The brown eyes with their slight tendency to bulge remained fixed upon Mr. Oakley's face, a habit very disconcerting to even the most innocent witness. Martin Oakley could by no means flatter himself that there was any disposition to regard him in this light. His mind, at first possessed by a frantic sense of incredulity, had now to struggle against the feeling that he was being rushed towards a precipice at a speed which precluded intelligent thought. He had expressed his willingness to make a statement, and was now regretting it. He had been cautioned, but could not resist the temptation to explain his actions.

Lamb's voice struck robustly on his ear.

"Pearson's account of your telephone conversation with Mr. Carroll is substantially correct?"

"I think so."

"Would you like to look at it again?"

"No—it's all right—that's what he said."

"Well now, how long was it before you made up your mind to come and see him?"

"Oh, almost at once."

"Who rang off—you or Carroll?"

"He did. He banged down the receiver. I only hung up my end for long enough to get the exchange again."

This was something new. Frank Abbott looked up from his notes, Miss Silver from her knitting, which had for the moment required a somewhat closer attention than she usually gave it.

Lamb's "What did you want the exchange for?" rang sharply.

"I wanted to get on to Carroll to tell him I was coming over."

"Did you get him?"

"Yes."

"He knew you were coming over?"

"Yes."

"What did you say to him?"

"I said, 'Look here, you can't leave it like that. If you think you saw anything you'll have to tell me what it was. I'm coming over.'"

"What did he say?"

"He laughed, and I hung up." The urge to explain drove him. "That's why I went round to the side of the house—I thought he was calling me—I thought I heard my name. I came up to the front door. He was expecting me—I thought perhaps he'd be there to let me in. But when I heard my name—"

Miss Silver gave the slight cough with which she was wont to demand attention.

"Mr. Oakley, are you sure you heard your name?"

He turned a ravaged face on her.

"I'm not sure about anything. I thought I heard it. That's what took me round to the side of the house. Don't you see I must have had some reason for going there?"

The Chief Inspector said without any expression at all,

"We don't know what reason Mr. Carroll had for going there. But he did go there. The person who murdered him would have that motive for following or accompanying him."

There was a pause during which, and not for the first time, Mr. Oakley became convinced that he would have done better to hold his tongue. He was dismissed to the company of the other guests assembled in the drawing-room under the solemn gaze of a large local constable. If this young man had had any thoughts to spare from his job he might have reflected that the company presented some strange contrasts, but beyond concluding that it was a rum start he was conscious of little else than that this was a murder case, and that one of these people was probably a murderer. That being so, it did not matter to him that Mr. Tote was wearing blue serge trousers and a tweed overcoat; that Mrs. Tote had got back into the tight black cloth dress which she had worn for dinner, a garment rather ostentatiously smart in the hand but reduced by her to a sort of limp dowdiness; or that the other elderly lady had come down in a thick, old-fashioned grey dressing-gown, in spite of which she sat there shivering and looking as if she would never be warm again. Of the two young ladies, Miss Brown was in a tweed skirt and jumper, and Miss Lane in a very fancy dressing-gown, poppy-red and as flimsy as they come. Mr. Masterman was in a dressing-gown too, a very handsome garment and quite new.

Well, there they all were, and there they sat, not one of them with a word to throw to anyone else. And time went on.

In the study Lamb said,

"He was struck on the head with something that broke his skull. There's no sign of the weapon. It's got to be somewhere. There's no sign of it in the house. I don't say it couldn't have been cleaned and put back wherever it came from, because it could. There's fire-irons, flat irons, golf-clubs, and all manner of things, but getting things clean and putting them back takes time, and there was precious little time. The man could have been no more than just dead when Frank got here. Take it any way you like, that telephone conversation was over by a quarter past ten, because that's when Pearson finished locking up and saw Carroll go up-stairs. At five-and-twenty past Miss Silver is ringing the Ram. Frank gets going by the half hour, and bumps into Oakley six or seven minutes later. Now if Oakley left the Mill House after his second telephone call he wouldn't get here before half past—not walking in the dark—I don't see how he could. If he killed Carroll he had about six minutes to do it in and get back down the drive to where Frank met him. I don't say it couldn't be done, because of course it could, but he'd got to meet Carroll who was quite probably looking out for him, induce him to go round to the side of the house—why?—quarrel with him to the point of murder, hit him over the head, and make off down the drive. If it was Mr. Oakley, he may have brought the weapon with him, or he may have picked up something on his way. A big stone would have done it, or a brickbat, in which case he must have thrown it away as he ran, and we shall find it when we can make a thorough search by daylight. He won't, of course, have been able to do anything about cleaning it up, so unless there's something very heavy in the way of rain we shall be able to identify it all right. What puzzles me is why either Carroll or the murderer should have been where the body was found."

Miss Silver coughed in a tentative manner.

"Mr. Carroll's bedroom windows look out that way."

Lamb grunted.

"Yes, but they were shut and the curtains drawn."

Her needles clicked above the pale pink vest.

"If someone had desired to attract Mr. Carroll's attention, a handful of gravel might have been thrown up at one of the closed windows. Mr. Carroll would then have looked out. That he was persuaded to a meeting with his murderer is certain. There is nothing improbable in the supposition that he may have closed the window again and drawn the curtains."

Frank Abbott broke in with "How did Oakley know which was Carroll's window? He'd never been to the house until he dined here on Saturday night, and he hadn't been here since. That is to say, he'd never been here by daylight. Yet we're asked to believe that he made a bee line for Carroll's window and got it with the first shot. I can't swallow it myself."

His Chief had a frown for this.

"A bit free with your opinions, aren't you, my lad? I'll ask for them when I want them. I don't say there isn't a point there, but I'm quite able to see it myself. And here's an answer. Who says Oakley didn't know the house? Who says he'd only been here once? Who says he didn't fix it up with Carroll on the telephone to come round under his window?" He hit his knee with the flat of his hand. "Oakley—Oakley—Oakley every time!"

Frank Abbott had an impenitent frown.

"I just can't see why, sir."

"What do you mean?"

"I can't see why Oakley should have chosen such a place for a private conversation. At that hour everyone would be upstairs. Five of the upstairs windows look down on to that court, two in each of the small wings, and one in the middle of the side wall of the house, all double casements. The two on the left belong to Carroll's room, the two on the right to the bedroom shared by Mr. and Mrs. Tote. The one in the end wall lights the passage. Now, would Oakley, who had every reason to desire privacy, choose a place like this for the sort of conversation he was going to have with Carroll? To my thinking it's all wrong. How could he know that the Totes wouldn't have their windows open? If they had, they could have listened to everything that was said. Oakley was obviously in a fever about his wife—he'd have wanted to talk privately between four walls—"

This time Lamb hit the table.

"What makes you think he wanted to talk? If he'd got his mind made up for the murder he wouldn't come into the house—he'd get Carroll to come out!"

"And take him round under the Totes' windows? It doesn't make sense."

"Look here," said Lamb—"suppose it was this way.

He throws his gravel up at the window—I'll have that looked for—or makes some other signal, and Carroll comes down. Well, suppose he gets out of one of those ground-floor windows—no, that won't do, because they were all fastened on the inside, and Oakley couldn't have fastened them."

"Suppose it wasn't Oakley, Chief."

"Well?"

"Suppose it was someone in the house. He could have got back by the open window and shut it after him, couldn't he?"

Lamb's colour had deepened.

"And what would he be doing, meeting Carroll out there? And why should Carroll go outside to meet anyone who was living in the house? They could pick any room they liked to talk in, couldn't they? Everyone had gone to bed. Now you look here—facts are what we've got to stick to. Carroll left the house and went to that court. It's no good asking why he did it, or saying it's not the sort of thing he would have done—he did it. The same applies to Oakley. It's no good saying, 'Why should he choose a place like that to meet Carroll?' He went there, and he left Carroll lying dead. There's no evidence to show whether he found him alive. He says no. That'll be for a jury to decide—unless any of these people we've got boxed up in the drawing-room has got something useful to say. I'm going to start with Mrs. Tote."

During the first part of this conversation Miss Silver had appeared very much abstracted. Those rapid needles of hers slowed down and came to a standstill, her hands resting upon the pale pink wool. Towards the end she was giving her attention to what was being said, but with the air of one who has something to say and is waiting for the first opportunity of saying it. She now coughed in a very definite manner and said,

"Just a moment, Chief Inspector—"

It was almost as if he had forgotten she was there. Or perhaps the surprise in his look was intended to remind her that her presence was so very far from being official that the less said about it the better. He would not have used the word sufferance, but it may have been in his mind. It is certain that there was a graceful feminine deference in voice and manner as she said,

"I wonder if you would be so very good as to allow me to put a question to Mr. Pearson in your presence. It may prove to be of no importance at all, in which case I shall have to apologize for taking up your time. Or it may prove to be very important indeed."

She had all his attention now. It had a quality of frowning displeasure.

"I'm seeing Mrs. Tote next—if you *don't* mind."

Frank Abbott pressed his lips together. The Chief being sarcastic was not the Chief at his best. The simile of the hippopotamus presented itself to an irreverent mind. Miss Silver, on the contrary, evoked admiration. She appeared to have withdrawn to so considerable a distance that one might almost imagine her to have retreated into the Victorian age. From this distance she smiled and addressed the Chief Inspector.

"Then you will perhaps permit me to be your messenger. I will inform Mrs. Tote that you are ready to see her."

When the door had closed behind her Lamb rustled the papers on the blotting-pad. Frank's eyes travelled to the fluff of pale pink wool poised amongst its needles upon the arm of a just vacated chair. He had an idea that Maudie had turned the tables, and that it was his respected Chief who was feeling snubbed. He looked at the infant's vest, the ball of pink wool, and the knitting-needles, and was comfortably assured that Maudie meant to come back. He allowed himself a very faint smile, and had his head bitten off for an idle, insubordinate young pup.

"And I tell you what, my lad, if you don't watch your step you'll be getting into trouble one of these days—sniggering and sneering when you think I don't see you! Answering back too, and in French as likely as not! And perhaps just as well!"

Frank bowed to the storm in his most respectful manner. It would blow itself out.

CHAPTER 33

Miss Silver did her errand.
The hall was empty as she came through. If there had been anyone there, she might have been observed to go over to the hearth and, standing there, give some moments of close attention to what remained of the fire. The logs of which it had been composed were sunk together upon a deep bed of ash. They were not wholly consumed, but so charred and eaten away as to be mere frail shells, almost as light and insubstantial as the ash upon which they lay. They still looked like logs, but at a touch they would crumble and fall apart—with one exception. Tossed in upon the back of the burned-out fire was just such a log as might have served for the sign of one of those old inns which take their name from the Crooked Billet—a roughly L-shaped faggot, heavy and gnarled. It lay tilted against a pile of banked-up ash.

Miss Silver bent forward and looked at it closely. The heat had died out of the fire, but there was still a glow from the ash. She put out a hand and drew it back again, after which she shook her head slightly, pursed her lips, and proceeded to the drawing-room to summon Mrs. Tote.

They came back to the study together, and found the Chief Inspector restored. He addressed Mrs. Tote in as genial a manner as he thought proper.

"Come in and sit down. I'm sorry to keep you up so late, but I am sure you see the necessity. I suppose you have no objection to Miss Silver being present while I ask you a few questions? She is representing Miss Brown."

Mrs. Tote said, "Oh, no."

She folded her hands in her lap, fixed her red-rimmed eyes upon him, and thought with anguished longing of the days when a policeman used to be a pleasant sight. If only anything didn't come out about Albert—if only she could be sure that there wasn't anything to come out. Getting rich quick in ways you oughtn't to was bad enough, but there might be worse than that. Murder would be worse. When the word came into her mind it made her feel as if she was shrinking up smaller and smaller and smaller, until presently she wouldn't be there at all—and then she wouldn't see Allie again—

Lamb's voice sounded like a great gong.

"Now, Mrs. Tote—about tonight. What time did you go upstairs?"

"Ten minutes to ten."

"Rather early?"

"We'd all had enough of it."

Something about the way she said this gave him quite a good idea of what the evening had been like. He took her through it, getting her angle on what had already been very accurately described by Miss Maud Silver. She agreed that Mr. Carroll had had a good deal to drink—"Not drunk, of course, but he'd had more than was good for him. He'd never have said the things he said, nor behaved the way he did if he hadn't—trying to make everyone think he knew something—well, it isn't the way anyone would behave if they'd any sense in them. Downright foolish, I thought it was, and likely to lead to trouble."

"What do you mean by that?"

She was frightened. She oughtn't to have said it. It was only what she thought. You can't just say what you think in a murder case—it isn't safe. She spoke quickly.

"No one likes to be hinted at. That's what he was doing—hinting. I was afraid one of the gentlemen would take it up and there would be words."

Perhaps she oughtn't to have said that either. She threw a nervous glance at Miss Silver. There was something reassuring about the pink wool and the steady click of the needles.

Lamb recalled her attention.

"Well, you went upstairs at ten minutes to ten. Did you go to bed at once?"

"No."

"What did you do?"

"We talked a bit."

"About Mr. Carroll—about the scene downstairs?"

"Well, there was something said."

Lamb laughed.

"Well, I suppose there would be! And I suppose your husband wasn't best pleased?"

"Nobody would be," said Mrs. Tote.

"I don't suppose they would. I'm not blaming him. And I suppose you were trying to soothe him down?"

"Well, I was."

"And then?"

"He went off to his dressing-room."

"What time was that?"

"Twenty past ten."

"Look at your watch?"

"Yes. I wanted to see if I'd write a line to my daughter. My husband takes his time undressing."

"Did you write to your daughter?"

"No—I thought I wouldn't. I was feeling upset—I didn't want to upset her. I thought I would undress."

Lamb leaned forward.

"Now, Mrs. Tote—your room has two windows looking on to the courtyard where Mr. Carroll's body was found. Were those windows shut or open?"

She said, "Shut," looked round at Miss Silver, looked back, opened her mouth as if she was going to say something, and then closed it again.

"Yes, Mrs. Tote?"

She sat there, twisting her hands in her lap, pressing her lips together.

"Come, Mrs. Tote—something about those windows, isn't there? Did you open one of them—did you look out?"

Her fingers went on twisting. You couldn't exactly say she nodded, but there was some small reluctant movement of the head. Lamb looked at her with a gravity which was impressive in its way.

"Mrs. Tote, if you heard anything or saw anything tonight, you know as well as I do that you've got a duty. It isn't pleasant giving evidence which may lead to a man being hanged, but murder's murder, and if you know anything, it's your duty to speak."

Her red-rimmed eyes were sad but acquiescent.

"I opened the window."

"Yes. Why?"

"I heard something."

"What?"

"Something rattling—as if there was someone throwing stones up against a window."

"Your window?"

She shook her head.

"Oh, no—not mine. So I thought I'd look out."

"Yes?"

"I put out my light and opened the window. I couldn't see anything at first, but I could hear someone moving down there in the court. And then all at once Mr. Carroll opened his window just over the way and stood there looking out with the lighted room behind him."

"See him?"

"Oh, yes—quite plainly. He leaned out and said, 'Who's there?' and someone moved below and said, 'Come along down—I want to speak to you.'"

"Yes—go on."

"Mr. Carroll said, 'Is that you, Oakley?' and the man in the court said, 'It might be worth your while to keep a still tongue. Suppose you come down and talk it over.'"

"What did Carroll say to that?"

"He laughed. It was all very quiet, you know. I've got very quick hearing. It was just so I could hear it and no more. He laughed, and he said, 'I'll come down and let you in by one of those groundfloor windows,' and he shut his window and pulled the curtains over it."

"What did you do?"

"I shut my window and went back into the room and put the light on. I didn't think it was any of my business, and I didn't want them to know I'd been listening."

"Did you hear anything after that?"

"No—"

"Nothing that might have been a blow, or a fall?"

"I was moving about, you see—pouring out water and having a wash. You don't hear things when you're washing—" There was something hesitating about her manner.

"But Carroll said, 'Is that you, Oakley?' You're sure about that?"

She had a shrinking look, but she said quite firmly,

"Yes, I'm sure about that. He said the name quite loud."

"And you heard nothing more—nothing more at all after you shut your window?"

She seemed distressed.

"I don't know—it isn't fair to say if you're not sure."

"Then you did hear something?"

Her fingers twisted.

"Not to say hear. I was washing. I thought there was something—like someone calling."

"What did you think when you heard it?"

"I thought it was Mr. Carroll calling out to Mr. Oakley. Just the name—that's what I thought it was—the way he said it before, only louder. It must have been louder, or I wouldn't have thought I heard it—but the water was running—I couldn't swear to anything."

He let her go.

When the door had closed behind her he threw himself back in his chair.

"Well, that puts a noose round Oakley's neck all right!"

Miss Silver coughed delicately.

"Mrs. Tote will not swear that the person she saw in the court was Mr. Oakley."

She sustained the full impact of a formidable frown.

"She heard Carroll address him as Oakley—she'll swear to that."

"That is not quite the same thing. Mr. Carroll may

have been mistaken. In fact the final point you so skil-
fully elicited from Mrs. Tote confirms Mr. Oakley's
story. He explains his presence in the court by saying
that he thought someone was calling him and hastened
in the direction from which he believed the sound to
come."

Lamb gave a short annoyed laugh.

"And isn't that just what he *had* to say? Carroll has
shouted his name—anyone may have heard him. He's
got to put some kind of a gloss on it, so he uses it to
account for his going round to that side of the house."

With his frowning gaze upon Miss Silver, he was
struck by the birdlike quality of her regard, the head a
little on one side, the eyes very bright. He had seen her
look like that before, and it meant something. In fact,
the bird with its eye on a highly promising worm.

"If I might just put that question to Mr. Pearson,
Chief Inspector—"

"It won't keep?"

"I believe not."

He jerked round in his chair.

"Ring, Frank!"

Pearson came in all agog. His nerves had received a
severe shock, but he was being a good deal buoyed up
by the fact that it was entirely due to his zeal that the
police had arrived in time to arrest the murderer upon
the very scene of his crime. That the circumstances of
this case would provide him with the most interesting
reminiscences, he was already aware. But this solace
could not entirely prevent a nostalgic yearning for a future in which two murders would have become merely
the subject of a tale. As he was subsequently to put it to
his wife, "It's all very well when it's a has-been as you
might say, but very upsetting to the nerves when it's
going on and you don't know who's going to be the

next corpse." Since murders do not commonly take place in the presence of two police officers, to say nothing of one of them being a Chief Inspector, he found the study a very comfortable place, and would have been quite willing to stay there all night.

Miss Silver's words were therefore rather a disappointment.

"I only want to ask you one question, Mr. Pearson."

He assumed the butler.

"Yes, madam?"

"When you came through the hall after locking up, did you put any wood on the fire?"

If anyone had been watching Frank Abbott he would have been observed to start.

"Oh, no, madam—I shouldn't do that."

"So I supposed. Did you notice the condition of the fire?"

"It is part of my duty to do so, as you might say. I wouldn't go upstairs and leave a big fire, or anything that might fall out."

"And the fire was low?"

"Three or four bits lying flat and quite charred through."

"And you have put no wood on since?"

"Oh, no, madam."

"Or anyone else?"

"No one has had the opportunity—not since the alarm was given."

Miss Silver turned a look of extreme gravity upon the Chief Inspector.

"When I came downstairs after the murder I noticed a heavy crooked log at the back of the fire. It was not there when we all retired just before ten o'clock. When you began to speak about the weapon used in tonight's murder, the fire as I had seen it when I went upstairs and as I saw it when I came down again came very strongly to my thought. At first it only seemed that there was some incongruity, but whilst you were talking to Sergeant Abbott I became aware that this extra piece of wood might very well be the missing weapon. I can only hope that the smouldering ash has not been hot enough to destroy possible evidences."

Before she had finished speaking Frank Abbott was at the door.

CHAPTER 34

Ten minutes later Lamb said, "Well, Miss Silver, we are very much obliged to you. There's no doubt we've got the weapon. Fortunately Oakley must have been in too much of a hurry to do more than pitch that log in on the back of the fire without waiting to see where it landed. If it hadn't rolled off what was left of the fire it would probably have caught. As it is, there's no mistake about what it was used for."

"Oakley?" Miss Silver coughed in rather a definite manner. "Mr. Oakley, Chief Inspector?"

He stared. Frank Abbott gave a slight start.

Miss Silver was knitting rapidly. She said,

"If that log was the weapon, Mr. Oakley was not the murderer. It is not possible."

She got a grunt and a curt "Your reasons?"

"When Mr. Pearson came to tell me of the telephone conversation he had just overheard he mentioned that he had been shutting up the house. Every window on the ground floor was shut and fastened, every door locked and bolted—your men can confirm this. Even apart from the question of how Mr. Oakley could have left the house completely shut up after disposing of the weapon as you suggest, we are faced with another problem. Mr. Carroll did leave the house. He left it after it had been shut up for the night—since Pearson saw him going upstairs when he himself had finished locking up. He must have come down again. He must have opened some door or window in order to leave the house. Yet no door or window was found to be open or unlatched. Someone inside the house must have shut Mr. Carroll out. Is it not natural to suppose that it was the murderer? Mr. Oakley could not have done it."

There was a pause. Lamb's surface irritation was all gone. His mind, slower than Miss Silver's, but eminently competent and impartial, bent itself to weighing the arguments she had used. He did not allow himself to be hurried. He knew his own pace and kept to it. In the end he said,

"That's right—it wasn't Oakley—he couldn't have done it." He spoke as to an equal, quite without rancour, and continued in the same tone. "Any idea who did do it?"

She said gravely, "Someone who knew that Mr. Oakley was coming over."

He whistled.

"How do you make that out?"

"I think it follows. I feel sure that the murderer knew of the telephone conversation between Mr. Oakley and Mr. Carroll—I think it quite apparent."

Lamb's eyes bulged.

"You're not going to tell me you think it's Pearson! I can't swallow that."

Miss Silver smiled.

"I shall not ask you to do so. We know that Pearson was listening to the first of the two conversations, the one which was terminated by Mr. Carroll. He did not, however, hear the second, when Mr. Oakley rang up to say that he was coming over. I considered it practically certain that there would be a second extension, to Mr. Porlock's bedroom, and I have ascertained that this is the case. Now consider for a moment. Mr. Carroll had been playing upon the nerves and upon the fears of the whole company. How tightly strained must the murderer's nerves have been—how intensely he must have been wondering whether Mr. Carroll really had any hold over him, and how he meant to use it. The party begins to separate for the night. He sees Mr. Carroll enter the study and shut the door. He may even hear him calling the exchange. Do you not think that he would wonder whether Mr. Carroll was about to impart his information to the police? If he could slip into Mr. Porlock's room he could listen in on the extension and find out. I suggest that this instrument should be examined for fingerprints without delay. If they correspond—and I think they will correspond—with the prints taken early this evening from the mantelpiece in the hall and from the panelled side of the staircase, there will be a good deal of support for my theory."

"Whose prints do you expect to find?"

Miss Silver shook her head.

"Pray allow me to continue. The murderer hears Mr. Oakley say that he is coming over. I think it possible, in fact probable, that he only reached the extension in time to hear this second conversation. He would have had to get upstairs and watch for an opportunity of penetrating into Mr. Porlock's room."

Lamb gave another of his grunts, usually a sign of interest.

"Well, what did he do next? I suppose you can give us an eyewitness account!"

Miss Silver continued to knit.

"I fear not. I can only tell you what I believe may have happened. He would, of course, immediately realize that Mr. Oakley might be used as a scapegoat. The circumstances of Mr. Porlock's murder make it quite clear that the murderer is quick-witted and resourceful. He would, I think, see his chance of disposing of Mr. Carroll with very little risk to himself. He would calculate how long it would take Mr. Oakley to get here, and he would have to allow for his coming by car. The distance between the two houses being a good deal less than a mile, the difference between driving and walking would not be very great. Since the garage at the Mill House is at some little distance, I should suppose that he would wait for not more than five minutes before descending to the billiard-room, probably by the back stair."

"The billiard-room?"

"I think so. Part of it lies under Mr. Carroll's room, and it therefore has windows giving upon the court where the body was found. These windows, like the ones above, are all casements, and they are not very far from the ground. Having climbed out, he would have to go as far as the edge of the gravel sweep and provide himself with a handful of pebbles. He throws these up at Mr. Carroll's window. As the window below was probably open at the time, it is possible that traces of gravel may be found on the billiard-room floor."

Lamb jerked round on his subordinate.

"Go and have a look! Get Hughes, and tell him to try the telephone extension in Porlock's room for prints—door-handles inside and out—window-fastenings in the billiard-room. Tell him to look slippy. He'd better start with the telephone. Let me see—where's Jones? Put him in the billiard-room till it's been gone over. And tell

Jackson no one's to leave the drawing-room till I come."

Sergeant Abbott departed with regret. He would have preferred to stay and hear whether Miss Silver had anything more to say. This being the case, he did his errands in remarkably good time and returned with an air of vicarious triumph to report two or three pieces of small gravel just inside the billiard-room window.

Lamb grunted.

"Well, Miss Silver, it seems you've hit the nail on the head. Perhaps you will tell us now whose prints you think we're going to find?"

Her needles clicked, the pink ball revolved. The triumph had been all Sergeant Abbott's. She spoke gravely.

"I have been a very short time in this house. I have not, therefore, had my usual opportunities of making contacts or coming to conclusions. But, even on a very short acquaintance, there are things which cannot be overlooked. At any time before nine o'clock—"

Lamb picked her up sharply.

"Nine o'clock?"

She inclined her head.

"Coffee was brought into the drawing-room just before nine o'clock. The gentlemen joined us very shortly afterwards. Up till then, if I had been asked which of the guests in the house was the one most likely to have murdered Mr. Porlock, I should have been very much inclined to indicate Mr. Carroll. He made a very disagreeable impression on me. I thought him crooked and unscrupulous, and when it came to a question of motive he seemed to have a stronger one than anyone else. Proof that he had been concerned in treasonable correspondence with the enemy would certainly have meant a serious term of imprisonment, if not the death penalty. Even if the charge were not fully substantiated, he would be ruined professionally."

Lamb was leaning forward, heavily intent.

"And what happened after nine o'clock? He wasn't murdered for another hour and a half."

"My suspicions became directed elsewhere. When Mr. Carroll began what he was pleased to call his entertainment I naturally kept a very close watch upon everyone. Let me remind you of my position. I was in the sofa corner next to the fire and therefore very well placed for observation. On my right, sharing the sofa, was Mrs. Tote. In prolongation of the end of it, and rather out of the circle, was Miss Masterman. Mr. Carroll stood in the space between her and the armchair occupied by Mr. Tote. Miss Lane, Mr. Justin Leigh, and Dorinda Brown were on the sofa opposite mine. Miss Brown had the coffee-table in front of her. Mr. Masterman was standing up before the fire—"

"Yes, yes—we've had all that!"

Miss Silver continued to knit.

"As you will see, I was most advantageously placed. It is true that I should have had to crane my head rather uncomfortably in order to watch Mr. Masterman's face, but as it was not necessary for me to do so, this did not signify. Almost at once my attention became fixed upon Miss Masterman."

Frank Abbott moved so sharply as to suggest protest. The Chief Inspector stiffened, his whole mass seeming to become more solid.

Miss Silver went on placidly.

"I had been a very short time in the house, when I realized that it contained two very unhappy women. Both Mrs. Tote and Miss Masterman were carrying a heavy load of anxiety and grief. In Mrs. Tote's case, I discovered that she was unhappy about her husband's sudden rise to wealth and her separation from her much loved only child. She spoke quite frankly on these subjects, but I discerned a deep uneasiness as to the methods by which so large a fortune had been made. I thought that she was not quite sure whether there had been a step farther—into crime. I did not myself consider Mr. Tote very seriously. I think he probably went upstairs after his interview with Mr. Porlock and talked violently to his wife about what he would like to do to him. She made a half-admission to this effect. I did not think that the man who had planned to murder Mr. Porlock would have been so foolish as to threaten him, or to advertize his bad temper as Mr. Tote did on that Saturday evening. I therefore set the Totes on one side. Miss Masterman was unhappy in quite a different way. When I first saw her she seemed to be living within herself—there seemed to be no contact with the outer world. She looked strained and ill, and I received the impression that she was waiting for something. After I had seen and talked with Sergeant Abbott I thought her frame of mind consistent with the supposition that she and her brother had inherited money to which she felt they had no claim. She seemed quite sunk into herself, quite abstracted, as if even a murder could not disturb what had become a habit of thought. When we came into the drawing-room after dinner she drew away from the circle about the fire and took up a newspaper, which screened her face. I do not think she was reading. I watched her, and she never turned a page. But when Mr. Carroll began his so-called entertainment she was, I think, startled out of her apathy. He had a very vivid and dramatic manner—everyone was watching him. I watched Miss Masterman. She did not lay the newspaper down, but she lowered it a little. She did not look at Mr. Carroll. Her right hand tightened on the paper so hard that it tore. She did not notice that I was looking at her. Her attention was wholly fixed upon something else. I followed the direction of her eyes and saw that she was looking at her brother. He had set his coffee-cup down upon the mantelpiece—I was in time to see him do so. As I have already remarked, I could not see his face without making an effort, but it was quite easy to see his hand setting down the coffee cup—quite easy and, I thought, quite sufficient. Mr. Carroll had been addressing a series of highly provocative remarks to Mr. Tote. I did not take them very seriously. He was, in my opinion, merely baiting the person most likely to respond. After I had intervened with some light remark Mr. Carroll turned his attention to Mr. Masterman. He said much less to him than he had done to Mr. Tote, and there was much less apparent reaction, yet it was at this moment that Miss Masterman's attention and my own became engaged. Currents flowing beneath the surface are sometimes very strongly felt. Miss Masterman felt something which roused her. I was myself aware of a sudden extreme tension. It might have been difficult to trace this tension to its source if it had not been for one thing, a slight but curious physical reaction. The hand with which Mr. Masterman put down his coffee-cup was perfectly steady. It was his left hand. The cup was put down without the slightest jar. The right hand, which was hanging by his side, was steady too. But both thumbs twitched uncontrollably. It was one of those involuntary movements of which a person may be hardly aware. I am quite sure that Mr. Masterman was not aware of the twitching until he looked down and saw it. He showed great presence of mind, sliding one hand down into his pocket, and putting the other behind him as if spreading it to the fire. It was all very smoothly and naturally done, but instead of allay-

ing my suspicions it heightened them. I found myself
believing that Miss Masterman had seen what I had
seen, and that she placed the same construction on it. In
these circumstances, I thought it probable that she
would seek an interview with her brother. I do not
know if you remember that her room is opposite mine.
The gallery which runs round three sides of the hall
gives access to two distinct bedroom wings. Miss
Brown, Miss Masterman, and I have rooms in the right
wing on this side of the house. The room used by Mr.
Porlock is in the left wing, on the same side as the drawing-room and billiard-room, as are also the rooms occupied by the Totes, Mr. Carroll, and Mr. Masterman.
I did not undress. I waited with my door a little ajar to
see whether Miss Masterman would leave her room and
go round the gallery to the other wing. She did so almost immediately. By going to the end of the passage I
could see that she went as far as Mr. Masterman's door.
She knocked on it and waited."

Lamb said, "The two passages are directly opposite
one another. You were looking right across the hall into
the passage which runs over the drawing-room. I suppose it was lighted?"

"There was a light at the end, opposite Mr. Carroll's
room. I could see the whole of the passage. Miss Masterman knocked again, then she turned the handle and
went in. She left the door open behind her. I went to the
end of my own passage and turned out the light so that
I could continue to watch without being seen. I had
hardly done this before Miss Masterman came out
again, still leaving the door open. She stood there in a
very undecided manner, and I formed the opinion that
Mr. Masterman was not in his room. After a little while
she went back into the room, coming to the door every
now and then and looking out. It was obvious that she

intended to wait for her brother's return. There did not then seem to be any reason for me to continue my watch. I went back to my room, and a few minutes later Pearson came to report Mr. Carroll's telephone conversation with Mr. Oakley. I did not see Miss Masterman again till after the alarm had been given, when she came out of her room in her dressing-gown."

"You think she may have seen something?"

Miss Silver coughed.

"I think she must have done so. Consider, Chief Inspector. She was there in her brother's room, watching for him and very much on the alert. The door of the room was open. If anyone came out of Mr. Porlock's room, she could scarcely avoid knowing who it was. A back stair comes up between Mr. Masterman's room and that occupied by Mr. Carroll. If Mr. Masterman went down that stair, she must have seen him go. If Mr. Carroll used it, she probably saw him too. She was, in my opinion, almost at breaking-point after a long period of strain. She was desperately anxious to see her brother—perhaps desperately hoping that he would be able to reassure her. In these circumstances, do you think that anything would escape her?"

Lamb grunted.

"What's she doing now?"

"When I went in to fetch Mrs. Tote she was sitting shivering by the fire. The room is very hot and she is warmly dressed, but she cannot stop shivering. If you question her, I think she will break down. The man is her brother, but he has murdered two men who stood in his way. When you come to inquire into the death of the old cousin from whom he inherited, it may be found that there is a third murder on his conscience. Miss Masterman's trouble lies deep and is of long standing. She may have suspected what she did not dare to let herself believe. Now, I think, she knows, and if she knows she must speak, for everyone's sake—even for her own. If Mr. Masterman suspected her knowledge, I believe that she would be in great danger. The man is a killer. He is crafty and skilful. No one who threatens his safety is safe. I believe that you will find his fingerprints on the telephone extension and on the billiard-room window below. I believe that they will correspond with those taken in the hall from the mantelpiece and staircase."

Frank Abbott said, "She was right about those, sir. Hughes told me just now—they're Masterman's."

Lamb turned a stolid gaze in his direction.

"And they don't prove a thing," he said.

CHAPTER 35

The Chief Inspector shifted his gaze to Miss Silver, who continued to knit. After a moment he repeated his last remark.

"They don't prove a thing, and you know it. Anyone staying in the house could have left those prints without having anything more to do with the murder than you—or me. Think of trying them on a jury—" he gave a short bark of laughter—"well, I see myself! I'll go a step further. Say we find his prints on the extension in Porlock's room—what does it prove? That he went in there and put through a call. Most likely everyone in the house telephoned some time today or yesterday. Masterman will say he used the nearest instrument. Say we find his prints on the billiard-room window—by all accounts he's spent most of his time in that room since he came—he'll say he opened the window to get a breath of air."

Frank Abbott said, "It accumulates—doesn't it, Chief? Even a jury might begin to think that there was rather too much Masterman."

The gaze came back to him and became a repressive stare.

"If you're going to count on a jury thinking, you'll be heading for trouble. I've told you before, and I suppose I shall have to tell you again, that what a jury wants is facts—plain solid facts, with plain solid witnesses to swear to them. Juries don't want to think, because they know just as well as you and me that they're liable to think wrong. They don't want to wake up in the night and wonder whether they were right or wrong when they voted guilty in a murder case—it's the sort of thing that gets a man down. Juries want facts, so they can go home and say, 'Well, he did it all right—there's no doubt about that.' " He pushed back his chair. "Now what I'm going to do is this. There's evidence enough against Oakley to justify taking him down to the station and charging him—"

"But, Chief, you said he couldn't have done it."

Lamb got to his feet.

"Never you mind what I said—I'm saying different now."

Afterwards Frank Abbott was to wonder how much difference there had really been. Lamb could be deep when he liked. Frank came to the conclusion that he might, in retrospect, regard his Chief and Maudie as two minds with but a single thought.

Meanwhile the Chief Inspector was staring at Miss Silver, who responded with a faint, intelligent smile.

"It is considered a woman's prerogative to change her mind, but I have never been able to see why a gentleman should not have the same privilege."

She was putting away her knitting as she spoke, in

the flowered chintz bag which had been a birthday gift from her niece Ethel. Ignoring Frank Abbott's raised eyebrow, she followed the Chief Inspector from the room and across the hall.

In the drawing-room there was one of those silences. It must have been a quarter of an hour since anyone had spoken. Mr. Tote was in the armchair which he had occupied after dinner. He had a newspaper across his knees, but it was a long time since he had looked at it. Moira and Dorinda were on the sofa to the right of the fire, with Justin Leigh half sitting, half leaning, on the end next to Dorinda. On the opposite sofa Miss Masterman was in the place formerly occupied by Miss Silver, her thick duffle dressing-gown clutched about her. She held it to her in a straining clasp, as if to steady herself against a strong recurrent shudder.

In the other corner Mrs. Tote leaned back with her eyes shut. There was no colour in her face except in the reddened eyelids. She kept thinking of Mrs. Oakley screaming out about Glen. It wouldn't be hard to break her. If the police arrested Mr. Oakley and he was tried and hanged, she'd break all to bits—"And I'd have to stand up and swear to what I heard." It was worse than the worst bad dream she had ever had. She kept her eyes tight shut so as not to look at Martin Oakley, who walked continually to and fro in the room like a creature in a cage.

Mr. Masterman was in the chair where his sister had sat after dinner shielding her face and thinking her thoughts. He sat easily and smoked one cigarette after another but without haste.

Moira Lane was smoking too. A little pile of cigarette stubs lay in the ash-tray balanced beside her on the padded sofa arm. Her colour was bright and high. Dorinda was very pale. She leaned into the corner, and was glad when Justin dropped his hand to her shoulder and left it there. It was warm, and it felt strong.

Police Constable Jackson, on a stiff upright chair by the door, was thinking about his sweet peas. He had sown them in the autumn in a sunk trench and they were all of four inches high, very hearty and promising. He was going to train each plant up a single string, and he aimed at taking a prize at the flower-show in July. Five on a stem, you got them that way—great strong stalks as thick as whipcord and twelve to fourteen inches long—whacking great flowers too. His imagination toyed with a gargantuan growth.

It was when he was wondering what the record number of flowers to a stem might be that the door opened and Chief Inspector Lamb came in followed by the little lady who had fetched Mrs. Tote, and by Sergeant Abbott who you could pick out anywhere for a Londoner and la-di-da at that. Pretty well see your face in his hair, you could, and a pretty penny it must run him in for hair-oil—posh stuff too. . . . His thoughts broke off. He got to his feet automatically as the Chief Inspector came in.

Everyone had started to attention. Mrs. Tote had opened her eyes. Mr. Oakley had just reached the far end of the room and turned. He stood where he was like a stock. Everyone waited.

Lamb walked straight across the room and tapped Martin Oakley on the shoulder.

"I must ask you to accompany me to the station. I have a witness to the fact that subsequent to your telephone conversation with Mr. Carroll, in the course of which you said you were coming over to see him, someone came into the courtyard and threw gravel up at Carroll's bedroom window. He opened it and called out, 'Is that you, Oakley?' The reply was, 'It might be worth your while to keep a still tongue. Suppose you come down and talk it over.' You can make a statement if you like, but I'm warning you that anything you say will be taken down and may be used in evidence against you."

Martin Oakley stared at him. In the past three days he had become a haggard caricature of his former self. He stared, and said, "Are you arresting me? My God— you can't! I didn't do it! It will kill my wife!"

With everyone else in the room Miss Masterman had turned and was looking at the two men, leaning with her right arm upon the back of the sofa, clutching at the neck of her dressing-gown with her other hand. At the word *arrest* Miss Silver saw her start. When Martin Oakley said, 'It will kill my wife!' she said something under her breath and stood up, jerking herself to her feet all in one piece like a figure made of wood.

Miss Silver thought that the murmured words were "Oh, *no*—I can't!" If this was so, she repeated them— before Lamb had time to speak, and this time in so loud and harsh a voice as to divert everyone's attention to herself.

"Oh, no! Oh, no! I can't!"

She had taken a step forward, the arm which had lain along the back of the sofa outstretched as if she were feeling her way in the dark.

Geoffrey Masterman said, "She's ill!"

He got to his feet, but before he could take a forward step there was someone in his way—Frank Abbott, with a hand on his arm and a quiet, drawled "Do you think so?"

Miss Masterman walked past them. She looked once at her brother and said,

"It's no good."

If he made a movement, the hand on his arm checked it. He said,

"She's always been a bit unbalanced, you know. I've been afraid of this for years. You'd better let me get her up to her room quietly."

No one took any notice. It came home to him then that he was separated from the people round him—not as yet by bolts and bars, by prison walls, or by the sentence of the law, but by the intangible barriers which have separated the murderer from his kind ever since the mark was set on Cain. Nobody listened to him or regarded his words. Only Jackson, catching Sergeant Abbott's eye, moved up on his other side.

Miss Masterman came to a standstill midway between the fireplace and the window. In that harsh, strained voice she spoke to Lamb.

"You mustn't arrest him! He didn't do it!"

He seemed very solid and safe, standing there. Law and order. Thou shalt not kill. All the barriers that have been built up through slow ages to keep out the unnameable things of the jungle. If you let them in, too many people pay the price. She heard him say, "Do you want to make a statement, Miss Masterman?" Her breath lifted in a long sigh. She said,

"Yes—"

CHAPTER 36

Agnes Masterman's state- ment:

"I am making this statement because there is nothing else I can do. Mr. Porlock and Mr. Carroll were bad men. Perhaps they deserved to die—I don't know. My old cousin never did anyone any harm. You can't kill people just because they are bad, or because they are in your way. You can't let innocent people suffer. I can't let Mr. Oakley be arrested, because I know that he is innocent. There are things you can do, and things you can't. I can't let him be arrested.

"We went upstairs at about ten minutes to ten. I didn't know what to do. I had to talk to my brother, but I was afraid—I was very much afraid. I had been thinking about the money—my old cousin's money. She didn't mean us to have it—at least she didn't mean Geoffrey to have it—and she made another will, but he kept it back. I ought to have gone to the lawyer at once, and all the time I couldn't be sure whether he had frightened her—or something worse. She was old and frail, and very easily frightened. I couldn't get it out of my head. I don't know how Mr. Porlock got to know anything about it, but he did. He made us come down here because he wanted to get money out of Geoffrey. When he was stabbed like that I was afraid, but I didn't think it was Geoffrey. I thought it was Mr. Carroll. I think most of us did. But Geoffrey said he thought it was Mr. Tote. He really did make me feel that he hadn't anything to do with it himself. And he gave in about the money and said he would produce the will. He told me she'd left fifty thousand to me, and I said he could have it. I thought I would make sure that he didn't change his mind, so I wrote to the lawyer and said we had found a later will, and I walked down to the village and posted the letter on Sunday evening. After that I didn't feel I minded about anything else. I was just waiting for the answer.

"Then tonight something happened. It was like waking up, only instead of waking out of a nightmare it was like waking into one. It happened when Mr. Carroll was talking. I think he was bad and cruel. He was trying to make us believe that he knew who had murdered Mr. Porlock. He kept hinting that he had seen something when the lights came on. I don't know whether he really did or not. I looked across at Geoffrey, and I saw his thumbs twitching. That was when I woke up. He'd done it all his life when he was very much afraid. My father was very severe with him. I've seen his thumbs jerk like that when he went in to be caned. I saw them jerk and twitch when my old cousin died. He doesn't know it's happening. When I looked across and saw it this evening I knew what it meant. I couldn't help knowing. I had to talk to him and tell him that I knew, but I was very much afraid.

"As we came through the hall, Mr. Carroll said, 'I've got a call to put through.' He went into the study. Geoffrey looked dreadful. He left me and went upstairs. The others had gone already. I went to my room, but I felt I had to speak to him. I came out again and went round the gallery and down the other passage to his room, but he wasn't there. I thought perhaps he had gone to the bathroom, and I waited. I left the door half open. Presently I heard a door open and I looked out. It was the door of Mr. Porlock's room, and Geoffrey was coming out of it. I didn't want him to see me watching him, so I drew back. He didn't see me. He went past his own room and down the back stairs. I waited a little, and then I went down too. I thought perhaps it would be better if we had our talk downstairs where no one could hear us and wonder why we were talking. When I got down the billiard-room door was open and there was a cold draught blowing. It was all dark, but I felt my way in, and the window on the left was open. I stood there for quite a little time. I thought something bad was happening, but I didn't know what it was. I was afraid to go on, and I was afraid to go back. Then all at once I heard footsteps outside in the court, and a pattering sound. One or two pebbles came in through the window. Then I heard Mr. Carroll open his window upstairs. He called out, 'Is that you, Oakley?' and I wondered what Mr. Oakley was doing there. I went behind a curtain and looked out. I could just see someone in the middle of the court. He said, 'It might be worth your while to keep a still tongue. Suppose you come down and talk it over.'

"As soon as he spoke I knew that it was Geoffrey. He was talking in a sort of whispering way, but you can't mistake your own brother's voice. I stood behind the curtain. Mr. Carroll came down, feeling his way like I had done. He climbed out of the window and went to where Geoffrey was. Geoffrey said very quick, 'What's that behind you?' Mr. Carroll turned round, and Geoffrey hit him. I couldn't see what he had in his hand. He hit him, and Mr. Carroll fell down. He called out Mr. Oakley's name and he fell down. After that he didn't make a sound and he didn't move. Geoffrey came running to the window and got in. He shut it, and he drew the curtain over it, all in the dark. I thought he would touch me, and then he would kill me too, but he just pulled the curtain and went out of the door and along the passage to the hall. I don't know why he went there, because he came back almost at once. I heard him go up the back stairs. I didn't move for a long time. I think I fainted, because when I began to think again I was half sitting, half kneeling on the window-seat and there was someone out in the court with a torch in his hand. I went along the passage to the hall and upstairs to my room. I took off my dress and put on my dressing-gown because it was warm—but I can't get warm."

CHAPTER 37

The inquest was over. Ver-
dict, wilful murder by Geoffrey Masterman. Dispersal
of the guests at the Grange. Miss Masterman to a
nursing-home. The Totes to the expensive and uncomfortable house in which she always felt a stranger.
Moira Lane to the three-roomed flat which she shared
with a friend. Miss Silver would stay to keep Dorinda
company until after the funeral, when she too would
return to town.

It was Dorinda's destination which was in doubt.
She could return to the Heather Club and look for another job. But on the other hand why should she? Two
murders and a legacy which she had no intention of
keeping didn't really interfere with the fact that she was
Mrs. Oakley's secretary. She put the point to Moira
Lane, and Moira blew a smoke-ring and said,

"Too right." Then she laughed and said, "Ask Justin!"

Dorinda asked him. At least that is not quite the way
to put it. She just said of course there wasn't any reason
why she shouldn't go back to the Oakleys, and he said,
"What a mind!" and walked out of the room. He didn't
slam the door, because Pearson was coming in with the
tea-tray, but Dorinda got the impression that if it hadn't
been for that, he might have banged it quite hard.

After tea she walked up to the Mill House and was
ushered by Doris into the pink boudoir, where the Oakleys had been having tea. Doris took the tray. Martin
Oakley shook hands and edged out of the room. She
was left with Linnet, in one of her rose-coloured neg-

ligées, reclining on the sofa propped up with pink and blue cushions. Dorinda thought she resembled a Dresden china figure, a little the worse for wear but obviously cheering up. The stamp of tragedy, so ill-suited to her type, was gone. The shadow under the forget-me-not blue eyes no longer suggested a bruise. Some slight natural colour was evident beneath a delicate artificial tint. She was affectionate to the point of warmth. She held Dorinda's hand for quite a long time whilst she gazed at her with swimming eyes and said how dreadful it had all been.

Dorinda agreed, and came straight to the point.

"I could come back any day now—"

It was at this moment that her hand was released. A lace-bordered handkerchief came into play. Between dabs Mrs. Oakley murmured that it was all so difficult.

"You don't want me to come?"

There were more dabs.

"Oh, it isn't that—"

"Won't you tell me what it is?"

It took quite a long time. Dorinda was reminded of trying to catch a bird with a damaged wing—just as you thought you had got it, it flapped off and you had to start all over again. But in the end out it came. There was a lot of "Martin thinks," and "Painful associations," and a very fluttery bit about "the dead past." But, in much plainer and more brutal English than Linnet Oakley would permit herself, what it amounted to was that Dorinda knew too much. There were little sobs, and little gasps, and little dabs, but it all came down to that.

"Of course, we shall get married again at once, and nobody need ever know. The Scotland Yard Inspector promised us that, unless it was necessary for the case against the murderer. And it couldn't be, could it? So as

Martin says, it's just to go through the ceremony again, and then we can forget all about it. I'm sure you'll understand that. You see, it's been so dreadful, because I did think perhaps Martin had done it—not Mr. Carroll, you know, but Glen. And Martin thought perhaps I had, which was very, very stupid of him, because I shouldn't have had the strength, besides not being so dreadfully wicked. And you know, there was a time when I was very, very fond of Glen—I really was—and I couldn't ever have done anything to hurt him. I can't say that to Martin, because he has a very, very jealous temperament—that was why I was so frightened."

She gave a last dab and reached for her powder compact.

"I mustn't cry—it makes me look such a fright. And I really ought to be thankful—the way it's turned out, I mean—its not being Martin. Because if it had been—" The hand with the powder-puff drooped. The blue eyes swam with tears again. A sobbing breath caught in her throat. "If you've been in love with anyone and been married to him you can't feel just the same as if he was anyone else. And I *was* in love with Glen—anyone could have been. There was something about him, you know, though he wasn't even kind to me after all the money had gone. And he went away and didn't care whether I starved or not—and I very nearly did. But there was something about him—"

Dorinda remembered Aunt Mary dying grimly and saying with a bitter tang in her voice, "What's the good of asking why? I was a fool—but there was something about him." There couldn't be two more different women anywhere in the world, but they had this one thing in common—neither of them had known how to say no to the man who was Glen Porteous and Gregory Porlock. She said in a calm, soothing voice,

"I wouldn't go on thinking about it—and you're making your eyes red. You haven't really told me whether you want me to come back to you. I don't think you do, but it's better to get it quite clear, isn't it?"

Mrs. Oakley dabbed with the powder-puff and said, "Oh, *yes.*"

"You see, I must know, because of getting another job."

Linnet stared.

"But Glen left you all his money."

"There isn't very much, and anyhow I *can't* keep it. All I want to know is whether you want me—and I think you don't."

It seemed that she was right.

"Not because we don't like you and all that, because we do. But you see, *you know,* and we should always know that you knew, and I don't think we could bear it. So if you don't *mind*—"

Dorinda came back to the Grange and informed Mr. Justin Leigh that she was out of a job.

"I shall go back to the Heather Club and look about me. I've got a month's salary in hand, and as I shan't have done a stroke of work for it, it's not too bad. In a way it's a relief that the Oakleys don't want me back, because I think it would be nice to go where no one had ever heard of Uncle Glen. It's stupid of me, but I've rather got that feeling."

Mr. Leigh, extended full length in the easiest of the study chairs, neither raised his head nor fully opened his eyes. He might have been asleep, only Dorinda felt perfectly sure that he was not. After a short lapse of time he murmured enquiringly,

"Declaration of Independence?"

She said with dignity,

"Miss Silver and I can go up to town after breakfast tomorrow."

"Yes, I should have breakfast first. Never travel on an empty stomach."

"I wasn't going to. Now I'm going upstairs to pack."

He opened his eyes enough to let her see that they were smiling.

"You don't need six or seven hours to pack. Come and talk to me."

"I don't think I want to."

"Think again. Think of all the things you'll think about afterwards and wish you'd said them to me. If you can't think of them for yourself, I'll be noble and oblige." The smile had spread to his lips. "Come along, darling, and relax." He reached out and pulled up another chair until it touched his own. "I'll say this for the late Gregory, he knew how to pick a house with good chairs. And what have we been doing for days, and days, and days? Sitting on the edge of them as taut as bowstrings talking to policemen! No way to treat decent furniture. Come along and tell me all about the new job."

Dorinda weakened. She had a horrid conviction that she would always weaken if Justin looked at her like that. But of course there wouldn't be a great many more opportunities, because they would both be going back to work, and they wouldn't be seeing nearly so much of each other.

She came and sat down in the chair, and the very first moment after she had done it she knew just what a mistake it was. It is a great, great deal easier to be proud and independent when you are standing up. Soft well-sprung chairs are hideously undermining. Instead of being buoyed-up with feeling how right it was to be self-supporting and independent, she could only feel how dreadfully dull and flat it was going to be. And as if that wasn't enough, her mind filled with pictures and images which she had been firmly resolved to banish. There was the moment in the hall on Saturday night when Justin had put his arm round her and of course it meant nothing at all because they were cousins and someone had just been murdered. And there was the moment which really filled her with shame when she had pressed her face into his coat and clung to him with all her might. That was when the police were arresting Geoffrey Masterman and he had broken away and taken a running jump at the end window. The horrid sound of the struggle—men's feet stamping and sliding on the polished floor, the clamour of voices, the clatter of breaking glass, came back like the sound-track of a film. Justin had pulled away from her and gone to help. It made her feel hot all over to think that he had had to push her away. That was why she mustn't let go of herself now.

His hand came over the arm of the chair and touched her cheek.

"You're not relaxing a bit—you're all stiff and keyed-up. What's the matter?"

Dorinda said soberly, "I think I'm tired."

She heard him laugh softly.

"I think you are. And of course that's a magnificent reason for sitting up as stiff as a board."

"I get like that when I'm tired. Justin, please let me go!"

"In a minute. Move a bit so that I can get my arm round you. . . . That's better. Now listen! I'm thinking of getting married."

She couldn't help starting, but after that one uncontrollable movement something poured into her—some flood of feeling which carried her right away from all the things which had been troubling her. They didn't seem to matter any more—they were drowned and swept away. She didn't know what the feeling was. If it was pain it wasn't hurting yet. What it was doing was to make her feel that nothing else mattered.

She turned so that she could look at him.

"Is it Moira Lane?"

"Would you like it to be?"

"If it made you happy—"

"It wouldn't. Anyhow she wouldn't have me as a gift."

"How do you know?"

"I don't think she'd care about taking someone else's property."

He spoke, unconscious of incongruity, and, incongruous or not, it was the truth. Moira had stolen a bracelet, but she wouldn't take another girl's lover. Queer patchy sort of thing human nature.

Dorinda said, "Someone else?" And then, "Who is it, Justin?"

She was looking straight at him. His arm had slipped from her shoulders. He took her hands and said,

"Don't you think it would be a good thing? I've seen a flat that would do. I've got furniture. Will it amuse you to help me choose carpets and curtains? All my mother's things are in store, but I expect they will have perished. I'll get a day off and we'll go down and see if there are any survivors."

"Who are you going to marry?"

"I haven't asked her yet, darling."

"Why?"

"Just the feeling that I didn't want to get it mixed up with policemen and inquests and funerals."

Dorinda said, "The funerals are over."

"That's what I was thinking. Are you going to marry me?"

"Do you want me to?"

"Oh, Dorinda!"

She saw that his eyes were wet. It did something to her. He was still holding her hands. All of a sudden he jumped up pulling her with him, and put his arms round her. It wasn't until he let go of her hands that she knew how tight he had been holding them. They felt quite stiff and numb. She set them against the rough stuff of his coat and held him off. But she didn't feel that the stuff was rough. She knew it was, but she couldn't feel anything because her hands were numb. She held him off, and said what she had to say.

"I'm not the right person for you—I've always known that. I don't know enough about how things ought to be done. You ought to marry someone like Moira. I thought you were going to marry her—I've thought so for a long time."

"Think again, my sweet. Think about saying yes. Did I tell you I loved you? I do, you know. It's been coming on for months. I thought you'd understand when I gave you my mother's brooch."

Her eyes widened.

"I thought you were fond of me—"

He gave an odd shaky laugh.

"I've gone in off the deep end. Are you coming in too? *Dorinda*—"

She took her hands away and put up her face like a child.

"If you want me to."

CHAPTER 38

After dinner that evening a party of four sat comfortably round the study fire. Frank Abbott made the fourth. The Chief Inspector having departed leaving him to tidy up, he had most thankfully accepted an invitation to stay at the Grange. Tomorrow they would all have gone their separate ways. Tonight they sat peacefully round the fire and talked like friends. The sense of strain had gone from the house. Old houses have seen many deaths, many births, many courtships, much joy and sorrow, much good and evil. In more than three hundred years this house had known them all. Gregory Porlock and Leonard Carroll had joined themselves to the past. They were no more to the house now than Richard Pomeroy who had stabbed a serving-man in 1650 and been hanged for it under the Lord Protector, or than Isabel Scaife who married James Pomeroy some fifty years later and threw herself out of a window of the very room occupied by Mr. Carroll. For what reason was never clearly known. She fell on the stones of the court-yard and was taken up dead. Men looked askance at James Pomeroy, but he lived out his life, and it was his son who was known as good Sir James and endowed a foundation to provide twelve old men and twelve old women of the parish with a decent lodging and wearing apparel, together with food sufficient for their needs "for as long as they shall live, with decent Buriall afterwards."

There were other stories, other minglings of good and bad—men who thought little of their own lives, risking them in battle, throwing them away to bring a wounded comrade safe; men who sinned and men who suffered; men who did well and men who did ill; men who died riotously abroad, or piously abed. The house had outlived them all. Gregory Porlock and Leonard Carroll were neither here nor there. The house could live them down.

The fire burned bright. The room was comfortable and warm. Miss Silver had finished the vest she had been knitting and had begun another. An inch of ribbing ruffled on the needles in a pale pink frill. She looked at Justin and Dorinda with a benignant smile. Nothing pleased her better than to see young people happy.

She turned her glance on Frank, and met one from him which was cool and a little cynical.

"Well, revered preceptress, are you going to perpend?"

"My dear Frank! What do you want me to say?"

The cynical look changed to a smile.

"Anything you like."

She smiled too, but only for a moment. She was grave again as she said,

"I shall not ask you to be indiscreet, but I assume that since Mr. Masterman was brought up before the magistrates this morning on the charge of having murdered Leonard Carroll, there does not seem to be enough evidence to charge him with Gregory Porlock's death, although it must be clear to everyone that he committed both these crimes."

Frank nodded.

"Those handprints you put us on to and the trace of luminous paint on the edge of his dinner-jacket sleeve are the only things you can begin to call evidence in the Porlock case, and counsel would make short work of them. He could have put his hand on the mantelpiece for a dozen innocent reasons. He could have touched the staircase panelling during the charade. They all came down the stairs, turned at the newel, and went through the spotlight towards the back of the hall. That left-handed print on the panelling occurs just where he would have been leaving the spotlight and passing into the dark again. Quite a natural action to put out a hand and touch the wall."

Miss Silver coughed.

"But in that case the hand would have been pointing towards the back of the hall. The print was, I understand, very nearly upright, but with some inclination in the other direction—in fact just as one would expect to find it if, as I suggested, Mr. Masterman had been crossing from the hearth in the dark with a hand out in front of him to let him know when he reached the staircase. I expected a left-hand print, because the right hand would be held ready to use the dagger."

Frank nodded.

"Oh, that's how it happened. But we couldn't go into court with it—a clever barrister would tear it to shreds. No, we've got him for Carroll—I think that's a cert. His prints on the telephone extension in Porlock's room and on the billiard-room door and window, *and* Miss Masterman's statement—"

Dorinda said quickly, "I'm so dreadfully, dreadfully sorry for her."

Miss Silver looked at her kindly.

"She has been through a terrible time. I think there is no doubt that she has suspected her brother of causing their old cousin's death. Not necessarily by poison or actual violence. She was, I understand, in no state to be frightened or shocked. I think Miss Masterman fears that she was frightened and died of it. That is a terrible thing for her to have had on her mind, quite apart from the suppression of the will, which did not actually benefit her since she received the same amount under the will which has now been produced. I cannot help wondering how long Miss Masterman herself would have survived if her brother's guilt had not come to light. Suppose Mr. Oakley had been arrested. Suppose her to have held her tongue—I do not think it possible that she could have concealed her remorse and distress from her brother. And he must have become aware of the danger he would be in should she break down, as she did in fact break down. He had just killed two men—do you think he would have hesitated to kill again? I think we should have had a very convincing suicide. I feel sure that Miss Masterman saved her own life when her conscience would not allow her to stand by and see an innocent man arrested."

Justin raised his eyebrows.

"I wonder whether she thinks it was worth saving."

Miss Silver's needles clicked with vigour.

"I must disagree with you there, Mr. Leigh. Life is always worth saving. Miss Masterman is a conscientious woman. She has good religious principles. She will have a large fortune. She can be encouraged to look forward to the good she can do. There will be painful times for her to go through, but I shall try to keep in touch with her. I believe that she will come through and take up her life again as a trust for others. I shall do my best to encourage her. You know, as Lord Tennyson says:

No life that breathes with human breath
Has ever truly longed for death."

Justin restrained himself.

"An echo from the great Victorian Utopia, where the

more articulate portion of the population made believe that all was for the best in the best of all possible worlds."

Miss Silver coughed in a reproving manner.

"It was an age which produced great men and women. Pray do not forget those who toiled tirelessly for the better social conditions which we are beginning to see realized. But to return to Lord Tennyson's aphorism. I do not believe that faith and hope can be separated from life, and where these linger, however faintly, they can be revived. A real longing for death could only follow upon their complete extinction."

Frank's bright, cool glance held a spark of unaffected admiration. Maudie, so practical, so resolute, so intelligent, so inflexible in her morality, so kindly, and so prim—in all these aspects she delighted him. He blew her an impudent, affectionate kiss and said,

"You don't know what a lot of uplift I get from being on a case with you. My moral tone fairly shoots to the top of the thermometer. But go on telling us. There's quite a lot I want to know, and most of it will never come out in court." He turned to Justin. "Strictly off the record, I don't mind telling you something of a highly confidential nature." He dropped his voice to a whisper and said, "She knows everything."

"My dear Frank!"

He nodded emphatically.

"Don't take any notice of her. She was brought up modest—a Victorian failing. You can take it from me that as far as she is concerned the human race is glass-fronted. She looks right through the shop-window into the back premises and detects the skeleton in the cupboard. So next time you think of committing a crime you'd better give her a wide berth. You have been warned. It is only the fact that I have a perfectly blameless conscience that enables me to meet her eye."

Miss Silver pulled at her pale pink ball.

"My dear Frank, I really do wish you would stop talking nonsense. Pray, what is it that you wish me to tell you?"

"Well, I should very much like to know whether Carroll was bluffing—all that talk of his about what he might have seen when the lights came on. There's no doubt that he was very advantageously placed. From the top of those stairs—well, three steps from the top, which comes to very much the same thing—he would be looking right down on all those people round the hearth. If there was anything to see, he'd have seen it all right. But was there anything? If there was, what was it?"

Miss Silver coughed in a gentle, thoughtful manner.

"I think that there was something. I have given some consideration to what it may have been. There is no possibility that Mr. Carroll could have seen the blow struck, or the removal of fingerprints from the handle of the dagger. After hearing Mr. Porlock call out and fall, Mr. Leigh had to push Miss Dorinda back against the wall and then feel his way along it to the front door and turn on the lights. The murderer had ample time to wipe the handle of the dagger and remove it from the vicinity of the corpse. I think there is only one thing which Mr. Carroll could have seen. In stabbing Mr. Porlock, the sleeve of Mr. Masterman's dinner-jacket came in contact with the luminous paint with which he had marked his victim. He would not notice it until he had gained the position where he intended to be found when the lights came on. But once there, he might very naturally glance down at his hand and arm and see in the darkness a faint glow from the smear of paint. To try and remove the smear would be instinctive. If the lights went on whilst he was rubbing the edge of his sleeve, this is what Mr. Carroll may have seen, and I think he was too clever not to draw his own deductions. You will remember that Mr. Masterman subsequently took the opportunity of brushing against Miss Lane, who had some of the paint on her sleeve, and that he then drew everyone's attention to the fact that he had stained his cuff. Now this stain was right on the edge of the cloth sleeve and nowhere else. It would be very difficult to acquire a stain of this sort by brushing against a lady in a light frock—so difficult that I cannot believe it happened. Whereas it would, I think, be extremely difficult for a man to stab someone up to the hilt in the middle of a luminous patch without getting some of the paint on the edge of a shirt cuff or coat sleeve. I have asked everyone whether there was anything noticeable about Mr. Masterman's dinner-jacket. Four of them, including Mr. Leigh, remarked that the sleeves were too long, practically hiding the shirt cuff. This would account for the smear being on the cloth."

Justin Leigh said, "That's very interesting, Miss Silver. But if Carroll thought Masterman was the murderer, why didn't he blackmail him instead of going for Oakley?"

Miss Silver shook her head. There was some suggestion that a pupil was not being quite as bright as she expected.

"Did Mr. Carroll strike you as a courageous person? He did not make at all that impression upon me."

Justin gave a half laugh.

"Oh, no."

"I do not think that he would have approached anyone whom he knew to be a murderer directly. He would certainly not have gone to meet Mr. Masterman in that deserted courtyard. But Mr. Oakley was a different matter. Like everyone else, Mr. Carroll had seen Mrs. Oakley on her knees beside the dead man and heard her call him Glen. He could hardly fail to guess at Mr. Oakley's state of mind, or to suspect that he might be terribly afraid of his wife having some part in the crime. He was prepared to play upon those fears. He rang up, dropped his malicious hint, and rang off again. When Mr. Oakley rang him up and said he was coming over, Mr. Carroll must have felt confident of success. That his purpose was blackmail is certain from the words overheard by Mrs. Tote when Masterman, pretending to be Oakley, said, 'It might be worth your while to keep a still tongue. Come down and talk it over.' Mr. Carroll laughed and came. That was his moment of triumph. But the triumphing of the wicked is short."

Justin said, "Yes, you're right—it would have been like that. Very satisfying. It all fits in. Well, we're all off tomorrow, but I hope it isn't goodbye. You'll come and see us when we're married?"

She smiled graciously.

"It will be a pleasure to which I shall look forward. It is always delightful to look forward. As Lord Tennyson says,

> *How dull it is to pause, to make an end,*
> *To rust unburnished, not to shine in use!"*

There was a slightly awed silence. Dorinda produced rather a shy smile, but Frank Abbott rose to the occasion. There was laughter in his voice, but it was the laughter of real affection. He leaned over and kissed Miss Silver's hand, knitting-needles and all.

"Don't worry," he said. "Pure gold doesn't rust."

THE END

Agatha Christie's
DEADLY
DELIGHTS

- ❑ **The Mirror Crack'd From Side to Side** 100285-2 . . $4.99
- ❑ **Poirot Investigates** 100287-9 . . . . $4.99
- ❑ **Endless Night** 100334-4 . . . . $4.99
- ❑ **Death on the Nile** 100369-7 . . . . $4.99
- ❑ **Passenger to Frankfurt** 100378-6 . . . . $4.99
- ❑ **Dead Man's Folly** 100367-0 . . . . $4.99
- ❑ **The Body in the Library** 100364-6 . . . . $4.99
- ❑ **Death Comes as the End** 100368-9 . . . . $4.99
- ❑ **Murder on the Orient Express** 100274-7 . . . . $4.99
- ❑ **Destination Unknown** 100381-6 . . . . $4.99
- ❑ **They Do it with Mirrors** 100376-X $4.99
- ❑ **Sleeping Murder** 100380-8 . . . . $4.99
- ❑ **Hickory Dickory Dock** 100372-7 . . . . $4.99
- ❑ **The Seven Dials Mystery** 100275-5 . . . . $4.99
- ❑ **Ordeal By Innocence** 100278-X $4.99
- ❑ **Sparkling Cyanide** 100379-4 . . . . $4.99
- ❑ **4:50 from Paddington** 100383-2 . . . . $4.99

Yes, please send me the books I have checked above.

MAIL TO: HarperCollins Publishers
P.O. Box 588, Dunmore, PA 18512-0588
OR CALL: (800) 331-3761

SUBTOTAL .... $_____

POSTAGE AND HANDLING. .... $ 2.00

SALES TAX (Add applicable sales tax) .... $_____

Name_____

Address_____

City_____ State_____ Zip_____

Allow up to 6 weeks for delivery. (Valid in U.S. only.) Prices subject to change.
Remit in U.S. funds. Do not send cash.   HO991

More
Agatha Christie
DEADLY
DELIGHTS

- ❏ **A Caribbean Mystery** 100365-4 . . . . $4.99
- ❏ **At Bertram's Hotel** 100363-8 . . . . $4.99
- ❏ **By the Pricking of My Thumbs** 100335-2 . . . . . . $4.99
- ❏ **Cat Among the Pigeons** 100284-4 . . . . $4.99
- ❏ **Crooked House** 100277-1 . . . . $4.99
- ❏ **Curtain** 100366-2 . . . . $4.99
- ❏ **After the Funeral** 100371-9 . . . . $4.99
- ❏ **Hercule Poirot's Christmas** 100373-5 . . . . $4.99
- ❏ **Mrs. McGinty's Dead** 100375-1 . . . . $4.99
- ❏ **Murder is Easy** 100370-0 . . . . $4.99
- ❏ **Nemesis** 100326-3 . . . . $4.99
- ❏ **Postern of Fate** 100276-3 . . . . $4.99
- ❏ **The Clocks** 100279-8 . . . . $4.99
- ❏ **The Mousetrap and Other Plays** 100374-3 . . . . . $5.99
- ❏ **The Murder of Roger Ackroyd** 100286-0 . . . . $4.99
- ❏ **The Pale Horse** 100377-8 . . . . $4.99
- ❏ **Third Girl** 100382-4 . . . . $4.99

Yes, please send me the books I have checked above.

MAIL TO: HarperCollins Publishers
P.O. Box 588, Dunmore, PA 18512-0588
OR CALL: (800) 331-3761

SUBTOTAL .... $_____

POSTAGE AND HANDLING. .... $ _2.00_

SALES TAX (Add applicable sales tax) .... $_____

Name_____

Address_____

City_____ State_____ Zip_____

Allow up to 6 weeks for delivery. (Valid in U.S. only.) Prices subject to change.
Remit in U.S. funds. Do not send cash.   H10011